Johnny Come Home
The Civil War in Northeast Missouri

Acknowledgements

The basis for the fictional characters that helped meld the story with facts about the Jenkins family came from Joan Sommers Jenkins of Colorado. Stories passed down by word of mouth and the written record from some who lived during the era enabled the author to bring out the emotions, political thinking, and environmental problems of that era. Kathleen Wilham of Shelbyville used her expertise as a genealogist to sharpen the accuracy of events and people.

Special thanks goes to Hazel Bates of Palmyra. From her publications on the Bates, the Howells, and others came much background material, especially the writings of Bennie Howell that enlivened realistically the people and setting near Paris, Missouri. Eldon Mette of Palmyra furnished a vast amount of wonderful material that described from different viewpoints the happenings in Palmyra.

The ranger at Athens State Park, Roger Boyd, was generous with his time and resources. Legends, some myths, and recorded material brought forth a virtual reality to the events at Athens, Missouri. Julia McKee Connelly, the granddaughter of John McKee, a participant in the Battle of Athens, gave many insights and stories of the lifestyle and events around Kahoka, Athens and surrounding area. Similarly Lucretia Craw, a great granddaughter of Willis Boulware, living on the John Newton Boulware property, furnished key information about Boulware history.

The staff of the State Historical Society at Columbia was invaluable in helping with many recorded events from official military records as well as state and county historical records. The map collection of Missouri, its counties and cities helped to depict accurately buildings, roads and topography of 1861 and 1862. Finally, I wish to thank my editor, Dr. Don Brenner. His expert eye and talents gave polish and clarity to the work, especially to the more complex events.

List of Fiction Characters

In order of appearance

1. Doctor Anthony Ogden Rollins
2. Mrs. Nancy Rollins
3. Johnny Jenkins
4. Zeke Slater
5. Blake Slater
6. Lieutenant Steed
7. Isaiah Flack
8. Ezra Flack
9. Elizabeth Flack
10. Sam Huett
11. Marney Huett (the shaman)
12. Sam's father

Introduction

Without railroads and steamships, the North would not have been able to bring its power to bear and probably would have lost the war (1).

Upon the election of Abraham Lincoln in November 1860, leaders in the southern states realized that a strong antislavery populace in the North had also sent antislavery congressmen and senators to Washington, notably three-fourths of the Republicans elected. James McPherson accurately portrayed the fears of the South when he quoted an article from the Richmond Examiner; "A party founded on a single sentiment...of hatred of African slavery, is now the controlling power (2)."

In the midst of this portentous time, on December 31, 1860, the 21st General Assembly of the State of Missouri opened in Jefferson City. The voters had given Lincoln only ten percent of the state's votes for president. They elected a pro-slavery governor, Claiborne Fox Jackson of Independence, who had led Missouri "ruffians" in the border war with Kansas (1854-1861), ironically, against a young Union Captain, Nathaniel Lyon, who would soon be the Governor's nemesis. And the majority of the 133 state representatives and 33 senators held beliefs similar to Jackson (3).

Two representatives elected from northeast Missouri, both conditional secessionists, played critical roles in the events of 1861. John McAfee was elected to the Legislature for the first time in 1844. He was elected to his fourth term in 1860 and won election as Speaker of the House. Born in

1

Clairborne Fox Jackson.
Used by permission, State Historical Society of Missouri, Columbia.

John McAfee.
Used by permission, State Historical Society of Missouri, Columbia.

Lexington, Kentucky in 1808, he moved to Marion County, Missouri, in 1832. In 1834 he ran for the legislature but his future father-in-law, Major Obediah Dickerson, defeated the outgoing, ambitious youngster. He moved to Monroe County the following year where he remained until 1840. During these years he married Emily Dickerson who was born in Paris, Kentucky, in 1818. Their first child, Caroline, was born in 1839. The next year the family removed to Shelby County where he engaged in law practice and merchandising. He played a conspicuous part as leader of the pro-slavery contingency (4,5).

John Newton Boulware was elected to the 21st General Assembly from Clark County, the most northeasterly county in Missouri. Born March 20, 1806, in Franklin County, Kentucky, he migrated to Missouri, marrying Nancy Gash in March of 1834 in Marion County. In 1821 Nancy's older sister Martha had married Moses D. Bates, the founder of Hannibal (6). John Newton and Nancy had five children, although two died before Nancy. After Nancy's death in 1844 John Newton moved the family to Clark County, where by 1860 he had a 1300-acre plantation with 16 slaves near Gregory landing. He fought in the Black Hawk War (7).

Newspapers throughout the state of Missouri reported the political maneuverings in Washington and the events around Fort Sumter. And Governor Jackson had access to the thinking of the "cotton states." In his inaugural speech given January third, 1861, Jackson said, "The destiny of the slaveholding states of this union is one and the same... Missouri will not be found to shrink from the duty which her position upon the border imposes; her honor, her interests, and her sympathies point alike in one direction and determine her to stand by the South (8)."

One important key to victory for the Union troops rested in their ability to control the railroads in western Virginia and in Missouri. The Baltimore and Ohio Railroad traversed along two hundred miles of the Ohio River on the western

Counties of Northeast Missouri - 1861

border of Virginia. The Hannibal-St. Joseph Railroad ran through the entire state of Missouri, dividing it into north and south. Success in gaining control of these land routes by the Union also would help gain control of the rivers, the Ohio, the Missouri, and the upper Mississippi.

Hence, except for Missouri, the allegiance of all of the upper-South states seemed settled by mid-year 1861. Virginia, North Carolina, Tennessee and Arkansas aligned with the Confederate States of America. Of these four, Virginia, even though it faced problems in the western part of the state, had been the most influential in leading others to the confederacy. July proved the month that made secession bittersweet for Virginia because northwest Virginia had set the stage when only five of thirty-one delegates voted for an ordinance of secession (2). Union troops moved into the area in May, and on June 21st George B. McClellan took command of troops in the area and amassed 20,000 men in western Virginia, using several thousand to guard the railroad. On July 11th he sent William S. Rosecrans's Ohio and Indiana regiments against the Confederates under Robert S. Garnett, killing 170 of the rebels. Rosecrans pursued the army of 3000 and struck their rear on July 13. This campaign freed northwest Virginia of organized Confederate forces (9). The Union controlled the Baltimore and Ohio Railroad and along with Kentucky's neutrality also controlled the Ohio River.

Eyes turned toward the west because Missouri occupied a strategic position for control of river traffic between the Ohio and Mississippi Rivers and the traffic on the Missouri to points west. The Hannibal-St. Joseph Railroad was a vital overland supply route to Kansas and Nebraska. But control of the Hannibal-St. Joseph Railroad demanded that the Union overcome strong sympathies for the Confederacy in northeast Missouri, manifested by sabotage of the Hannibal-St. Joseph and North Missouri Railroads as well as a growing rebel force.

Bitter and scurrilous, yet intimate and at times irrational, the numerous skirmishes and clandestine guerilla tactics put the war's scars on the landscape of a major portion of northeast Missouri. Beyond political and physical battles, the slavery issue cast an ominous cloud over the Bible belt by dividing the churches, an ugly division, a polemic that shredded the very spiritual fiber of its faithful.

The depiction of battles, skirmishes, and most other events in the work that follows is based on research and an amalgamation, in some cases, of historical data culled from newspaper accounts of that time and official military reports, as well as historical records of various counties. No attempt has been made to describe conflicts as a "battle" or a "skirmish" based on number of combatants. Loss of life and number of wounded as well as length of encounter certainly qualify many events as battle even when the number of combatants is not huge as in the eastern war zone.

Fictional characters, used by and large as the main characters, pull together the diverse events, allowing the use of family stories handed down by letter or word of mouth, as well as legends and even some myths. Great effort has been made to reflect as realistically as possible the emotional, social, religious, and political environment experienced by historical figures as well as the fictional characters.

The author

Prologue

Overview 1861

Following the skirmishes for control of western Virginia, Union and Confederate leaders prepared for a "ninety-day war." But with little discipline in the enlisted troops who were commanded by officers appointed on political merit and with little or no experience both sides made a slow start. The first real battle in the East, the battle of Bull Run, brought together on July 21st huge armies: 35,752 Union troops (Confederate authorities claimed 54,140) and 31,840 Confederate soldiers. The Union forces suffered 481 dead, 1011 wounded and 1216 missing. The Confederates had 387 killed, 1582 wounded and 632 missing. Although not a major victory for the rebels, the defeat caused the Federals to delay their invasion of Virginia (1). In the next significant conflict on the 21st of October, the Union forces tried to drive the Confederates from the Leesburg area, located forty miles north of Washington. Once again, political appointments and inexperience cost the Federal troops dearly. Crossing the Potomac River, they tried to take Ball's Bluff and lost almost half of their 1600 men, many drowning when they retreated back across the river (2).

The only bright light for Lincoln in the dismal war months of 1861 was the capture of Port Royal, South Carolina, the best natural harbor along the southern Atlantic coast. Utilizing clever tactics designed by Commanding Officer Samuel du Pont, Union ships on November 11th silenced the guns of the two forts guarding the entrance to Port Royal Bay. The four-hour battle demoralized the Confederates along the coast, because it forced them to recognize the superior sea power of the Union (3,4).

Outside of northeast Missouri, the war in Missouri in 1861 tilted toward the rebels. Citizens of Carthage, a town of 500 in southwest Missouri, saw the beginning of the confrontations on July 5th. Governor Jackson had amassed 4,000 men, moving them south to train and equip before returning to fight Union forces. Although only 2,000 rebels, clad in civilian clothes, were armed, they managed to outmaneuver the gray-clad Hessians under Colonel Franz Sigel. Outnumbered by four to one, Sigel with his seven cannon made the encounter a hotly contested battle that lasted all day. Eventually, Sigel was forced to retreat and Jackson continued his march south (5). On August 10th at the Battle of Wilson's Creek in southwest Missouri, the former Governor of Missouri, General Sterling Price, with a force of 13,000 men defeated a smaller Union force of 5,500 men under General Nathaniel Lyon. Each side suffered over 1300 casualties. The Federal troops retreated (5,6) and the victorious Price headed north, adding recruits to his army. On September 17th Price, with a force of 18,000, surrounded 2,800 Union soldiers from the Twenty-third Illinois Infantry and the Thirteenth Missouri Regiment at Lexington, located on the Missouri River between Kansas City and St. Louis (5,6). The entire Union force surrendered on September 20th.

On November 7th Colonel Ulysses Grant, commander of the Illinois 21st regiment, crossed the Mississippi River from Illinois and attacked a rebel camp at Belmont in southeast Missouri. Although he inflicted great casualties amongst the Confederates (642 casualties and 175 prisoners), he was forced to retreat, suffering 485 lost and having to leave the wounded behind as his undisciplined men made for the boats (6). In spite of another defeat for the Union forces in Missouri, the rebels failed to gain control of the railroads and rivers, due mostly to the Union strategy in northeast Missouri (4).

Capture of Camp Jackson
St. Louis, May 10, 1861

He was the only one in the entire camp in civilian clothes, but he did not feel the least bit self-conscious. The eyes, holding years of experience and trained from professional encounters, scrutinizing people, reading their obvious ailments, or interpreting subtle movements, scanned Lindell's Grove. Rows and rows of tents stretched among the trees, their white tops appearing in happy contrast to the surrounding green. A more fitting spot to soften the severities and increase the comforts of soldiers' lives could not have been chosen (7).

Doctor Anthony Ogden Rollins was named after his father, Anthony Wayne Rollins, who was born in Pennsylvania, attended Jefferson College in Philadelphia and became one of Missouri's pioneer physicians. He had six children, sons John and Robert never married, two sisters, Eliza and Sarah, married. Ogden's famous brother, James Sydney, elected to the U. S. Legislature in 1860, was father of the University of Missouri in Columbia (8). He wouldn't call his younger brother Anthony Junior, called him Ogden.

Slowly the wary physician let the harmonious view replace the after-image, the scene when they had entered Camp Jackson at three o'clock, a little over two hours previously. When the squad from Company B picked him up at noon, the boyish private waited in the medical supply wagon for him to placate the concerns of Mrs. Rollins. "Nancy, you needn't worry, I'm only a civilian consultant for Colonel Blair and Captain Lyon," he told her. "No danger," he had added, all the reassurances accompanied by a warm smile failing to erase the fear from her eyes. Their residence, on Locust near Beaumont Street, sat next to the Beaumont residence, a duplex built in 1855, two years after the death of the famous surgeon, William Beaumont, for whom the city fathers named the street. Doctor Beaumont's military friend since Prairie du Chien days in Wisconsin, Col. E. A. Hitchcock, had come to St. Louis in 1855 and helped the widow Beaumont. Some say he returned because of strong feelings for Sarah, the Beaumonts' thirty-three year-old daughter. Ogden knew how futile any serious relationship would be — Sarah had suffered through two mean marriages and was more interested in the security she found in her mother Deborah and little Lilly, her daughter (9).

Ogden had complained to the driver of the wagon, Private George Jenkins, that he need not fetch him to Lindell Grove, but the youth told him Colonel Blair insisted. While the short trip of less than a mile west on Olive, an early Plank Road, gave Ogden an opportunity to get acquainted with the boy of eighteen, the horde of citizens soon made him thankful he was riding, and under the protection of blue coats. People jammed Olive Street. Many loaded down Olive Street railcars (10).

Near Compton Street, the northeast end of Lindell Grove, they caught up with the 3rd Union volunteers under Colonel Franz Sigel. His force had started early in the morning from the Arsenal, marched north on Carondolet to Broadway, turned west on Olive, and from there moved to Compton. The artillery company with twenty pieces under Colonel Totten had accompanied Sigel and busied themselves with securing positions on elevations at Grand on the west end and along Olive on the north side, giving them command of the camp's entire length. Blair and Lyon had left the Arsenal and turned off Broadway at Market, marching their six thousand troops west. Traveling six miles in all, Colonel Boernstein had left the Marine Hospital, located just south of the Arsenal, with his staff and men of the 2nd volunteers and marched up Broadway and then headed west on Chouteau Avenue, turning north on Jefferson, where they took Laclede Avenue west, and stationed themselves so that

CAPTURE CAMP JACKSON

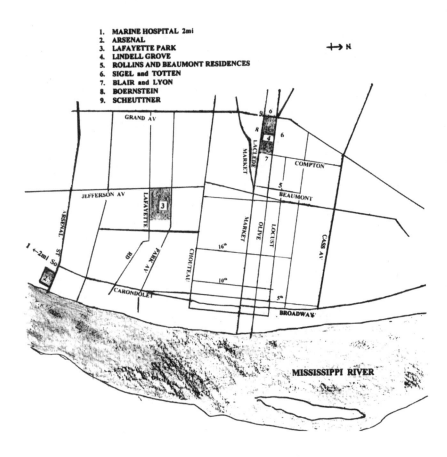

1. MARINE HOSPITAL 2mi
2. ARSENAL
3. LAFAYETTE PARK
4. LINDELL GROVE
5. ROLLINS AND BEAUMONT RESIDENCES
6. SIGEL and TOTTEN
7. BLAIR and LYON
8. BOERNSTEIN
9. SCHEUTTNER

they covered the entire south border of the grove. The 4th volunteers under Colonel Nic Scheuttner started from the Arsenal but branched off on Market Street and followed it until it turned southwest, continuing west on Laclede Avenue to occupy positions on the south side near the east end of Lindell Grove (11).

With the camp surrounded, Lyon issued an ultimatum to General Frost, Rebel commander, giving him twenty minutes to surrender or suffer an attack. Frost replied that he needed more time. Lyon denied the West Pointer's appeal, and at the last instant Frost surrendered. This power of men and arms descending on Lindell Grove portended a medical catastrophe of untold proportions, certain to be compounded by the immense crowd of people who arrived by carriage, buggies, railcars, baggage wagons, horseback, or on foot. Many men carried rifles, shotguns, or whatever weapons they could find. Their intent, obviously, was to rush to the assistance of the Rebel camp, but the Union Army obstructed them (10). Ogden let that image of hordes in the streets give way to the tents, the flags gently waving in the breeze. The surrender and the occupation of the camp had been orderly, peaceful.

"What does your family do? Where did you say home is, Private?" Ogden searched the light blue eyes. He realized he had been wrestling with his own emotions and had neglected the anxieties of this young greenhorn named George Jenkins.

"They were farmers in Clark County, Doctor — in California now. My mom and two sisters left for the west with my step-dad in '57 (12)."

"Left you behind?" Ogden puzzled at this, but figured whatever the reason it undoubtedly accounted for the young man's maturity.

"Brother Johnny — he was twelve then — was hurt bad the day before the caravan left. He couldn't travel, not even certain he'd live, and they had paid lots of money and waited months to get on the list, so I stayed behind to look after him. When he got better I was supposed to take him to California. By the time he was well enough to travel winter had set in. And the next spring we both decided we liked our new homes better than that of our step-father, so we never went to California."

"But that was four years ago."

"I stayed at my Uncle Robert's farm with a bunch of cousins. I helped on the farm. Brother Johnny worked for Doc McKee, stayed with a Quaker family."

"So your young brother is a Quaker. And you, your family?"

"My cousins' family has always gone to the Christian Church in Alexandria (13). Rev. Matlock gives interesting sermons about the war and slavery," George said and stared at Ogden.

"For or against both?" Ogden turned and saw consternation cross George's face.

"Well...." George paused while he eased back on the reins to let a squad of soldiers cross their path. "You know, he never tells the congregation. He seems to give arguments both ways and challenges the people to believe what they think God wants them to believe."

"Clever. My family has been Presbyterian for ages. In 1837 the Presbyterian Church split over the slavery issue, resulting in Old and New School Churches. And in 1857 the New School Church in Missouri was so anti-slavery that the action of the General Assembly on slavery drove all the slave holding states to withdraw."

"How did the churches in St. Louis react?"

"Little discussion on the subject was held in the Old School Churches (14). In fact, the sentiment of the whole state, not just St. Louis, was that nothing should be said against slavery, so my wife and I started to attend the Unitarian Church of the Messiah. The pastor, William Eliot, is an excellent preacher, an outspoken Union Loyalist (15).

Brother James and wife are very active in the Presbyterian Church in Columbia. All the Rollins are loyal...."

"It seems to me that most people in my area are loyal to the Union," George interjected, but stared at Ogden, paused before adding, "Even those with slaves, church people as well as those who don't bother with going to church."

"A secessionist representative and the fire-eater, former U.S. Senator Green, are from that part of the state, from Canton."

Jenkins cleared his throat. "Senator Green is from Monticello, eleven miles west of Canton. Judge Boulware, the legislator, lives about ten miles from us. The farm I've been living on is close to the Des Moines River, near a village you never heard of, St. Francisville."

Ogden chuckled. "Heard of it." Ogden watched as Jenkins broke into a smile.

"Doctor McKee said I should apply to McDowell. But I needed money so in January I joined the Canton Guard for six months. Colonel Moore sent me down here to get training as a surgeon's helper."

"Doctor McKee's mother is a Lapsley, sister to my wife. Good folk." Ogden recognized the Captain approaching, the one who brought Jenkins and the squad to his house five hours earlier. He smiled.

Captain Constantine Blandowski, the son of a Polish immigrant, took great pride in his Union captaincy. He had told Ogden on the way to the camp that his family already thought he was a hero because as a foreigner he had been promoted to the rank of Captain (16). The horse stopped beside the wagon. Ogden could see black hair under the blue cap, its shiny black bill reflecting the rays that meandered through the overhead green canopy. Dark blue eyes sat in a round face, the clean-shaven face nonetheless dark from the heavy beard and swarthy complexion.

"Doctor, you can't teach Jenkins much medicine from today's encounter." He glanced over his shoulder at the crowd of gray uniformed men starting to form a line three abreast.

Ogden watched while General Daniel M. Frost rode a horse to the head of the column, followed by his staff. "Luckily the boss of the U.S. Army in St. Louis, General Harney, went east. He wouldn't have been as forceful as Captain Lyon (17)."

Suddenly, with colors flying and drums beating, the captured Confederate column, bordered on each side by Federals, marched through the woods skirting the road and went through a hole cut in the fence near the turnpike (10). Blandowski told Ogden they would stay off to the side and fall in at the rear and once out of the grove head for the Rollins house.

"Still my job to secure your safe return home, Doctor," he announced, and with his cap pointed to the end of the column.

Finally, about half past five the Rebel column of prisoners, the single file of their captors stretching along each side, entered the road. Rhythmical tromp-tromp of hundreds of boots resounded throughout the grove and generated opaque brown dust that hung as a shroud over the procession. Within minutes, however, the atmosphere was shredded. A cacophony of rifle shots engulfed Ogden. His heart jumped in his chest. The shattering blasts seemed to come from every side, from high windows and at ground level — probably from Rebel sympathizers he surmised as he squinted at women, men, and children running helter-skelter, some falling to the sod of the grove (10). He felt a breeze pass his cheek and his hat flew over the side of the wagon just as Blandowski lurched forward and then fell from his saddle (16). The horse bolted but struck the wagon and froze.

"Doctor Rollins," Jenkins shrieked.

Ogden jumped from the wagon, crawled under the horse's belly and reached Blandowski's side. He groped for a pulse in the Union officer's bloody neck, put his hand behind the head to examine the pupils and fought back the urge to vomit. He removed his hand from the hole in back of Blandowski's head, and feeling Jenkins pressing his side, wiped the brain tissue and blood on his shirt and stared at the panic-struck face. He fought back nausea, swallowed gastric contents that welled in his throat.

Jenkins gasped and Ogden repressed the impulse to tell him about the hole in Blandowski's head. He surveyed the surroundings. Wounded and dead on both sides — including many civilian Rebel sympathizers — had turned the beautiful grove into a battlefield. Ogden spied a girl reclining against a tree stump, her ghost-white face immobile with the mask of death (10).

"No!" He screamed, hurdled over a man struggling to his feet, and grabbed the limp body, a girl of fourteen. He felt for a pulse in her neck and searched the eyes. "My God, no," he shrieked at the skies and clutched the cold figure to his chest, blood from her mouth spilling on his chest.

A tug at his shoulder turned him to peer in Jenkins' face. "You know her," the pale-faced youth said.

"Emily Sommers. Her parents live on Carr around 17th street (10)," he said and gingerly placed the girl by the stump. The cries of pain from writhing forms nearby transformed the man of sorrow to the professional physician.

Anthony Ogden Rollins stood tall, straightened his tie and held Jenkins in his gaze by grasping both shoulders. "The dead do not need us. But many here do. Go get the bandages and laudanum. We have much work to do." He forced a warm, half smile.

Close to midnight Jenkins stopped the buggy in front of the Rollins residence. Three Union soldiers, now minus their captain, hovered around. Ogden saw the glow of a lantern in the front doorway. Of course, Nancy would wait, wouldn't be able to sleep. Perhaps her faith could assure her he was alive, but most likely the years of caring, understanding the emotional, the spiritual, suffering he must endure kept her awake.

Ogden turned to the soldiers and asked, "Where you headed?"

"The Arsenal, Sir," the older soldier replied.

"Better go south on Grand and down Arsenal to go back," he said, smiled at Jenkins and added, "Safe from the street mobs."

On the porch he grabbed at his wife. She, with her eyes looking at the bloody shirt, illuminated orange-red from the lantern, restrained him, then grabbed a hand and led him into the kitchen. Nancy placed the lantern on the table, spun about, wiped her moist cheeks and leaned over to administer a peck. Ogden raised his eyes from his chest, realizing what had inhibited the normally administered emotional hug. He smiled and leaned over. Her lips were hot and her eyes pools of liquid. With help she sat, and he pulled up a chair and sat near for their usual séance when he suffered and she, the seasoned high school teacher and his personal pacifier, soothed his soul.

Staring at the shirt and then his red chest, an eerie sight in the subdued lantern glow, she said, "Bad, huh?"

Jolted by the lingering after-image of the grove battlefield, he struggled. Words wouldn't form, only tears. Nancy clutched a hand and squeezed. Silence. Unashamedly, he let the stream run onto his chest, sending a pink stream into his bellybutton. "Two soldiers dead; one, that nice Captain that came for me, shot in the head." He sobbed and pointed to the blood. "That's his. Two more will die before morning. Sixteen civilians died in Lindell Grove, four more later at the City Hospital (10). Many wounded cared for there and at the Good Samaritan Hospital where our friend, Reverend Nollau, is superintendent (10). Wounded soldiers treated by Doctor Bill McPheeters, chief surgeon at the Marine Hospital (13)." Ogden scooted the chair around the corner of the table and hugged Nancy, fixed soft eyes on her. "The

THE ARSENAL AT ST. LOUIS, MISSOURI.—[Sketched by Alexander Simplot.]

The Arsenal at St. Louis.
Used by permission, State Historical Society of Missouri, Columbia.

civilians. One was Emily Sommers, the one you had in class this year. Killed instantly. She…" He stopped, frozen by the most distorted face he had ever seen portrayed by his wife of twenty years. Convulsive gasps escaped as a rhythmical moan. Ogden helped Nancy out of the chair, picked up the lantern, and led her to the bedroom.

Nancy Lapsley had taught in elementary school in Lexington, Kentucky, in 1844 when Ogden studied medicine at Transylvania University. They met at a forum, a debate about slavery. Soon after, they married and moved to St. Louis, Ogden joining the faculty at McDowell Medical College and Nancy teaching at an elementary school. When the first high school west of the Mississippi River, moved to the corner of 15th and Olive Streets on January 6, 1856, Nancy secured a position teaching English and was the only married teacher in the entire city (18). The building with a hundred-foot high tower sat on the western limits of the city at that time, but now it rested well within the city.

After he had washed the blood from his body, he returned to the dark bedroom and climbed under the covers. A hand grappled for him, found his hand, and held tightly. "Nancy, I thought I would die in '49 when daughter Amy got cholera. After she died and for a week while you hovered on the brink, I knew I would never face such agony again." He waited.

"I know. She was only three when she passed on, and I didn't want to live. You told me I had to or else you'd die and lots of cholera victims wouldn't live without your help."

Ogden felt her warmth when she rolled on her side against him. Peace flowed over him, her body seemed to melt.

"Emily and her parents were three of many you saved that year."

He reached over and scratched her back. "They had her twelve more years than we had Amy. But the nonsense is what hurts. This evening when the streets filled with angry people, Mayor Taylor spoke at Planters House trying to explain to the mob (10). If Chief McDonough hadn't brought out some twenty policemen (10), who knows how many more would be dead."

He felt a wet peck on his cheek and the bed crunched as she rolled over, her back to him. As though the soft words reached his ears by reverberating from the wall, he heard, "For years I've felt badly I couldn't give you another daughter or a son. With this madness, I'm happy not to have a child to send to fight."

"There wasn't supposed to be a fight. The surrender was peaceful." The words spawned ugly images. Blandowski so young, Emily a child, he muttered to the pillow. *The young can't die. Lord, I can help by..."* Sleep obliterated more ugly scenes.

Chapter 1

Battle at Monroe Station
July 10

Johnny Jenkins tried to act interested in his companion's details about the Salt River Road they had taken from St. Francisville, but an old resolve kept prodding his brain. He blurted, "I got to get in med school, Dr. McKee."

Dr. Robert S. McKee, the twenty-nine year old son of Robert A. McKee, had attended Keokuk College of Physicians and Surgeons, first for ten months in 1855-56. He had to interrupt his medical education and return to the family farm outside of St. Francisville for a year until his father's health improved. In 1858 he completed his medical education and immediately joined Doctor O. B. Payne in St. Francisville (1). Dr. McKee grinned. "I know, Johnny. That's why we will stop in Palmyra before heading for Hannibal." He paused as Red lurched up the far bank.

Johnny held the reins tight for he knew Red was fidgety from the clatter of his hoofs and the thunder the heavy wagon made on the old wooden bridge. He wiped the dust-laden sweat from his face with his shirt, but mulled over his outburst. He peeked at McKee, intently surveying the river, looking upriver and then down. "Tell me about Palmyra. I took a steamer to Hannibal. Never been to Palmyra."

McKee gestured with an arm, "This is the North River. Palmyra sits on high ground between this stream and the South River. It's known as 'Two Rivers Country,' famed for its beautiful, rich valleys, its wild game, and its faithful springs (2,3). See, down there the Quincy Railroad Bridge crosses the river and joins the Hannibal-St. Joseph Railroad in Palmyra. It's only 12 miles west of Hannibal and only four miles from the Mississippi River. Martin Alley Gash, one of Palmyra's first settlers along with John Palmer, moved from Buncombe County, North Carolina, in 1821 and built a log cabin on the banks of the South River (3). His oldest daughter, Martha, married Moses D. Bates, founder of Hannibal, and another daughter, Nancy, married John Newton Boulware, our rebel legislator."

"Been a year since I finished all high school courses they offer at the school in St. Francisville. Mr. Civer, my teacher all these years (4), got me some advanced books, like they have in colleges. I read them and..." Johnny smiled at McKee and continued. "I have read everything Lincoln wrote, all his speeches that's been in the papers."

The wagon moved along Main Street. Headquarters for many Union soldiers from Iowa and Illinois, Palmyra, a town of 3000 in 1861 (4), teemed with frenetic activity, soldiers on horseback and supply wagons clogging Main Street and stirring up clouds of dust. Johnny guided Red south on Main Street amongst the horde of wagons and horses. McKee pointed to the hitching post in front of the courthouse. Before disappearing into the courthouse he told Johnny that in 1855 this structure replaced the original one built in 1835 after it burned to the ground (5). But McKee's last words rang in his ears, "I heard that a professor from St. Louis is here in Palmyra, Johnny. Dr. Anthony Rollins is married to my mother's sister. He was on the faculty at McDowell Medical College before the war began. Now he trains army surgeons for the Union. I am told he is up in these parts, helping outfit the medial teams for units from Iowa and Illinois, the troops stationed here and Hannibal to protect the railroad. I won't be long. I'll find out if he is here or in Hannibal. He'll be a good connection for medical school."

Johnny waved and with a cat like swiftness swatted a fly that landed on his cheek. He climbed down, stood next to Red, held the bit firmly, and kept up a steady stream of chatter to soothe the jumpy horse, nervous and tossing its head with each wagon that rumbled close by. Red watched Johnny out the corner of his left eye and raked a hoof along the dirt street. Through the brown vapor that slowly rose to the sky, Johnny caught a glimpse of the white ball perched on top of the courthouse. He let a grin creep across his face when he conjured up an image of older brother George. *I'm goin' to get in med school like you, George,* he muttered, but threw back his head when a gust of air carried street dust and a strong scent of horse. A shadow fell on Red and blocked the shrouded sunlight. Hairs on Johnny's neck bristled.

"Hey, Blake, it's owl eyes," a squeaky voice sounded behind him.

"Nah, Zeke, the nigger lover."

That voice sounded all too familiar. Johnny Hamilton Jenkins recognized the voice of his archenemy, its mounting volume drowning out the street hubbub. The clamor failed to mask the racing pulse in his head. He slowly turned, nonchalantly leaning against the wagon while he rested an arm on the removable side of the wagon, letting his hand dangle under the seat. He pinched the end of his straight, pointed nose, then removed the tattered, black hat, shook his long blonde hair, and fanned his face with the floppy.

"Whew. I declare. This here town suffers with so many ruffians." He raised his eyes and stared first at Zeke, the baby-faced sixteen year-old Slater his age. Zeke fixed his gaze to his right, his mouth uttering sounds too faint for Johnny's ears so he watched for the reaction of Blake Slater, Zeke's older brother. Blake's square face, its black stubble making him appear more than his twenty years, seemed to threaten Zeke. "What brings two of St. Francisville's worst rebs way down here into Union territory?" Johnny said.

Blake snapped his head toward Johnny, raised in the saddle, and peered past him. A grin eased over his face. "Doctor McKee's wagon? You Doc's slave, ain't you?"

Johnny noted Blake's heel press into his horse's flank. He

stretched his arm under the seat of the dray and said, "Blake, you been stupid long as I knowed ya. I'm Doc McKee's assistant. We come to pick up medical supplies and take back to the Union troops at Athens. I'm goin' to be a surgeon's helper. Doctor McKee says that'll get me into medical school. Some day I'll be a doctor."

Blake threw his head back and howled. "A poor, ugly kid. 'Sides, you might get crippled more or even killed." His horse inched closer, and when its head bobbed up Johnny saw Blake's hand grab a whip from the pommel. He sidestepped toward Zeke's paint, dragging a rifle from under the seat. He poked it in Zeke's belly and threw a twisted smile at Blake. "There ain't medicine for the indigestion I'm 'bout to give."

Zeke's eyes shut. Blake reined back his horse and replaced the whip. Johnny spotted the white scar on Zeke's forehead and aimed the rifle at it. "Maybe I could make the scar I give you disappear, Zeke."

Blake raised both hands, dropped them, and parted his cracked lips as Zeke mouthed, "Not you. That ol' nigger done it."

"What's up, boys?" Dr. McKee's voice from the other side of the wagon froze Blake's lips and relaxed Johnny's muscles. His pulse slowed. He glanced over his shoulder and watched Dr. McKee, accompanied by a gray-haired man in a dark suit, stride around the wagon and stop between Johnny and the Slaters.

Johnny wiped the sweat from his forehead with his hat. "Not all the pigs got rendered in La Grange, Dr. McKee." All the while he watched the other man as he walked toward the buggy tied to the far end of the hitching post. At the buggy he removed his stiff black hat, wiped his forehead with a red kerchief he removed from his coat pocket. Eyes fixed on Blake, he flipped his head toward the buggy, a commanding motion for the Slaters to ease their horses for the man.

Johnny stuck the rifle under the seat, felt a firm arm

around his shoulder. The six-foot two-inch doctor stood six inches above Johnny. His steel blue eyes danced at Johnny, his dark brown hair blew over the left side of his face. "A good Quaker wouldn't do that." The eyes warmed with each word.

"I ain't no Quaker," Johnny said.

"If you don't want to act like one, behave like a doctor," McKee said. He watched momentarily until a squad of Union soldiers, approaching the courthouse, replaced the view of the disappearing buggy and two horses. Accompanied by a far-away look, he said, "Imagine that, Judge Boulware here and meeting with Speaker of the House McAfee. Says he and the Speaker were here to support the Union, put the secessionist legislature days behind them. Maybe."

"I recognized him. His two nephews ain't about to put the past behind. The Judge's dumb — thinks Zeke is the bad one. Blake told him Zeke was responsible for my beating. Said he came upon the fight and stopped it. Ha! Blake's a mean polecat, the one what beat me near to death."

"The Judge is very popular and powerful in Clark County and not dumb, just deceived by that rascal Blake," McKee said.

Johnny turned and stared into McKee's eyes. "Did you find Dr. Rollins?"

"He's at the depot. Been a lot of rebel activity around Monroe Station. He's going with the troop train." McKee climbed up, wiped dust off the seat and sat.

"Will I be able to meet him? Brother George wrote me that he was an assistant to a Dr. Rollins at Camp Jackson and the Battle of Boonville." Johnny rubbed the side of Red's neck and climbed in the driver's seat.

They drove south past the yellow Gardner house and four blocks further approached the depot, where a beehive of activity greeted them. McKee motioned for Johnny to stop in front of the large building across the street. A steady

John Newton Boulware.
Courtesy of Joan Jenkins, Windsor, Colorado.

stream of uniformed men carried boxes of supplies from
Holtzclaw's warehouse and store across the street to the
train (4).

"Stay with the wagon. I'm going over to the train and see
if I can find Dr. Rollins," McKee said and crossed the street.

Johnny secured the reins to the hitching post and watched
soldiers lead horses to the train, bemused by the stubborn
behavior of the animals, spooked by the moaning boiler and
the hissing steam from the locomotive.

"This is Colonel Rollins. He teaches young medical students how to act like professionals. Colonel, this is Johnny
Jenkins."

Johnny caught the subtle message from McKee. Having
worked for the young physician for the past four years tend-

ing his horses and running errands, Johnny easily recognized McKee's teaching mode with the facial signs, arm gestures, penetrating eyes. How many times had he told Johnny he needed not only learn medical things, but proper behavior. Johnny struggled to compose himself under the scrutiny of two physicians, his thoughts still rattled from the barbs hurled by the Slaters. "Colonel, I try…"

Rollins stepped forward, extended his hand and said, "Your brother George told me all about you." He cast a piercing look and added, "Call me Doctor Rollins or plain Doctor, Johnny."

McKee moved to Johnny's side and rested a hand on Johnny's shoulder. "Johnny just had a run in with the Slater boys, the nephews of our secessionist legislator — ex-legislator, John Newton Boulware, Ogden. They are the ones that beat Johnny nearly to death four years ago." He paused, rolled his head toward Ogden.

Rollins addressed Johnny, "Destruction of track and sniper fire on passing trains along the Hannibal-St. Joseph tracks has heightened. General Fremont, Commander of Union forces in Missouri, has placed General Hurlbut in charge of protecting the entire length of the Hannibal-St. Joseph Railroad. His headquarters is in Macon City. He has ordered Companies H and F of the Sixteenth Illinois Infantry, Companies A, F, and K of the 3rd Iowa Regiment, along with Company A of the Hannibal Home Guard to move from Palmyra to Monroe Station, the hot bed of anti-Union activity (6). I want you to come and be my surgical team helper."

Stunned, Johnny turned to McKee, his glee uncontainable. He stuffed his hands in his pockets while searching for a way to say yes without offending McKee. His mouth opened, but no words came out.

"It's okay, Johnny. They'll only be gone from here a couple days. While you begin your training as a surgical helper, I'll go to Hannibal and organize the medical supplies for

Colonel Moore." He grinned at Johnny, nodded to Rollins and said, "Johnny is an expert on the use of plants and herbs to treat wounds and ailments, Ogden. We were sent here to gather medical supplies for Moore's Northeast Army and take them to headquarters at Athens, some twenty miles up the Des Moines River from St. Francisville."

Johnny grabbed his bedroll from the wagon and followed Rollins to the second car behind the locomotive. At the steps stood a red-haired young man in a new looking, blue uniform.

"Lieutenant Steed, this is George's brother, Johnny Jenkins. He's training to be a surgical helper for the Northeast Union Army. Take him under your wing. He's going to be with us a couple days while we check out the situation at Monroe Station." Rollins entered the car, followed by Steed.

Johnny watched Steed, trying to mimic his every move. Steed sat in the row behind Rollins. When he scooted to the window, Johnny threw his roll in the overhead rack and eased next to him.

"Since the Illinois 16th was without a surgeon, Doctor Rollins assumed responsibility for Colonel Robert F. Smith's force and brought me as his surgical assistant. Colonel David P. Bigger, surgeon for the Illinois 9th, and the other surgical assistants that arrived with Doctor Rollins, remained at Headquarters' Hospital in Hannibal (7)," Steed said, studying Johnny all the while.

Johnny listened intently while Steed told him about brother George and his experiences at Camp Jackson (6). Steed stared longingly out the window, seemed to speak to the glass. "Agatha and I going to get married. Doctor Rollins says this fighting is supposed to be over in three months. Then I'll get hitched, maybe work in St. Louis. Your brother and I worked with a Doctor Cornyn in the battle of Boonville, the first battle of the war in Missouri. That was June 17th. Cornyn will be a good connection for George because he worked at the City Hospital in St. Louis before the war."

"Tell me about the fightin' in Boonville. Did George get any medical experience?"

Steed removed his cap and stroked his hair. "General Lyon took us from St. Louis on three steamers. He planned on capturing our rebel governor in Jefferson City, but when we got there we found Jackson gone. Upon hearing that Jackson's General, former Governor Price, had gone to Boonville and was training a rebel army, we headed up river, spending the night at Rocheport, some fifteen miles downstream from Boonville (6)."

"Was bother George excited or afraid?"

Steed smiled and replaced his cap. "Nah. He got broken

Thespian Hall, Boonville. The theatre is restored to its appearance when used as a hospital for the battle.
Photo by the author.

in at Camp Jackson. Besides, Boonville wasn't much of a fight. At dawn we landed six miles below the town and General Totten took a ship with artillery upstream and anchored opposite the rebel camp. Barely twenty minutes of gunfire and the battled ended. Your brother helped me and Doctor Rollins treat many wounded, mostly our boys. Some fifty rebs received medical care from the three town doctors at the Thespian, a theater in town."

"Did you capture Price? How about the dead?"

"Price took sick the day before and went to Glasgow. Marmaduke was the field commander. Two Union killed and fifteen Confederates. Many more rebs wounded (6). Seems of the three thousand only half had weapons — a ragtag outfit," Steed replied, shaking his head.

At Monroe Station, nineteen miles from Palmyra, the troops disembarked and headed south. Union loyalists told Captain Smith that a band of rebels camped in Florida. Late that afternoon fifty mounted secessionists commanded by Captain Clay Price ambushed the Union forces twelve miles south of Monroe Station. Captain Smith and his surprised men, along with Ogden and the surgical team, took refuge for the night at Hagar's farm, located three to four miles north of Florida. Early in the morning of the tenth they retreated to Monroe Station. Nearing the town, Johnny noted that the station house and the outhouses, seventeen passenger cars, freight cars, and other railroad property were in flames. Three to four hundred enemy soldiers collected from all directions, but a few rounds from Smith's forces routed them. Smith's troops holed up in a two-story academy building called the "Seminary," a perfect place for Ogden's green surgical team to establish a temporary hospital. While they cared for the few wounded, the troops rested and regrouped in the sturdy building (6).

However, by noon on the eleventh, the Confederates had surrounded the "Seminary". Governor Jackson had appointed Thomas A. Harris, a representative from Marion County,

Brigadier General and commander of all Confederate forces in North Missouri. Harris had established headquarters first in Paris and then in Florida. With 1000 men he joined Price's force, making a force of over fifteen hundred. Having spotted the fort-like "Seminary", Harris sent for a cannon hidden in a haystack north of Palmyra and another in the possession of Dr. William Kneisley. From a mile away the nine-pounder and six-pounder boomed, but no shells landed close.

Smith sent word to General Fremont about the siege, requesting reinforcements. Johnny observed the hundreds of spectators who dotted the hillside overlooking the academy, in a picnic atmosphere, enjoying the shelling of the brick building. The cannon fired from closer range, maybe four hundred yards, Johnny figured. The scene soon deteriorated when a load crashed through a window and exploded the wooden furniture and flooring in the area of the hospital.

Lost in the intensity of caring for five soldiers, peppered by splinters and debris from the shelling, with a couple patients already receiving attention for wounds, Johnny ignored an oppressive feeling. He coughed at the irritating smoke in the back room where he and Steed had most of the acute problems under control. Steed dragged Johnny to the front room. They found Rollins working on casualties from the Iowa 3rd.

After Steed reported that all wounds had been treated in the back room, Rollins said, "Good work. Go back and check the bandages for fresh bleeding, signs of shock." He slowly turned and looked about. "Take Jenkins. Teach him what to look for. And stay away from the windows. They might get lucky again."

By late afternoon Major Hays arrived by train from Hannibal with reinforcements for the beleaguered Union force. From a flatbed car the brass cannon opened fire with loads of grape. Unrelenting, the fire from two other cannon scattered the Confederates, but not before they got off a last barrage, three of the twenty-seven shots finding their mark, hitting the back of the "Seminary" (6).

In the front room the Iowa surgical team reviewed their casualties with Rollins. Suddenly, Johnny, his ghostly pale face smeared with sweat and black soot, appeared in the front room where he approached Rollins. "Sir, come, please. It's Lieutenant Steed." His lip quivered. "The back room took a direct hit."

While the Iowa surgeon, Dr. Charles Thompkins, directed the care of the others injured in the back room, Rollins employed Jenkins in Steed's care. The blast had knocked Steed unconscious, so Ogden used the opportunity to remove large splinters impaled in the mangled face.

"Eyes look worrisome, Doctor," Johnny blurted when Ogden had the bleeding controlled.

Ogden put an index finger over his lips and glared at the tense face. Carefully, he applied a head wrap that covered Steed's entire head except the face below the nose, leaving his mouth uncovered for breathing. Johnny felt tears welling up. He lowered his head so Rollins couldn't see the tears. Telling himself to be tough, he felt Steed's pulse. A hand raised his head. Johnny stared into the watery eyes of Rollins.

Over the thunder of the brass cannon from Hays's reinforcements Rollins said, "It's okay, Johnny. Compassion is the soul of a great physician."

The steady barrage from Union cannon sent the rebels fleeing, allowing Smith's force to return safely to Palmyra (6). Rollins transported the wounded on a flatbed, but kept Steed in a coach car stretched out on two adjoining seats. Holtzclaw's warehouse in Palmyra served as a temporary hospital for further care and observation of the wounded before being moved to the main military hospital in Hannibal.

General Fremont had responded to Smith's call. He ordered Colonel Williams from St. Joseph to board his forces on a train and make haste for Monroe Station, but Williams was detained at Brookfield by a burned out railway bridge. Of the other two forces Fremont sent to relieve

Battle of Monroe Station

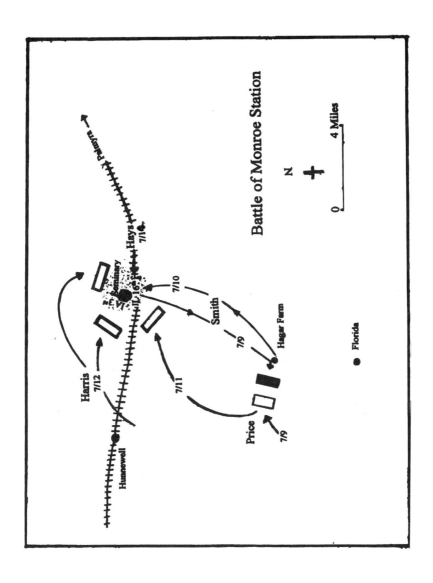

Smith, Gen. S. A. Hurlbut arrived the evening Smith escaped. Colonel U. S. Grant, in St. Louis from his reconnaissance in southeast Missouri, had boarded his men on the North Missouri Railroad at St. Charles. They arrived the following day. During the next week skirmishes occurred in Fulton, Millersville, Mexico, and Wentzville (8).

Melancholy, not fatigue, possessed Johnny after helping Rollins care for Steed over the next two days. Colonels Bigger and Thompkins cared for the other hospital patients while the assistant surgeons took care of morning sick call and outpatient follow-up care of wounded. Steed had moved and groaned the past two days but hadn't opened his eyes at the last dressing change.

Johnny saw pus oozing from both eye sockets. "Do you have medicine for that, Doctor?" He pointed at the yellow on the old bandage.

Ogden ushered him outside the room and stopped at the front door of the warehouse, his eyes narrowed, searching Johnny's. "None. I have no medicine. Do you pray?" Ogden turned for the train depot.

"I have been praying for Steed. I pray every day, Doctor," Johnny shouted over the clatter of a carriage that rumbled by.

Ogden paused to let it pass and at the opposite side of the street he turned and smiled at Johnny. "We doctors do what little we can. God does the healing. That you must believe, Johnny."

Johnny watched Ogden enter the depot. A gentle breeze ruffled his hair. He looked up at the treetops and muttered, "I believe, God."

Harassment of the North Missouri Railroad continued and Major Hays began scouring the woods in Callaway County for rebels. The Department of the Army made changes at the top; Major General John C. Fremont assumed command of the Western department for the Union Army, and Brig. General John Pope was appointed the new commander of all the forces in North Missouri (8). Lyon continued to move troops southwest to prepare for the massing of Southern troops in northwestern Arkansas. He assigned General Hurlbut the command of all forces for the entire length of the Hannibal-St. Joseph and the North Missouri Railroads (6). Hurlbut placed officers in strategic spots along the railroad where each set up headquarters at Warrenton, Macon, Renick, Sturgeon, and Mexico. Hurlbut, annoyed by the continued firing on trains and the destruction of track, ordered that anyone caught in such activities be arrested (2).

Outside Steed's room the morning McKee said he and Johnny must depart for Athens, Ogden grabbed Johnny by the collar, loosened his grip when alarm in the blue eyes matched the alarm on the lean face. "Johnny, you've done a good job. Talk too much, though." He let go and cast a warm smile. "The Lieutenant is fully conscious. His first dressing change as far as he knows. I don't know how much he can see." He moved to within an inch. "Do you read me?"

Johnny nodded his head.

Ogden sat on the edge of Steed's bed and said, "Michael, it's Professor Rollins."

Frantically, a hand groped the air for Ogden. "Thank God, you're my doctor. Jenkins tells me I've been unconscious for three days. That…the soldier I was caring for?"

"He died. Absorbed most of the blast. You got a blow to the face and head. Lots of inflammation," Rollins answered.

"I can move all extremities. Scars? Please tell me."

Ogden swallowed hard. Squinted at Johnny. "Small. Agatha will see them as hero's badges." Slowly, as he talked he removed the dressing, leaning over with the last layer so his head blocked the bright overhead light from Steed's eyes.

Ogden handed the mass of bandages to Johnny who took them but kept his eyes glued on Steed. Heartbeats thumped in Johnny's throat. Silence. One eyelid, then the other raised. One blink, two, repeated. Two red eyes stared straight at

Ogden's face. Heavy breathing filled the room.

"You still here, Professor?" Steed rubbed an index finger over his bare forehead, over eyebrows, eyelids slowly.

"Here," Ogden managed, jabbing a finger in Johnny's chest to stop the gush of air, and leaned back so the full brightness of the light shone in Steed's eyes.

"Lots of inflammation, Sir? Can't we turn on a dim lantern so I can see? Is it too early?"

"A bit, Michael. Don't fret. Remember this scripture from the first epistle of Peter, chapter five, verse seven, 'Casting all your care upon him; for he careth for you.' Healing takes time, Michael."

Ogden patted Steed's shoulder, motioned for Johnny to bandage Steed's face and departed. After Johnny finished the dressing, he told Steed to rest. With hurried steps Johnny headed for the door, walked behind the warehouse and cowered behind a rain barrel to avoid scrutiny. He sat, pulled both legs up, wrapped his arms around them and cried. "He's so young, God — so terribly young — for what?" His refuge blocked out the street noises and the sounds of the activity at the train station. A chirping snapped up his head. Johnny searched the nearby bushes, but the blurred images obscured his view. He used his shirttail to wipe his eyes and spotted a brown speckled sparrow perched on a woodpile. One of the favorite scriptures the Quakers taught him came to mind. A second sparrow with a black throat landed next to the chirping bird. He spoke to his feathered audience, "Behold the fowls of the air: for they sow not, neither do they reap, nor gather into barns, yet your heavenly Father feeds them." He bowed his head and prayed, "Lord, send Jesus here to take spittle with some dirt and put it on Steed's eyes." Johnny bit his lip when he recalled how Rollins quoted scripture to Steed. He mumbled, "I can't quote where those verses are found in the Bible." The birds chirped. He smiled and, pointing a finger at the bushes, said, "I wish I could fly home to St. Francisville. No war up there."

Chapter 2

Battle at Athens
August 5

Wagons filled with supplies for the Union army in Athens rattled down Main Street in St. Francisville. Johnny gazed past the town square, filled with gawking town folk, past Fort Pike, a small blockhouse that guarded the opening of the square to the Des Moines River (1). He spied the river-bank, cluttered with piles of supplies, men trudging from the steamer, a scene that made him chuckle, "Guess the war's reached way up here."

"You still set on fighting, Johnny?"

The brassy voice of Dr. O. B. Payne (2) interrupted his daydreaming. He turned, peered at the figured seated on the wagon called a dray because by removing it's side it served as an ambulance. He smiled at the eager, lean face of the most popular doctor in northeastern Missouri, the most successful of the three in St. Francisville. The town folks said he was better than the two in Athens and the three in Alexandria.

"Nope. But I'm goin' to be your assistant. Aren't I?"

"Pretty young for even that, Johnny."

"I'm soon seventeen. If you don't want my help, I'll just take this here steamer to Canton." Johnny pointed past Fort Pike toward a small side-wheeler resting in the shallows of the Des Moines River. "I'm goin' to join George after Athens, anyhow." He watched the doctor wrinkle his nose, then turn to a horse and rider to his right.

"This is John McKee. No relation to my partner. His pa's a farmer, businessman in Athens (3).

Johnny nodded and studied the stranger. "I'm Johnny," he said to McKee who sat on a sleek-appearing brown, its coat plastered down, shiny from sweat.

"Young McKee just sped here from Athens. Tell this eager boy what you heard, John."

"Just about supper time last night old man Hiller, who lives a couple miles from Athens, came running into town. Seems his two-year-old daughter, Hattie, got bad sick with the croup so he headed for the pharmacy. Near town he cut through a thicket where he overheard a group of men talking about Green's troops. He heard them say that Green had moved to Chambersburg, planned to attack Athens at first light (4)."

"You mean tomorrow? The meeting at Benning's house in Athens didn't count for much, Doctor Payne?" Johnny said.

"If you mean the end of July? It was the southern sympathizers who tried to get Moore to leave Athens with his Union troops, leave the tons of supplies for Green's rebel army. Moore told them if Green was aching for a fight he was about to get a licking (5). Well, if we don't muster up some help, Moore will get the licking. We need to make sure others know to be in Athens this night," Payne said. "McKee is going to Henshaw's tavern in Alexandria, straight west on the road to Winchester, then north to Union and Kahoka to bring in help. I'll take this dray, and my horse along the Main Divide (1) to Athens so I can alert Waterloo, Peaksville, Revere, and Sweet Home. It'll be safe from any nearby rebs."

"So there's goin' to be a real fight?" Johnny said.

"Afraid so," Payne answered and looked in the back of the dray, peering at its load. "These all the medical supplies you and my partner brought from Hannibal?"

Johnny's eye caught a glimpse of Dr. McKee's father, Robert A. McKee (5), in the front window of the McKee Mercantile. He waved and absent-mindedly said, "Yeah."

"You will soon be dealing with officers, doctors, Johnny.

Say, yes sir. What's in the gunnysack?"

"Sorry, sir. Lots of stuff to make poultices for wounds. Marney says the inner bark of the witch hazel tree is good for inflammations (6). I figured we could use it with dressing right off." He paused but Payne just nodded his head. "Also lots of sassafras for tea to help them get back energy (6)."

"Other than calomel, quinine and laudanum, herbs are the best the army has, the only for wounds," Payne said, paused, chuckled. "Johnny, I use those herbs in my practice." He looked in a small feed sack. "What's the powder?"

"Dried roots of the spotted geranium. Marney says its good to put in cuts to stop bleeding (6). Calomel is for the flux (7). Right?"

"Only for more mild to moderate diarrhea or dysentery. For the severe I add laudanum. Besides good relief of pain, opium drugs slow up the bowels. Army quinine isn't like Doctor Sappington's pills (8). His is easy to figure dosage. Sometimes the usual dose of army quinine makes patients toxic."

Johnny watched as Payne and young McKee headed out of town, the thought of the coming battle slowly moving a shiver up his back. "This town is my life, my people," he muttered, patted Red's neck and climbed up.

Though St. Francisville only had 1100 people, Johnny loved the location on the Des Moines River. It was six miles south and east of Waterloo and nine north of Alexandria, a bustling town of 1400 just below the point where the Des Moines dumped into the Mississippi. There the ferry crossed the Mississippi River to Warsaw, Illinois (5). At sixteen years of age, Johnny found plenty of excitement in St. Francisville.

He had not meant to stop, but he heard the familiar hacking sound from the store across the street from McKee's Mercantile. A frail, bent-over man, appearing to be in his fifties, although Johnny knew he was forty-four, stepped from behind a tall pile of sacks, stamped "SUGAR" with black letters. Isaiah Flack coughed into a ragged bandanna, wiped his lips, and smiled at Johnny with sunken eyes. "Kinda looks like them rumors are true," he said and fiddled with the collar of his faded black shirt tucked neatly in his patched, black denim trousers.

Johnny scrutinized the figure and wondered how Elizabeth Flack could be happy with a man twenty or twenty-one years older? He recalled he was twelve when they took him in — he had thought to be a companion for Mr. Flack's son, Ezra, but the last year made him wonder. He waited until the dust from another wagon, heading out of town on the road for Athens, had settled. Mr. Flack's breathing eased and he replaced the bandanna in his rear pants pocket.

Mr. Flack was a strict Quaker, and Johnny knew his remark about the rumors was his gentle way of telling him he shouldn't go to Athens. The night before he had involved Johnny in a long discussion about Quaker beliefs, especially their position as conscientious objectors during wartime. He told Johnny that since the Quakers had first settled in Pennsylvania their beliefs had caused problems whenever men were needed to fight. Johnny was surprised to learn that while most Quaker men didn't believe in killing, their actions varied considerably. Although some refused to join the army, most joined but would not carry a gun so they were usually assigned the role of caring for the sick and wounded. A few others carried guns and engaged in combat (9).

Johnny had listened intently to Flack and then told him he did not intend to carry a gun. "I'm goin' to do like you in the Indian wars and join to help the sick and hurt," he had told Flack.

"Thee must be careful. Little Ezra needs you." Flack threw a finger over his shoulder at the store across the street, intermittently visible between dust clouds. "Doc McKee says you pulled a gun on the Slater boys in Palmyra."

Johnny frowned at Flack, now slouched against the door jam. He recognized the use of formal Quaker address and knew it was an expression of love from the simple man. "I wouldn't have used it. Just a scare so's Blake would put away the whip." He straightened in the saddle.

"Many a righteous man held a gun he didn't intend to use. But got frightened and hurt someone, killed, even if'n he didn't believe in killin'."

"Nothin' will ever make me kill, bird, animal, never a bein'."

"I pray God keeps it so for thee."

On the way home Johnny guided Red past the yellow Baptist church. He turned when a voice called his name and spied Rev. Turner (2) rounding the corner of the church. Baptists came to Missouri in 1803 and this church was built in 1853, a feat since the town had so few people. Johnny waved at the pastor, smiling when he recalled him telling the small congregation one Sunday, "Baptists are like the Canada Thistle: given a favorable Spirit-laden breeze and they may be wafted to the remotest parts of the earth and wherever they light they take root (10)."

"Promise you'll come home soon as it's over in Athens, Johnny. Promise me."

John Hamilton Jenkins peered across the rough-hewn table and munched on a biscuit topped with sorghum. A cough made him raise his eyes to the pastel blue eyes that penetrated his mental armor. The look emanating from a cool shiny face with its drawn features melted into warmth that stirred his thoughts. He smiled. "Can't. I already told George I was goin' to meet him in Canton." He stopped when the pretty face drooped.

"My grandpa settled this town. It's my life and yours. So come home when the fighting is over." Elizabeth Flack's eyes narrowed above ruddy cheeks. She wrinkled her thin nose, turned up at the end. Johnny stared and worked on the hard bread. She went to the fireplace and stirred the kettle of

Baptist Church, St. Francisville. As it appears today. Photo by the author.

corn mash. He watched. She was all of five-feet tall with a full figure.

Johnny knew the story by heart. Although "General" Harrison, a trapper, had camped in the area regularly, Jacob Weaver, the proprietor of the first mercantile in St. Francisville, was the first permanent settler in northeast Missouri. In September 1829 he had arrived from Kentucky with his wife and five children. That same year others joined them. John Sackett, Jeremiah Wayland, George Haywood and Samuel Bartlett, all came from the same general area in Kentucky. Jeremiah Wayland had built a cabin north of St. Francisville about the time the Weavers arrived, but the flood washed it away (5). And late in 1831 to early 1832, William Henshaw settled in the Alexandria area and John S. Lapsley on the Des Moines River four miles northwest of St. Francisville, joined by Robert McKee (5). The last of the biscuit slid down on the sorghum as he recounted the story to himself.

Probably every man in Vernon Township knew Elizabeth. Since her mother had died when she was a toddler, Grandma Weaver had raised her. While people couldn't help noticing her small but cute figure, it was her untiring, restless ways, just like Grandpa Jacob's, that drew attention.

Very likely, this same enthusiasm and eagerness to help drove Elizabeth to marry Isaiah Flack when she was sixteen. The frail man, twenty years her senior, had appeared in town with a three year-old boy named Ezra. He came from Salem, Iowa, a stronghold of Quakers, twenty-two miles north of St. Francisville. Johnny had attended Friends' meetings there many times and had been in the Lewelling House, known as a depot for the underground railroad.

More slaves escaped into southwestern Iowa, because the denser population in northeast Missouri made capture more likely. But in spite of the roads from Athens to Keokuk being heavily guarded by proslavery men of northeast Missouri, many slaves found their way to Salem. In 1848, nine escaped slaves of an owner, Ruell Daggs from Clark County, hid in Salem (11). When a posse of Missourians appeared, a confrontation occurred and Mrs. Flack with the newborn baby in her arms was accidentally shot and died the following day.

Flack, a shy man who practiced Quaker beliefs, was devastated, and after three years he left the bad memories of his wife's death, settled at St. Francisville where he proved a big help to Jacob Weaver with his store. His assistance was sorely needed because the region had witnessed a sudden surge of growth. Shortly after Flack and Elizabeth married, Jacob Weaver moved his family to western Clark County, leaving his store for Mr. Flack.

One year after her marriage to Flack she went into labor. After two exhausting days, she delivered a dead baby and hemorrhaged so badly she almost died. The town folks said she lived because of Dr. O. B. Payne, the only town doctor at the time, and the work of a black woman they called a shaman.

Johnny reasoned it was the loss of a baby that made her insist in 1857 that the badly beaten twelve-year-old boy, Johnny Hamilton Jenkins, be allowed to recover in their small cabin and then live there permanently.

Johnny overheard the village women say it was another miracle administered by Dr. Payne and Elizabeth. Johnny figured differently, for one of the first things he remembered after his beating was a visit from the shaman, the mother of a colored boy, Sam Huett. He and Sam, his best friend, fished and swam in the Fox River near the place where he grew up, north and five miles west of St. Francisville, not far from Waterloo, the county seat (1).

Elizabeth returned to the wobbly table with a glass of milk and put it in front of him. "Well. You could come home after the fighting in Athens just for a bit so I'd know you are okay."

Johnny gulped some milk. "I'll come back after Athens. But then I'm goin' to Canton," he said and pushed away from the table, avoiding her eyes. He carried the tin plate to the table that held the pail for washing dishes. Though distracted by the sounds of wagons passing down the main street two blocks away, he felt her warmth, before she pressed against his arm. He eased his head around, his eyes drawn to her eyes like a magnet — they were watery. The faded robin's egg blue dress hid her youthful figure. Of the six buttons that closed the top part of the loosely draped homespun cotton dress from the waist up, three were unbuttoned. Early, when he began to notice such things, Johnny realized that Elizabeth never buttoned her dresses up tight at her neck and didn't wear many layers under her dress, customs of every woman he had ever seen.

With a quick parry he knocked her hand off his shoulder and drew her close. He pecked her forehead. Her little round belly pushed against him and rubbed upward as she stretched on tiptoes. Wet, hot lips hit his.

She leaned back. "I'll miss you so." Tears wound down her cheeks.

"I love you, Elizabeth," he sputtered and wrenched free. At the door a hand turned him. She was beaming.

"I know, my Johnny. I love you, too." She wiped tears with a forearm. She grinned, giggled. "Don't you ever tell no one." She wagged a finger at him. "And don't you forget it neither, so's you hurry back."

Flustered, he dashed for his room. The Flack cabin had a large room with a wooden floor and a small bedroom off to the left. The only window was near the front door and made of an oiled, thin opaque skin that let in a decent amount of light. This room served as kitchen and general family room as well as a space for Ezra's straw bed, hidden in the corner by a bunch of cowhides sewn together. They made a partition that blocked out light from the generous fireplace, the source of heat in the winter for the entire cabin. It was located in the right wall and against the back wall rested a large table with a small tub that held water for drinking and a larger one for washing dishes.

One of Johnny's chores to pay for his keep was to go to the well at the village square and fetch the water to keep the tubs full. After Johnny recovered, Isaiah Flack had partitioned the shed that was attached to the wall holding the fireplace. The small area's back wall, the outside wall of the fireplace, emitted heat in the winter, meager since it was the only source. The dirt floor was packed hard, and the door for the room opened into the shed. The other walls of Johnny's bedroom let through light and so much cold that after the first winter Elizabeth had helped Johnny line the wooden walls with gunnysacks and stuff straw between them and the wood. Only one linsey blanket and a bearskin were needed in the cold winter months after that. He grabbed his savings pouch and started to back out the door, consuming the view.

Elizabeth's hot breath struck his right ear. "The message's my whole life." She stepped back and with his hand pulled him out the door, waving a book. "It's Grandma Weaver's very own book of the gospels. Take it with you. It'll keep you safe and make me happy." She ran around the corner and disappeared into the kitchen.

Heading for the street he stuffed the Bible in his bedroll. With the bedroll secured behind the saddle, he mounted Red and turned him south on Main Street. Past the last home, a log cabin with a room made of weather-board attached to the far side, Johnny turned right, down a path, and after forty yards stopped at Wolf cemetery. In the stillness, he felt the weight of ancestral pressure, for in the graveyard rested the Jenkins's who settled Missouri. Johnny's grandparents, George Jenkins and Catherine Hamilton Jenkins, had originally resided in Lancaster County and then Chester County, Pennsylvania. They had thirteen children. The oldest, a girl Elizabeth, stayed in Chester County, but the second, Margaret, moved west as did four of her brothers (12). His Uncle Robert, his uncle George Washington Jenkins, and his father, James H. Jenkins, settled in Clark County. The fourth brother, Benjamin Amzi, continued farther west, turned northwest at Athens and went thirty miles into Iowa, where he built a cabin in Fairfield, a frontier village through which the Mormon Trail would pass in the future (13). Soon after their arrival in Indian Territory, Margaret married for the second time a Mr. Hendricks. Her first husband Elisha Wilson had died in Pennsylvania the year before they departed. When Hendricks died, Margaret moved in with her brother Robert.

Mid-way in the cemetery, Johnny passed the large gravestone that said Campbell and knelt at the second, a grave that said Martha Schee Jenkins. Martha was the second wife of Uncle Robert. She died in 1857.

Johnny brushed the dirt from the knees of his faded denim trousers and turned to search for the gravestone that read, Margaret Jenkins Hendricks. When she died, he cried the hardest ever in his life because after his near-fatal beating in '57 she had paid special attention to him. During summers, when school was not in session, he rode Red, the horse Dr.

McKee gave him for tending his horses, the four miles from St. Francisville to the farm and worked at various chores. Uncle Robert had bought the farm in 1853 from Doctor Trabue and moved the family from western Clark County. Most days, before he headed back home, she would sit him down at the huge oak kitchen table and push a glass of milk and biscuits at him. Sometimes, she would give him an article of clothing. Though not new, the faded denim pants he wore came from her. He had felt dressed up and harboring some guilt, he would talk her into giving him something for Ezra.

Other times she would peck his forehead with a jolly purring and use the gesture to stick a coin in his pocket. He never told anyone and had hid every one in a pouch behind the gunnysack batting of his bedroom. But most importantly, she healed his inner scars from the beating. Owl eyes, one of the twins had called him the summer after the near fatal beating. In the farmhouse kitchen — where a huge fireplace with cranes to hold big kettles for cooking opened into the adjoining room, the living room, as the only source of heat for the entire house (12) — Johnny took the mirror hanging over the wash bucket and proceeded to make faces at it. Margaret caught him, and after much coaxing he told her the kids in the one-room school in St. Francisville called him "owl eyes" and, now that one of the girl cousins did it, he wanted to see. Sure enough, when he wrinkled his forehead to raise his eyebrows the left one lifted so slowly his eyes did look like a picture in schoolbooks of an owl perched on a tree limb with one big eye and the other half that size. "I don't pay no attention to kids. I keep my hat pulled down low so's nobody can tease me," he told her. Margaret had hugged him and had him make every conceivable face he could at the mirror. In each one, the left eyebrow and eyelid moved slowly. Vividly, he recalled the next half-hour because he repeated and lived it so he'd never forget. Stiff face or slow face he told himself, for that way the eyebrows and eyelids were alike.

He felt the area under the left eye with a little finger and then compared it with the right side, the more sunken left side obvious to the touch and also visible under certain shadows. "Don't let people ruin your happiness by their teasing," she said and then taught him how to make the expressions look weird, or mean, or funny. "Use those to your advantage, to alert people, to frighten maybe, or puzzle the curious. Make up outlandish stories. Have fun with the thoughtless people," she said. He loved her, for after that he never wore his hat down to his eyebrows or felt self-conscious about his deformity.

"Thanks, Aunt Margaret," Johnny said, pushed off her grave, and dropped to his knees on the grave of Uncle Robert, who had died in 1858. His heart skipped a beat, for Uncle Robert, though he took in brother George in 1857 and wouldn't take Johnny in his home, he had watched over Johnny from a distance. He learned after Uncle Robert's death that Uncle Robert had given a tidy sum to Flack to help him fix the old Weaver store, an obvious payment for the Quaker's kindness to Johnny.

He stood and glanced over the gravestone to the row behind. With an imperceptible quiver of his lips he brushed by Robert Jenkins's stone and knelt next to an older gravestone, located one row to the south. Trembling and with reticence, he rubbed his fingers over the weather-worn inscription:

JAMES H JENKINS
born June 1 1809 died April 4 1853

"Pa, I miss you. I ain't — I haven't had a real friend, someone to love and talk to, save for Aunt Margaret, since you left me." He wiped his wet cheeks with the back of his hand. "I'm headin' out on my own. George's already done it. He joined the Canton Guard this past January and is in St. Louis. Pa, he always took care of me like you told him. Anyway, he and I are still close, and I'm going to join the

Grave markers of Robert and James Jenkins, Wolf Cemetery,
St. Francisville. Photo by the author.

army with him in Canton here in a few days. Remember your brother's first son? John's older'n me and running the old homestead instead of going to the fightin' (12)." He cast a glance at Uncle Robert's grave over his left shoulder. "You probably met up with your brother since he died a couple years ago, and his wife Martha. And maybe your sister Margaret, if she's got there yet. She died about a year ago." He ran his hand through his hair, looked back at his pa's grave, leaned over, and pulled some ragweed and a thistle from the hard packed earth and muttered, "Pa, I wish you could speak with me. I got some burning questions about girls — I mean about lovin' women." He wagged his head from side to side and shuffled for the road, but his second step brought him face to face with a smiling black face.

"You takin' to lovin' women, Johnny? Maybe you could use another beatin'."

Johnny squinted until the stiff black metallic face stretched into a grin that looked to be mostly white teeth. He stepped back and sized up the burly black figure, his muscular arms big around as one of Johnny's legs. The dirty flour-sack shirt without arms revealed shoulders that rippled as he gestured with a stubby finger. Like a sleek cat Johnny sprung for the square statue of a man and soon found himself catapulted to the ground, covered by a hulk, the stink of perspiration wrinkling his nose. He wrapped both legs around Sam's waist and squeezed, at the same time thumping his back. Sam pulled back his head and laughed aloud, but his flashing eyes spoke a message from years of shared emotions, ones that pricked the souls of both bodies enjoying the sting of the thistles on Robert's grave.

"Sam, I been by the place, but it's empty. Not even Marney there."

"We moved. With the fussin' about slaves past year, Judge Lapsley moved us into the shack on the south part of his farm. We was there once. It's the old Indian village couple miles south of here."

"Why you hidin'? Your pa been free for some time."

"Judge says there are over four hundred us colored in the county and we the only free. Guess some white folks don't take to it."

"So where's your pa?"

Sam stiffened and sat up. "He was beat like me...." Tears, big silent ones, rolled down his cheeks. He opened his mouth but only sputtered as the teardrops landed on his lips. He peeled off the ragged shirt and turned his back. Johnny gasped and then yanked Sam's trousers down until they caught on his muscular butt. He froze. And began to count aloud, his finger hitting a raised thick scar with each number, the telltale secret of the lashings. Johnny crushed his eyelids together to stop a flood of tears. The picture, a nightmare replayed too many times over four years, forced a sob. He was only twelve when he strolled along the banks of the Fox, heading for the rustic log shack on the Fox, home to Sam, his mother, and Sam's father. Finding the shack empty, he went to their favorite fishing hole because he needed to talk to Sam, his best friend. When he complained about his stepfather, Sam would tell him about the abuse his relatives had suffered as slaves.

Johnny's pa had died in 1853 after two years of coughing and hacking just like Mr. Flack was doing now. Johnny loved his mom, but his dad understood him. When his mom scolded him for sneaking off to read a book, his pa would take him aside and ask him what he had learned. He was the source of the books — didn't matter most were used — bringing one about every six months. Eiler, his stepfather, badgered him about reading and not doing his share of the work. That hot July four years ago, Eiler went in a rage when he found Johnny reading a book about medicinal plants, a booklet Sam's mother, who was known as the local shaman, had given him. Eiler burned the book, cussed him out, and kicked his behind.

Johnny opened his eyes and gingerly rubbed the ugly, thick scars on Sam's back. "I reckin' that changed all our lives," he said.

"Yeah. But I was naked and tied to that tree. I had quit countin', each whip lashin' me want to die. You were like a rabid dog. When yer first thumpin' with that log drawed blood from — the young one — his name was Zeke, I couldn't believe what I seed. And then you and Blake Slater was rolling in the dust, down the bank. I struggled when the two held you down and thrashed you, kicked you, and started to pound the life from you."

"I saw light some days later — and it was the prettiest face in the world, prettier than my mom's. It was Mrs. Flack's."

"'Bout that time pa popped up — he left the plant at Athens and happened on the beatin'." Sam stopped, stared hard at Johnny and burst into laughter.

"Nothin' seems funny to me," Johnny said, his mouth joining his nose in a quizzical question, careful to hold his eyebrows still.

Sam swatted a mosquito and nodded. "Pa's wild look was

so doggone terrifyin' they up and run. But not before he give that Zeke a wollop to the head."

"How'd I get to Flack's?"

"Pa and I took you to our cabin first for Marney to fix you so's you could make it home. Pa fetched Doc Payne and he rode out to see you." Sam pushed up from the mound of Robert's grave, grabbed Johnny's hand, and jerked him upright. The afternoon sun sent a dash of yellow on his face. To Johnny it almost looked angelic. "You wasn't suppose to live. Many days later you got strong enough to be moved, but your folks had to keep their place on the wagon train headin' to California or lose lots of money, maybe never get there. Doc Payne told us to take you to Flack's. That Mrs. Flack done took mighty good care of you."

"And Marney's herbs." Johnny put his arm around Sam's waist and guided them toward the road, down the well-worn path, guarded on both sides by tall brown grass going to seed. "When I heard mom and my two sisters left with Eiler for California, I was sorta sad — 'til I learned George stayed to look after me." Johnny stopped at the road as a wagon rumbled by, heading down the road for Athens.

"Seems some beatins and miseries come to be for the better," Sam offered, but searched Johnny's face. "Is Mrs. Flack the lovin' problem?"

He turned to peer in Sam's black eyes. "What brings you to the cemetery?"

"I come to say bye. Goin' to Athens. William McKee — he ain't no relation to the ones in St. Francisville — is in charge of the cavalry for Colonel Moore. He said I could be the horse doctor."

"What's that?"

"It means I looks after the horses. I think 'cause I used some of ma's herbs on one of the Judge's sick mares and 'cause she got fine, peoples think I know somethin'."

Sam stopped by the brown mare standing next to Red as Johnny climbed on Red. "Let's go. I'm Doc Payne's assistant. I'm goin' to help the regular army docs take care of the ones hurt." He watched Sam climb on the mare.

At the first road heading northwest, the Alexandria-Bloomfield Road, Sam pulled up the mare and asked, "Do you know why this Green is attacking Athens?"

Johnny eased Red close to the mare. "This Confederate, Martin Green, organized a troop of some twelve hundred, maybe a few hundred more, with headquarters at Monticello and trained them, hoping to get rifles and the like when on July 21 Colonel Moore with five hundred of his men — the rest still on farms — and twenty from Warsaw, Illinois, chased Captain Shacklett's small band out of Etna. Moore's horsemen had a brief skirmish and one of Shacklett's men was wounded and later died in Keller's Tavern (5). The secessionists were enraged so Green traveled from Monticello to Edina, using the anger to recruit more troops. Now he wants Moore's supplies at Athens (5)."

Known as the "Main Divide," the Alexandria-Bloomfield Road traversed the bottoms surrounding Alexandria, and two miles outside St. Francisville climbed a hill to reach the ridge that it followed to Waterloo, the county seat, then to Revere, and on to Peaksville, a newly established village of two stores, a blacksmith shop, post office, and two churches. From there it turned north to Sweet Home, which rested on a peculiarly shaped hill that sloped from its crest some seventy feet to the Des Moines River (1). At river level, two stores served the village as a port of call, one of the first on the Des Moines River, established in the mid 1830s for the new steamboat line. North of Sweet Home the road descended to river level, passed the widow Gray's house on the riverbank, climbed a hill, and entered Athens, some six miles northwest of Sweet Home. Except for the mill that sat on Water Street, all of Athens rested on a narrow plateau twenty to thirty feet above the river. Upon leaving Athens the road ascended thirty feet to the ridge and continued north and west for fifty-one miles to Bloomfield, Iowa. Water north and east of the ridge drained into the Des Moines River or the Mississippi while water west and south drained into the Fox River, hence the name "Main Divide (1)."

Traversing the bottomlands that led from Sweet Home to Athens, they slowed their mounts to a walk. When they approached widow Gray's house at the edge of town (1), Johnny donned his cap and waved at a couple blue coats leaning on their Springfield rifles. At the top of the hill, they eased by several groups of men clustered along Spring Street. Past Spurgeon's long, brick store, located at the southwest corner of Thome and Spring Streets, they spotted Payne's dray, parked a block away in front of the white, two-story frame William McKee house at the corner of Spring and Virginia Streets (1). Johnny spied a group of officers on the porch, tied Red to the dray, and climbed the steps. Dr. Payne saw him instantly and waved him over. He was talking to a man of medium build but a ramrod posture and a bushy head of mixed gray and black hair. He watched Payne's lips move, his eyes cast in his direction. When he reached the two men, the brawny-skinned face of the stranger turned to him with a grin.

"So you're George Jenkins's kid brother. He told Colonel Moore you were merely a boy, shouldn't be a soldier."

Johnny's heart fluttered. He frowned, slowly. "I'm no fighter but I can help the army surgeons better than most."

Dr. William Aylward chuckled and extended his hand. "Welcome. I'm Doctor Aylward from Memphis (14), substituting for Moore's regular surgeon. With Green showing up early, some of Moore's troops haven't made it. Moore's surgeon, Wilfred M. Wiley from Edina, is helping Woodyard recruit. So is his assistant surgeon, Doctor Andrew Clark. He lives in Kahoka (14)." He straightened and threw his head toward Sam. "Who's the darkie?"

"Sam takes care of McKee's horses. He and I..."

Aylward's voice halted him. "We'll use Spurgeon's store as the main hospital." He swept his arm east down Spring

Restored houses in Athens State Park; Top: Thome-Benning house; Bottom: William McKee house. Photos by the author.

Street toward the store. "Better get some chow and rest up for tomorrow."

Johnny left. He and Sam crossed the street to the opposite corner where they found the chow, beans and ham with hard bread.

Sam pulled Johnny off a bale of hay. "You asked why you never saw my pa." He led Johnny north along Virginia Street to the Benning house (1), around the side to the back yard. "That's where he worked 'til a year ago when this mess of state's rights lined people up as if for a cock fight." Sam aimed a finger at the structure that sat on the Des Moines, thirty feet below the Thome-Benning house (1).

Johnny stared at the mill. Of the undershot variety, because the stream struck the paddles at the bottom, the mill was inefficient compared to the overshot variety, but cheaper to build. In 1845 when Arthur Thome came from Kentucky, he built the huge mill and to increase efficiency had made a dam of logs and stones. The huge wheel turned a vertical shaft that rotated the top grinding stone. The bottom remained fixed. The mill performed not only as a gristmill, but also as a flourmill and a sawmill, the upper floor serving as a woolen mill (1). Johnny remembered being there with his father when it had been open only six years. "Yeah, I saw it when I was six. The colored man must have been your pa." Under the glare of the full moon he stared at the four-story wooden structure, the upper floors resting on thirty feet of stone. Behind, the noise of rowdy soldiers tried to dampen the river sounds. He strained and smiled at the rhythmical beat, swoosh of the river turning the huge paddle wheel.

"Good job for a darky," Sam blurted and then turned back to their campsite, a clear spot under a hickory tree on the back of the Colton-Gordon property, located across St. Louis Street from the Thome-Benning house (1). "Pa's job was to keep the grinding stones 'picked' so…"

"Hold it. I don't know nothin' 'bout milling," Johnny said.

Sam smiled. "A good mill keeps its stones 'picked' sharp because dull stones grind coarse flour, what's called 'cakey' and tends to ferment faster (15)."

"No stalling. Your pa, what happened?"

"I know Mr. Lincoln weren't at fault, but when he was nominated, this town of southerners made bad times for pa. And Blake Slater swore he would get pa for hitting Zeke when he come to your rescue. Well, when a Federal Marshall come from Kentucky looking for runaways, he grabbed pa. In front of a judge here in Athens Slater ups and says he knowed everyone in Athens and never saw pa before. The Judge turns to the Marshall. 'This here man surely fits the description of your runaway.' Sam took a deep breath. "They whipped him somethin' awful. I ain't seen him since."

Sadness reflected from Sam's drawn face to Johnny's heart, seeming to paralyze his brain. "Night, Sam." Johnny rolled onto his side, fought a sudden chill when he realized he was in the middle of an adult mess.

John McKee's face practically touched his, its stubble not evident in the darkness. He thrust a cup of coffee in Johnny's hand when he sat up, and offered Sam one as well.

"I'm cooking breakfast for the officers but Doc Aylward asked me to find you first and have you report to Spurgeon's store." He peered at Sam. "My pa says he doesn't need you now for horses. Wants you to help Johnny get any wounded to the McKee house — for officers you understand — Spurgeon's for enlisted men (14)."

Johnny thanked young McKee, beckoned to Sam, and the three hustled south on Virginia Street, the dirt street hardly visible with the absence of moonlight.

"Your pa the only relative in the comin' fight?" Johnny tried to catch young McKee's expression.

"Yes, but pa's brother, Uncle David, is a major with Iowa Third. There's an Edwin McKee in the Iowa Volunteers but he's not related." He snickered. "Some relatives down south are in the Confederate army-a cousin Joel is a Captain. Besides your brother, any relatives in the war?"

"None, unless some of my dad's brothers that went to New Orleans from Pennsylvania got kids with the rebs.

On the porch at Spurgeon's, Aylward and Johnny sat on a bale of straw and sipped coffee. Sam sat on a step. "Johnny, I think God looks on us with favor. If Mr. Hiller hadn't come to town to get medicine for his sick child we wouldn't have a hundred men here. Our scouts tell us Green was joined by Colonel Cyrus Franklin during the night (5)."

A tall, handsome man looked dashing in his blue shirt, black trousers tucked in polished black riding boots, crossed the street. Capt. William Parker McKee, born in 1816, married Sandra Bartlow, and settled in southern Iowa before starting a farm four miles south of Athens (3). The successful farmer and businessman owned considerable property in western Clark County as well as the two-story house in

Athens. At the steps to the porch he stopped, turned, pointed north and said, "Just before midnight a messenger from Croton said two companies of the Home Guard from Keokuk were camped directly across the river, but they were going to honor the state line and not join the fight." McKee turned, stared down Spring Street, muttered, "Come on, Johnny, you too, Sam. They'll need you near the battle line when the bullets start flying."

Aylward entered the store. Sam and Johnny followed William McKee to the cavalry, camped across the street from the schoolhouse. Gray light streamed over the buildings and fell on the empty street, outlining gray forms of men scattered along the base of the hill from the old brick kiln on the west past Thome Street to the east. The tops of the trees west of town turned golden, the color slowly creeping down, transforming the dark green foliage into chartreuse and bright green all the way to the trunk. Johnny strained to catch a view of a yellow-orange crescent that was peeking over the eastern horizon defined by cemetery ridge.

"Father, breakfast is ready," John McKee said.

"Never mind about breakfast, the enemy is coming and we are going to have a fight (16). Johnny, you and Sam eat the fixings while we flush out the enemy." He ordered the men to get their horses and fall in line.

Johnny watched Payne take command and lead eighteen riders up the hill. He had finished about half his helping of bacon and flapjacks, prepared by John McKee, when he heard gunfire coming from over the hill. Within minutes the cavalry burst over the hill. Moore's men, some 320 formed a line. The cavalry rode through the line and drew up behind Moore's troops (16).

John McKee stopped his mount next to Johnny. "We got as far as the reb's house, Captain Baker, where we formed a line. Their cannons came first with lots of men behind them. When they unlimbered the big guns, we were ordered to retreat (16)."

Muffled sound of hoofs coming from over the hill interrupted McKee and shattered the hush of dawn.

"There, Johnny." McKee's finger pointed to what Johnny
had already seen, a fuzzy line of gray figures a quarter-mile
away, atop the hill that overlooked them. The ghost-like
forms grew in size as they advanced for Moore's line.

David Moore, born July 1817, of John and Sarah Clark
Moore, immigrants from Ireland, was a farmer, storekeeper,
and pork packer in Union. He married Diademia Schnabel
and after fighting in the war with Mexico in 1850, traveled
to Clark County by covered wagon with wife, four sons, and
a small daughter (14). General Lyon had ordered Moore to
form the First Northeast Missouri Regiment and Humphrey
M. Woodyard to form the Second Northeast Missouri
Regiment, all the men supposed to come from four counties,
Clark, Lewis, Scotland, and Pike. Moore shouted for his
men to hold their fire.

The gray line of men became more distinct as they left the
shadows of the trees at the top of the hill. With the light
slowly displacing the gray-blacks of dawn, Johnny could see
that a few men had on gray uniforms, the rest were in farm
clothes. Half way down the hill they passed the brick schoolhouse and their faces suddenly had features. They trudged
farther down the hill, the light now defining each human figure. McKee pointed to the crest of Cemetery Ridge and the
silhouettes of two cannons. Mr. Kneisley, who had been
postmaster at Palmyra until replaced by a Republican, was
in command of the six and nine pounders — one a wooden
relic (5). Moore's men waited, restless figures aiming rifles
up the hill. More foot soldiers left mounts in the trees behind
and flanked the artillery on both sides.

To his left, Johnny caught a glimpse of men running down
cemetery ridge toward the river east of Athens. He felt his
heart thump hard and then faster with each moment. His
palms were wet, his mouth dry. "It's Major Benjamin
Shacklett's men making their way through the field heading

upriver toward us," McKee told him (5).

Johnny pointed to the line that had moved from the timberline to the west and appeared from the deep ravine that contained Stallings Branch. "Looks like Captains Dull and Kimbrough will spread out to the river and come at us from the west," McKee said (5), and swept his arm back to the center where Green, poised above with the artillery, slowly pressed toward Moore. The sound of morning doves had disappeared. The sun crept up the sky. Suddenly, Green's cannons boomed from three hundred yards away, their aim right down Virginia Street. Shots whizzed overhead, some smashing through the Croton train station across the river (5). The rebels yelled and moved faster. The nine-pounder quit belching orange but the six-pounder continued spewing at them. Johnny heard the noise and turned to watch the smoke where a ball tore through the house of "Uncle" Joe Benning (5).

Honoring the state line, the Iowans fired from across the river, their fine marksmanship attested to by falling rebs, those advancing in the cornfield along the river's edge toward Athens from the east.

Moore sent Capt. Hackney and the fighting preacher, Capt. John H. Cox, with sixty men to the right to contain Dull and Kimbrough from the west. At the same time, Captains Callihan, Spellman, and Small moved slowly to face Shacklett's advance through the cornfield of the bottoms. His men fired as they advanced, unwavering under the fire from the Federals. Suddenly, the rebels yelled and appeared to run for the Union line. Callihan's and Spellman's companies panicked and fled across the Des Moines at the shallow part just below the miller's dam. Small, who weighed 350 pounds, stood straight up and shrieked encouragement to his men (5). John Hiller "crossed the river, rallied a small force, probably eighty to forty men, behind the fence when we drove the force from the cornfield and the old log house where they fought from the doors and the windows" (17).

Col. David Moore, U.S. Army.
Used by permission, State Historical Society of Missouri, Columbia.

Undaunted by the cannon shots whistling over their heads, Moore's men held firm. The sun rose higher, but the light over the battle seemed to fade, partially blocked by the smoke from cannons and rifles.

Amidst the flow of blood and vicious yells, the rebels advanced. The Federal men stood firm and kept firing, dazed and perturbed from the vigorous yells and steady advance. Near the Federal line, the Confederates faltered (5). The gray line now shimmering through the gun smoke stopped eighty yards from the Union line. It wavered. Catlike Colonel Moore jumped in front, turned to his men, and yelled to charge with bayonets (5). Men in a variety of farm trousers, topped by a blue coat, some with blue caps, others with straw or felt hats, fixed bayonets and, appearing as a dark wave, lurched toward the stunned rebels. Streaks of yellow sunlight that shot through the clouds of smoke struck the shiny bayonets, seeming to catapult at the hesitant rebels. Suddenly, their center broke and they fled up the hill for the timberline in disarray. The rebels on the flanks began to withdraw, slowly at first, and then panic struck. They ran, leaving writhing figures in their wake (5).

Emerging from the smoke, several shapes staggered backward while others clutched an arm, or head, and reeled toward the rear. A couple fell in the dust of Virginia Street. A red spot on one man's white shirt grew until it turned completely red. He fell in grass along the dusty road. Another stumbled toward the hospital, waving an arm, the stump of the other painting the road with a reddish zigzag line. Momentarily, the nearby Cavalry watched the mangled bodies writhe in the dust. Johnny bolted for stick-arm. The man fell on his face. Johnny rolled him on his back and took the bandanna from his pocket, wrapped it around the upper arm, and twisted. The arm stopped spurting. Sam appeared and they dragged the one-armed man into Spurgeon's. Aylward patted Johnny's back. The dazed man mumbled an indecipherable lament and raised the stump to the ceiling, the flesh falling back leaving a forearm bone to point as if a stick at the black man hovering over him. Sam bolted for the door and Johnny went to the corner and vomited. A continuous flow of men dragged bloody bodies into the store, a few noncommissioned officers into McKee's house where Dr. Thomas Hailan from Athens tended their wounds. Dr. Aylward and D. M. Scott from Athens with the help of assistants such as Johnny, the Athens schoolteacher, R.P. Slaughter, and Sam tended the wounded in Spurgeon's store.

"Shake it off, Johnny, and get busy," Aylward screamed. The smell of gunpowder burned Johnny's nostrils. He swallowed hard twice and began with the first body. He packed bleeding wounds, both on the shoulders of two Union men and applied herb poultices, securing them with tight bandages. Finally, with all the wounded in the store treated, he stepped to the doorway for air, to get the odor of flesh from his nostrils.

Moore had sent William McKee's mounts to pursue the fleeing rebels, while he ordered his men to help the wounded. In the panic many of the Confederates left their horses and disappeared into the woods. McKee corralled four hundred horses, a pile of guns and ammunition (5). At the same time men in blue scoured the approach to the town. The dead were placed at the side of Spurgeon's store.

Johnny slumped on a bale of straw, looking at his bloody shirt. Groans mingled with the last vapors of battle smoke. It hovered around the two dim lights and seemed to mock the efforts of the medical men along with screams mixed with prayers. An odor of death filled his nostrils. Nausea had long given way to fortitude. Johnny couldn't grasp the sense; brother had wounded brother. Sons shot at fathers and neighbors tried to kill neighbors. But the sadness and confusion slipped into the shadows when he realized he had stopped lethal bleeding, held grown men pleading for life, and bandaged moaning boys. Suddenly he felt a wave of joy and smiled when he realized he would soon see Elizabeth, happy he had promised to see her before going to Canton. "I'm a man now, Elizabeth. You'll see," he said quietly.

Chapter 3

Rebel camp
Winchester, August 5
Raid on Palmyra

Blake Slater groaned, the sharp pain in his left forearm forcing his eyelids open. He wiped off the grimace with a grin, a musing, for it was his own hand wrapped around the bandage on his forearm. He closed his eyes again. The scene playing behind his eyelids needed completion. He and little brother Zeke were charging the enemy, side-by-side, catching glimpses of the wagons and flickers of orange amid the unending pop, pop. His nose burned from smoke, his lungs singed from yelling during the slow advance, Colonel Green's shouts of encouragement a cattle prod. Suddenly, some crazy figure in light blue trousers and dark blue coat stood on a wagon, waved a sword and yelled, the words masked by the gunfire and yells from Zeke on his left and the farmer from near Monticello, known as "Uncle Pres" Walters (1), on the other side. Walters, several years older, had enlisted in the state guard at Monticello, a company formed by Captain Bill Richardson and Captain Carlin, serving under Colonel Joe Porter (2). They had slowed when their line eased to a crawl. Silver-yellow glitter of bayonets set off a murmur up and down the gray line. Dirt kicked up at his feet — more pop, pop — a sharp cramp grabbed his left arm. He looked from the blue line of flashing steel and saw a red streak grow on the arm. He looked up. The gray line to his left and right inched back, then exploded in reverse. He joined them and ran and ran. "Zeke. Zeke, for God's sake where are you?"

"Wake up, boy. You're dreaming."

Big hands shook his left knee. He opened one eye. Same bandage. He opened the other and looked into a grimy, bearded face, streaked with mud and spots of dried blood, the features a blur. As if the visual fields of binoculars, he watched the blurry image sharpen. The saddle nose with a flat tip sat between wide eyes, coal black beads. He smiled at Walters.

"Darn it, Uncle Pres, you woke me up too soon. I was about to find out where Zeke got to. We were in the center, alongside the road. Zeke on one side and you on the other. All the way from Athens here to Winchester I looked and asked."

The burly man crawled over beside him. "I ain't seen him."

Blake stood. "I got to look around once more." His heart began to feel like a rock. The bodies, some in gray jackets but most in farmer clothes, a few with gray caps, lay in the shade along the main street of Winchester. No one had information about Zeke. A group of officers stood around a buggy by the post office. He recognized Colonel Green. Martin E. Green, born in Virginia in June 1815, had moved to Lewis County in 1836 with his younger brother, the former U. S. Senator, James S. Green. Elected to represent Lewis County in 1854, he served in the 18th and the 19th General Assembly. General Price appointed him Colonel in charge of the Northeast Missouri Regiment of the State Guard (2).

Blake squinted west into the sun. A man in a dark suit and perched on a buggy seat pointed in his direction with a crop while he talked to a lean younger man in a gray coat and cap. Fatigue faded when he recognized his uncle, Judge John Newton Boulware, and his cousin Willis. The officers separated and withdrew to the side.

Ten feet from the buggy, Blake paused to stare at the black horse, its coat shiny and matted around the cinch strap

Col. Martin Green, Confederate Army of Missouri.
Used by permission, State Historical Society of Missouri, Columbia.

from sweat, its tail working from left to right flicking flies from its haunches.

"Thank God, you're fine." The Judge sat stiff-backed on the buggy seat, his eyes searching Blake from head to toe. "That wound bad, Son?" The eyes partially hidden by an intense squint, widened when they rested on his bandage.

Blake's face broke into a grin. His uncle always treated him special, better than he did his father, or even Zeke. Weariness gave way to new energy. "A scratch, Uncle John." He studied the old man's face. "I was supposed to take care of Zeke but in the panic, everybody ran us over. I been looking."

The gnarled index finger beckoned Blake beside the buggy. The veil that swept over the Judge's eyes wasn't good. Blake stepped to the back of the buggy. Cousin Willis, stone faced, pulled down the blanket. Zeke stared at him. The ashen gray face unchanged from early in the morning when he and Zeke laughed as they approached Athens. Even the thick scar on the left side of Zeke's forehead appeared the same, its normal white matched by the color of death. Blake leaned on the buggy, grabbed at the side when his knees turned to jelly.

"Your pa's going to be fierce." The judge sucked in air. "He won't understand. He thinks we're fighting to keep a bunch of niggers." The old man turned and kept a forlorn look on Zeke. "Don't you cry, Blake. Zeke's a brave young man, but he had bad blood — from your pa's side. He won't break your ma's heart anymore. I'm proud three of mine fought for our rights." The tired face smiled at the young, bearded face. "Willis is okay and so are you — only Zeke — he the youngest..." a faint gasp stopped at the Judge's lips. He looked deep into Blake's eyes. "You going home? I'm taking Zeke to Sweet Home. I'll give you a ride."

Blake wiped the water from his cheeks, opened his eyes. Zeke was a good brother he thought, the scar on Zeke's forehead jabbing his brain. Zeke whipped that nigger and beat up that Jenkins kid for fun. "I do mean things for what it gets me, Zeke," he muttered to the unresponsive face. A cough brought the question back to his attention. "No, Sir. I'm staying with the company. I'm not one of those farmers that think this is another harvest week. I joined Colonel Green's regiment 'til this war is over."

John Boulware reached back and circled the scar on Zeke's forehead. "In Athens I saw the boy who put that on your brother."

"Jenkins? The same one we saw in Palmyra?"

"Same. He made some devil face and told me that's what you and Zeke did. The uncouth young man seemed to take great pleasure when he told me Zeke finally got what he deserved for nearly killing him. He told me to get used to it 'cause you'd be next for me to fetch under a blanket."

"Jenkins's are nigger lovers. That one — Johnny — he's strange. After Zeke and I whupped him for calling us bad names just because we were having a little fun with some black gorilla, he lived with some Quaker. Our beating didn't pound any sense into his Welsh head. He's crazy as ever. I've seen his funny face couple times since then. Fits him proper." He grinned when the judge let out a high-pitched laugh.

"You got him figured. Because Doctors Payne and McKee have let him assist, he thinks he's going to be a doctor when this fracas is over." When Blake frowned, the wrinkled face stared down the street. "Don't worry. I aim to see that he never sees the inside of a medical school." He used the crop to push the blanket over Zeke's face, reached inside his coat and handed Blake a brown envelope. "That's for clothes. Act important — look important. Green knows you spent the last three years at Christian College in Canton. He's going to give you a responsible job. On the way to Monticello stop by the farm and pick yourself a good horse." The judge turned the buggy for the Salt River Road.

Blake removed his gray cap and wiped his wet forehead and yelled, "Tell mom and dad I love them. Not to worry. I'll be alright." He turned to go, but a young woman stepping from the post office steps jarred his memory. A welcome image momentarily lifted the weight from his chest. "Say, Uncle John." The judge reined up the black. "Last night when you dropped by camp, Zeke and I were sitting with our victuals. Do you remember seeing a girl — well, she had a floppy cap, sorta skinny. Did you happen to see her in Athens?"

"Nope. You take care. Make me proud, boy."

"See you." Blake put his head down, turned, and walked to the walnut tree again. Walters hadn't moved. He stared at the mulling crowd and as if announcing to the dust devils dancing down the street, said, "Zeke's dead."

"Thompson's dead," Walters said. He stood and added, "With Zeke that makes eleven." He threw a red bandanna at

a wagon parked in front of the leather shop. "They're there.
I hear twenty-five of our men were wounded. I mean bad so
they were taken to Keokuk on the train. Lots others have
scratches similar to your arm."

"How many Union?"

"Don't rightly know," Walters said.

Many of the combatants had fled in a panic, leaving their
horses to swell Moore's burgeoning supplies at Athens.
Most headed straight south through St. Patrick for
Monticello, but Blake and Walters rode in a wagon on the
Salt River Road for about eight miles where they got off at
John Newton's farm to find two horses. Blake selected a
black stallion called Jefferson after Jefferson Davis and a
brown mare for Walters. With reassurance by scouts that
Moore remained in Athens to guard the tons of supplies, and
Woodyard had made headquarters for the second regiment
in Canton, which served as a collection point for the new
recruits, they continued on the Salt River Road, making
excellent time to Monticello.

Located eleven miles west of Canton, Monticello sat on a
hill above the Wyaconda River. Settled in 1833, it served as
the county seat for Lewis County and boasted a populace of
350 (3). Since new recruits occupied the bottoms of the
Wyaconda River below the village to the west, Blake's
group camped behind the Baptist Church. Built in 1837, it
sat on large grounds, two blocks from Main Street and the
courthouse, the headquarters for Green's army. An equal
number of troops took up residence across the street on the
lawn beside the Methodist Church, constructed in 1839.

In the shade of the building, Walters asked Blake what he
knew about the Green family. Blake told him he knew from
his uncle that Martin Green was a prominent businessman, a
former state legislator. "Brother James was in the United
States Senate until this last election, defeated for being a
radical secessionist (2). Uncle John told me he was brilliant

but not so shrewd, 'cause his rhetoric stirred up the opposition. Do you know what he's doing now?"

Walters peered down, smiled. "In early July, he was accosted on the road from here to Canton by a company of Moore's men, taken prisoner back to their headquarters, and accused of all sorts of crimes."

Blake watched a Lieutenant working his way toward them after stopping at a group in front of the post office. A man in the crowd had stepped aside and pointed at them. "Crimes? He was a civilian, an ex-senator."

"He was accused of inciting insurrection by giving his fire-eater speeches around the county, raising money and recruits for his brother Martin. He took the oath and I'm told is a docile, broken man, ill, lives in St. Louis."

When the Lieutenant moved to within ten feet, both men stood, when five feet, they saluted. The auburn-haired man, appearing to be in his early thirties returned their salute. "You Blake Slater?" He gestured at Blake.

"Yes, Sir."

After the squinting eyes examined Blake from head to toe, he told him to follow, Colonel Green's orders. Blake felt a rush of blood, recalling his uncle's words, Green will give you an important job. He marched behind the long-legged officer, some eight inches taller than Blake's five-nine. They approached the brick courthouse. Built in 1844, the three-story structure stood on the highest point of ground, its white turreted tower commanding attention more than the church steeples (4). They mounted the large stone steps and entered. Blake saluted Colonel Green after the Lieutenant stopped, saluted, and departed. Green didn't return the salute. Instead, he put his arm around Blake and pulled him close to the other man in the room.

"Slater, your uncle, one of the most powerful men in the legal government of this state, told me all about you. You have the education and brains to be my personal courier, Private." Green's face erupted into a big grin.

"Private? I…"

Green raised a hand and frowned. "Dangerous role. Requires someone smart, cunning." He handed Blake some green bills. "I want you to go over to Hetzler's store and get some civvies."

Glum struck Blake. "But I'm a private, your courier."

"Indeed. But if caught in grays with messages from Confederate commanders they might shoot you. Your uncle's already lost one. You are a Quaker from Iowa. Judge Boulware tells me your father manages the pork plant at Sweet Home. Mr. Harlan, the owner, lives across the river and is a staunch unionist. He fought with Moore at Athens (5). When stopped, you tell them these connections and that as a Quaker you are gathering medicines, blankets, and food for wounded soldiers, especially the pathetic, poorly supplied rebels."

The intrigue and the importance of his task began to settle in. Blake narrowed his eyes and looked at Martin Green. "Do I really shop for supplies?"

"Although we had more men, Moore defeated us at Athens because our boys had no army issue guns, ammunition, bayonets. We desperately need supplies. The union forces control the railroads and rivers, the supply routes, so we must organize, steal, capture ours. You will help us obtain supplies, not just for the wounded, Blake."

"Thanks, Colonel. I can handle it," he gushed.

"Your first assignment. I need to inform Captain Stacy at Market Mills to proceed with our plans to harass the Germans, the union loyalists, in Palmyra by taking their food, blankets, and money. My spies tell me Hurlbut has been ordered to pull out of Palmyra for Hannibal (6). So you need to leave early in the morning."

Blake stuffed the bills in his shirt and said, "I hope I get to do some real fighting again, Colonel."

"You shall. Tell Stacy that after he raids Palmyra, he should take his force to Philadelphia. I will meet him there after I feign a march on Kirksville to get Moore and Woodyard moving in the wrong direction (2)." Green looked at Walters. "You go with Slater. Be his helper."

Blake saluted and bolted for the mercantile. Happiness permeated his whole being. I will deliver important messages, be free to find Serena, and at the same time find supplies to strengthen the army. He knew he was important.

Raid on Palmyra
August 8

Blake opened his pack and put on gray pants, tucked them in his boots and while he buttoned a pure white cotton shirt, said, "Three years of college taught me more than book knowledge. I can figure people by looking at them. You look tired. What happened after I left?"

"I never finished seventh grade, but give me an adze, a mallet and froe, a broadax with some augers, and I can make you anything," Walters said, removed his straw hat, stared at Blake. "I got some important news from my stay over in Monticello."

Blake searched the men walking across the camp and held up a gray jacket, tossed it on his bedroll. He spied Captain Tom Stacy of Shelby County ambling about with the troop surgeon (6).

He threw off a quick grin at Walters and stopped him in Stacy's path, made a semblance of a salute. "Captain, Sir. This is Uncle Pres Walters. He just came from Monticello where he spied on the Feds. Colonel Green was clever — sending troops to feign an attack on Kirksville and Memphis (6)." Blake turned to Walters, his face a blank. "Uncle Pres's my assistant, tell the Captain."

Walters stammered. Captain Stacy patted his shoulder, looked at Blake and said, "Thank you, Private Slater. Mr. Walters, tell me about Monticello. You're a brave man."

Walters rubbed the grass with a shoe and put his hands in his pants pockets. "Captain, weren't much. Outside the house I hid in, they had a talk. The Feds what searched the houses reported. Seems they scared a bunch, but didn't do no harm. Not to folks, though they carried off bank money and food and some horses. A blond-haired kid they called Johnny told a colonel he had some laudanum from the pharmacy."

Stacy studied Blake through narrowed eyes. Blake shifted

to one foot and studied a row of ants marching for a hunk of cornbread. "You know that one, Blake?"

"Maybe. Judge said he's the doctor's helper."

"Well, Woodyard told him they'd take the drugs to Moore. Said they were to join the main troop in Kirksville (6)." Walters paused and twisted the corner of his mouth at Stacy. "The postmaster told Woodyard that Green sent a bunch of rebs to raid Kirksville."

"Colonel assigned Uncle Pres to me in procuring supplies and information because he speaks German," Blake said.

Stacy told Walters to go with Blake and the raiding party about to depart for Palmyra seven miles north (6).

They dismounted in front of a white board house at the end of the main street and read the sign next to the door: Grudger Haus. Willkommen. Blake smiled and stopped at the door, motioning for Walters to follow behind.

The door opened before his fist could strike the door a third time. A pear-shaped woman appeared with enough dark fuzz on her face to make him scrutinize her clothes before he decided she must be the wife.

"Ja. I'm Frau Grudger."

"I'm Private Slater." He pushed her aside and strode into the room. To his right a door slammed shut. "You nigger lovers get all your meat, beans, and taters."

The woman piled several large pieces of smoked pork and two bags on the table. Blake yelled for Walters to come get the loot. He followed Walters to their horses. Walters tied each end of a two-foot piece of rope on the end of each sack and hung them over the horse's neck. They moved down the street. Blake spied a house that fit the description given him by Stacy, a two-story old brick house occupied by a German family with the name of Gash. An old woman told them to look around and take whatever they wanted, but there wasn't anything, she said, because the Union General Hurlbut had made his headquarters there and had taken everything when he left. She seemed cordial and stopped Blake at the

Gardner House, Palmyra. Photo by the author.

door. With only a suggestion of an accent, she asked Blake if he and his companion cared for a drink of whiskey. She stepped by him, reached under the porch steps and produced a jug.

"That General liked his whiskey. He stowed this when he left." She thrust it toward Blake, but Walters's hand grabbed it.

The heel of his boot ground into Walters's shoe while he smiled at her twisted face, the black eyes beady marbles. "We don't drink on duty, ma'am," he said and wrenched the jug from Walters. She took it from his extended arm and disappeared in the house.

On their horses, Walters grabbed his reins. "No girls. No whiskey."

Slowly, Blake extracted the rifle from its boot. Walters dropped the reins when the muzzle indented his cheek. Blake saw the tremor of Walters's hands, lowered the rifle, and leaned over close to Walters.

"Assistant, Stacy said if he heard about anyone raping women or drinking whiskey he'd lock them in the Palmyra jail and leave them for the blue-bellies." They passed a two-story board house painted yellow. It sat on the corner of the main street. "That's the Gardner house. Captain says they are friendly."

They turned left at the courthouse and spied the wagons parked in front of the jail. Most were loaded with sacks, sides of beef, and blankets so they rode over and put their sacks and smoked pork in the one half-full. Sergeant Henning, the supply officer, told Blake they should head back for Marshall's Mill, as Captain Stacy left already.

In camp the troops ate a feast while Captain Stacy and two assistants gathered before the fire. A lieutenant barked out orders of the day and the plans for the next day.

Stacy stepped beside the man and said, "You men did a great job. We picked on the German homes because the Germans are loyal Unionists and have been a considerable help to General Hurlbut. Many others in Palmyra are our friends. We make a quick trip to harass the Germans once more and thereby hopefully discourage those who are eager to help Lincoln's goons. Today, General Thomas Harris, Commanding officer of Forces of Northern Missouri, told me the plans the commander of southern troops for all of Missouri has..." He bit his lower lip and searched faces. "Where's Private Slater?"

"Here, Sir," Blake announced as he stood under the oak.

Stacy threw a gloved finger toward the shadows where Blake stood stiffly. His heart raced, because in front of so many men, Stacy had singled him out.

"The Private's uncle, same as Colonel Green's own brother, has stood and supported Governor Jackson. Slater, who is the commander of all Missouri forces for the Governor?"

Blake's legs felt rubbery when he stepped from the shadow of the oak into the dim light of the fire. "General Sterling

Price, Sir." The pork and beans began to rumble in his belly but the silence stung him so with all the eyes glued on him, he smiled, and threw out his chest.

"Thank you, Private. General Price at the moment is in southwest Missouri preparing for a battle that may preserve our forefathers' legacy — the right each state has to decide whether or not it shall have slaves rather than letting some strangers in Washington decide." Stacy took a cup thrust before his face and sipped. "After a brief raid on Palmyra early in the morning, we are ordered to join Colonel Green, who will meet us in Philadelphia after he leads the enemy on a wild goose chase. After we get together, the entire force will proceed to the Missouri River at Glasgow or Arrow Rock and cross to the south side of the river. I am proud of you men. We all suffer when we must fight against neighbors and relatives. Get a good night's sleep, men."

Sergeant Henning showed Blake how to organize the supply wagons for the trip to the Missouri River. Two of Captain Stacy's lieutenants hovered over maps during the entire time. At first Blake fretted because Walters got to return with the raiding party while he remained in camp. But you're important, Walters had teased. He tried to listen to Henning, a bald short man with white whiskers that offset a red bulbous nose. One leg was shorter so he gimped around the wagons. A beefy hand on his shoulder sidetracked his thoughts of Serena.

"Homesick, boy?"

"No. Just worried about my girl back in Canton," he lied, figuring the man from Boonville had never heard of Waterloo.

"Send her a letter. We won't get home for months. New Market has a post office. Stacy likes you. He told me..."

The sound of horses announced the return of the raiding party. Captain Stacy, who had led the raid, rode straight through camp, kicking up a cloud of dust. Passing by Blake, the heaving and snorting of the brown turned Blake's gaze from the wind-blown appearance of the rider to the lather on the brown's flanks. He spied two blue coats being helped from horses. Blake put the last sacks in the daily supply wagon and wound through groups of men, their bantering an octave above the usual. A bugle sounded assembly. He rolled up his gear and joined Walters at the back of the men.

Stacy addressed the group. "Hurlbut's on the march for Palmyra so we're going to move on the double. Move out."

"Private Slater. Get your horse and roll. I want you to get in your procurement clothes and take a message to Colonel Green. He ought to be somewhere west of Monticello, maybe heading back to Philadelphia."

Blake studied the warm face, that stared at Walters and muttered a low, "Yes, Sir."

Blake slipped into his civvies and handed his uniform to Walters. He mounted Jefferson and said, "Keep those for me. If the yanks stop me and find them, they'd shoot me for a spy."

Walters stuffed the clothes in his bedroll and cast a frown at Blake. "I know what you're thinkin'. I wouldn't go lookin' for that girl. Ain't worth getting' shot for."

Blake spurred on the mass of muscle under him and sped north toward Philadelphia, his thoughts focused on Serena. I must get her away from that Jenkins — without getting shot.

Chapter 4

Sugar Creek chase
Athens, August 5

After the smoke cleared, Johnny sat on the steps to Spurgeon's store. Inside, Dr. Aylward with Sam's help completed the last of many amputations. He felt the coolness of sweat on his back and wiggled both shoulders, his curiosity fixed on a sergeant, a tall, slender man in nondescript trousers, blue coat with large brass buttons, and battered headgear known as a forage cap. He came from the direction of the Gordon and Benning homes and had hold of the grimy collar of a slender boy, probably a couple years younger than Ezra, perhaps eleven (1).

"You Jenkins?" The sergeant spoke from a forest of red whiskers and shoved the boy toward the steps.

"I am." Johnny reached over and pulled the frightened creature onto the step next to him.

"You help him find his pa, says he works at the paint shop. I found him in the ravine northwest of town. Acts like he would just as soon kill a Yank as talk to him." The sergeant wheeled about and headed for the corral.

"I got a half-brother in St. Francisville 'bout your age. Got a name?" The black-haired, sunburned boy stared (1). "I don't believe in killin'. I sure 'nuf fixed up lots of Yanks and Rebs. Tell me your name and I'll get you to your father safe."

"A. M. Dowd. My pa runs the paint shop. Ma sent me to see if he was okay (1). She warned me not to get caught by no Yanks because they'd know we is for Green." Prodded by a scream, the boy turned his head to peer inside.

Aylward strode from the store, sat on the other side of Johnny, put his arm around him, and squeezed. "You're a man now. Nice job. Your help saved lives."

Just then a neatly dressed, graying man came around the corner of the store, uttered not a word, and took the boy down the street (1).

"Southern sympathizers, Johnny. Most of Athens just as soon have Green win, get all the supplies." Aylward stood and pulled Johnny by the arm around to the side of the store. Johnny's gaze took in the view. Main Street looked like a tornado had hit. Debris, smashed wagons interspersed with dazed men, some weeping, others praying, and yet others dancing. They stopped at the side of the store and Aylward counted sixteen forms (2), mounds covered with worn blankets that had been stained by blood mixed in dirt. He pulled the grimy rag of a blanket off the head of the first one, knelt beside it, and wiggled a finger at Johnny. Dried blood, dark maroon in color, and bits of flesh mixed with black hair sat where a face should have been. Johnny fought back nausea.

"Scuse me, doc," a voice from the corner interrupted the two. A man from the Keokuk Home Guard sat at an angle on his horse. He pointed to the row of mounds. "I hear forty-six dead, all toll, and forty-four seriously wounded, couple those likely to die, plus some fifty more slightly wounded (3)."

"Thanks, sergeant. I thought you Iowans decided to honor state lines," Aylward said, handed Johnny a jug of water and turned his attention to the bodies.

"Most all did. I'm Rev. G. C. Beans from Croton. When I heard what one of those slavers told his troops, 'You breakfast in Athens, dine in Croton, and supper in Farmington in hell (3),' I decided I'd see about that." The man glided for the Des Moines on a slouch-backed mare.

While Johnny gulped down much needed water, Aylward said, "Eleven Confederate and five Union here (4). Maybe worse, if you believe the preacher, Johnny. To tell if a man's dead you feel here." Aylward put an index finger on the man's neck, then grabbed Johnny's left index finger and put it on his own neck.

Johnny smiled when he felt the doctor's pulse nudging his finger. "Yeah." Then his finger searched the faceless man's neck. Cold and still, the skin sent no clues, only caused him to shudder fiercely like a dog trying to shake water off its coat. He diverted his heartache by looking past Aylward at the melee, mocking him from the streets, the late morning sun casting oblique shadows, making the disheveled bodies taunt him in derision. Loud, indecipherable voices took his eyes to the road in front of the store where Moore and a well-dressed man in a buggy, one with fringe around the top, pulled by a tall, spirited stallion, threw gestures at one another.

His captive gaze transformed when Aylward spun around and removed the sheet from the face of the body behind them. He pulled the left eyelid up.

"Look at the eyes if they have any," he told Johnny, who had scooted to the top of the man's head, the clean, ghostly white face appearing angelic compared to the first. Aylward caught the sun's rays with a small mirror he had retrieved from a pocket and directed the reflected rays onto the glassy eye and then into his own eyes. "See how big his pupil is, and how it doesn't move when light hits the eye? What did mine do?"

The youthful face, though ghostlike, battered Johnny's cool. The nightmarish scene tilted the face out of focus. Completely absorbed, he jerked his eyebrows up, the left hesitantly following the right.

"What, Johnny?" Aylward stared, lips a mile apart, his weary appearing eyes studying Johnny's twisted face.

"Owl." He forced a chuckle and froze a blank face.

"Owl. Too much blood and...."

With his best porcelain look he said, "My face. You saw my owl face." He looked and pointed to the pasty face. "That's Zeke Slater. The younger brother who helped give me an owl puss." Aylward grabbed his arm, closed his mouth, and questioned with his eyes, so Johnny continued, "Your eyes were big but shrunk when the light hit 'em. Zeke wasn't the mean weasel — he shouldn't die so young."

Aylward smiled, pulled the sheets up, and pushing off his knees stood straight and stiff with head bowed. After what Johnny figured was a prayer, Aylward turned for the front. Johnny cast a remorseful look at the still forms alongside the building, and turning to follow Aylward, felt a cold ripple run up his back.

In front, disturbed men halted their dialogue. The man in the buggy wore a black ribbon-tie, his gray hair now visible. He waved a riding crop at Col. Moore.

"Whoa, Buck," he sniped at the jerky horse. "You will release the American heroes to me," he railed at Moore.

"Easy, Judge. You can have the dead rebels," Moore paused after sneering "rebels." He motioned behind Aylward and Johnny to the side of the store. "Eleven boys. Died for an un-American, lost cause. Tell your boys to take 'em."

The man walked over to a wagon and spoke with a shriveled up form of a man. The Judge spun about, his look seeming to pass through Johnny. The visual encounter, the creeping sneer, and small black eyes peering from behind thick, bushy eyebrows registered like a gong in Johnny's brain. Aylward had seen the exchange and inched next to Johnny and, as if a ventriloquist, asked who was the old man.

"Judge Boulware. The dead youngun you showed me is his nephew." He watched Boulware and the man in the wagon stop at the line of dead bodies. He jerked on Aylward's sleeve. "What do you know about the Judge?"

"Judge John N. Boulware, they tell me, has a big plantation along Gregory Road. With sixteen slaves he argued for secession, naturally. Powerful man, he was Clark County's representative to the General Assembly." As he talked, Johnny watched them look at all eleven faces, then load Zeke in the back of the buggy. The bent-over man pulled the blanket over the form. The Judge blew is nose on a large red kerchief, set his stare on Johnny, and guided the buggy in his direction.

Motion behind Aylward caught Johnny's eye. He stared as Boulware reined in his horse so the buggy hovered by Johnny.

Sad, black eyes ripped at his calm. The Judge poked a finger at him. "You deserved the beating, boy. Your brother George..." His mouth froze, his words seeming to suck back when his mouth hung open. Johnny raised his eyebrows fast as he knew how, if anything helping the left lag more behind. Judge Boulware let out a small gasp, so Johnny took a second finger and pushed the lazy eyebrow even with the right and smiled with his mouth. "See that, Judge? I can control what your misfit nephews did to me. I learned it from Doc Payne," he threw his head toward the buggy, "Says it'll make me a better doctor." He watched Col. Moore stop by the Judge's buggy.

The Judge stiffened on the seat. "You got no family, except that no-account brother who you thought was going to get in the Home Guard at Canton. Boy, I got friends. Your brother's going to be sent to the real fighting where he'll get killed and you — what you did to Zeke, you won't get in any medical school if I have my way." He backed the horse around and postured as if he intended to be the honor guard for his dead relative.

"Old man," Johnny hollered after the buggy. And, ignoring Aylward's tossing head, raised his voice an octave. "Have fun burying Zeke. I'll send you Blake same way when I catch up with him."

Watching the buggy speed through the men scouring

Virginia Street, Aylward said, "Boulware's son Willis was out there. Not one of the eleven, so I guess he'll settle for one dead out of three kin."

Moore stepped between Johnny and Aylward.

"I understand two of your boys were out there with young Boulware — fighting against you," Aylward said as he cast a cold face at Moore, then locked on Johnny's eyes.

Without offering an answer, Moore sidled over to Johnny. He directed those of sound body to load the more seriously wounded on wagons, take them across the river to Croton for transport to Keokuk by train. Sam loaded one and stopped beside Johnny, started to speak but a commotion behind them halted his speech.

"In all, twenty-five Confederates were wounded and eighteen Federals, not counting those with splinters or scratches from debris and other injuries not severe enough to require attention from an army surgeon (2)," Moore told him.

"Sergeant Beans from Croton says lots more. They got some in Croton, going to take them on the Des Moines Valley Railroad to the Estes House, the hospital in Keokuk. I suppose many crawled into the brush or were carried off by comrades." Aylward nodded at Moore and hugged Johnny while telling him to be careful if he decided to go straight to Canton. He and Sam exchanged glances while Aylward entered the hospital and Moore walked to headquarters.

"Did you hear that mean judge, Sam?"

"Yeah. I hear most young men who get medical schooling have well-off family and connections. You can't do much about that, Johnny." Sam put a hand on Johnny's shoulder.

"No worry."

Suddenly, Sam waved an arm at the makeshift corral situated behind Smith's Hotel (1). "Hey. Peers to me one of the horses untied itself from the corral and is taking a hike for the timber."

At that moment a slight figure in a bright green shirt

leaped on a horse. Rider, a dark form hugging the animal's neck, dashed up the hill for the woods.

"Bye, Sam," Johnny shouted over his shoulder while he ran past McKee's house for Red, tied at the edge of the herd of horses. As he streaked by, he hollered over a shoulder at Moore who stood on the porch, "I'll get him, Colonel."

The wind in his hair with the cool on his cheeks felt exhilarating. He laughed while he kept the distant shape of the fleeing horse and rider in view, confident big Red would soon overrun the nag. Ten minutes, twenty, the weaving in and out of the woods made the chase long. Action, a salve for raw emotions evoked by the dead and mangled bodies at the store, he mused. He giggled, spurring Red for the darting horse and rider. Concern finally interrupted the thrill of the chase. The kid's good, winding in and out of trees, neutralizing Red's speed Johnny realized. Suddenly, the horse lurched over Sugar Creek, stumbled, and sent its rider flying through the air. Johnny reined in Red and cautiously approached the figure, motionless on his belly. The surge of blood to his head seemed to brighten the scene. He spotted blood on the broken sapling beside the body. He eased forward and when he bent over the guy jerked over, aimed a pistol at Johnny. A lunge and Johnny landed on the body, using his right hand to knock the pistol loose. He sat on the thrashing body and pinned both arms spread-eagle. The wrestling match was over. A whimper issued from under the floppy hat. Johnny kept his tight grip, bent down, and peered under the hat.

He blinked his eyes, loosened his grip, sat up, and pushed his hat to the back of his head. "A kid. A lousy kid stealing Federal horses."

A rush of air raised the brim of the hat a smidgen and a squeaky voice protested, "I ain't no kid. And I ain't no horse thief, jerk. I..." a pathetic groan replaced the dialogue. Johnny saw the problem. Blood soaked the left shoulder of the cotton shirt and began to stain the ground. "You're bleeding to death," he shouted. He ripped the green cotton shirt off the shoulder, hollering, "I'm a surgeon's assistant. I can stop it." He tore a piece from the top of the bloody shirt and jammed the wad against the gash and pushed.

A shriek joined wild kicks. "Get off, you animal."

Johnny took a flailing arm and pushed it against the wad of shirt. "You don't want to bleed to death. Hold tight while I fix something to hold the pressure. He tore off the front of the green shirt, stared, and fell back against the base of a maple tree.

"Bumps. You got bumps. You're a girl kid. Incredible." He kept shaking his head, the scene blunted by the shadows cast by a stand of maples along Sugar Creek, seeming more unreal with each passing second.

"Aw, shut up. You seen 'em before. I'm fifteen." The girl's squint changed to a belligerent face. "They're not bumps. They're breasts. Quit staring and make that bandage." She stopped.

Still wagging his head Johnny muttered, "Big soldier Johnny Jenkins subdues fifteen-year-old girl kid. Wow." He moved on his knees and scooted beside the thin form. Gently, he wrapped strips of cotton shirt around the shoulder. The bleeding stopped. He straightened and stared at her chest, then jerked off his blood-stained shirt, pulled it over her head and helped her wiggle both arms through. She shoved, a strong thrust, against his bare chest. He fell back against the tree and watched the enemy attempt to straighten her clothes and then the gnarled muddy hair. She fumbled with the shirttail, then her greasy black hair.

"Okay, what were you doing here, whatever your name is?"

She looked up, wiped her cheeks with the tail of the bloody shirt and said, "I'm Serena Hill. We have a farm south of Alexandria. My daddy — he's agent for American Express — came to fight. I came looking for him. I do not have a brother. I'm the oldest so it was my job. How can I find out if he's alive? You called yourself Johnny Jenkins. I know lots of Jenkins. I never heard of you. So you must be a big fib. If you are a Jenkins, you'd be in their school. I go there — never saw you..."

"You run off at the mouth so fast I can't remember all the questions, save the most important. Sixteen men died in the fight, eleven Confederate and five Federal." He stopped when she let out a gasp. He scanned the small glen, enveloped by maple and oak saplings and paused to enjoy the cool air on his hot, sweaty chest. His long, straight blond hair matted with blood and mud was soaked at his neck and at his forehead. "None named Hill."

"What about wounded?" Serena pushed up and bent closer to watch his eyes hidden in the shadow of his brows.

"There were over forty wounded. How am I supposed to know all them? Besides, they all left for Keokuk. Now what Jenkins do you figure you know?" He decided she wasn't the enemy and if she was being so brave to help her daddy that was a good cause, especially a girl, he figured.

James Amzi and I go to the same school and I've met his twin sisters and brothers Robert and George — a bother is George F. and there's a George W. also, a cousin, I think."

"My cousins, except the George W. is my brother. I been livin' in St. Francisville with the Quaker Flack." He reasoned being a blabber-mouthed girl she needn't even know about Elizabeth being almost his age.

"How can I find out about my daddy?" She sat back

Ignoring the question momentarily, he gave a shrill whistle. "I propose we go back to Athens. Get me a shirt, clean up, and get you a shirt ain't so bloody and a bandage that won't shake loose on a horse." He saw the corners of her mouth inch up. "They got a list of wounded there and I have to fetch my bed roll." He stood and walked twenty feet where big Red waited. At Red's side he paused until she stood beside him. She was only an inch shorter, but skinny.

After mounting Red, he extended his arm to her good one

and was amazed at her strength when she held on while he lifted her to a position behind him. She wrapped her good arm around his skinny waist and squeezed tightly. Once Red hit the road for Athens and the oppressive, steamy air of the swampy area around Sugar Creek and the Fox River had vanished, Johnny's spirits soared. Free. I'm free, and I love helping sick and injured. I will be a doctor some day, he resolved.

On the way he asked her how she got inside Athens. She told him she had sneaked in the night before on a wagon of supplies and spent the night at the schoolhouse. She told him that her mother's father, John Lapsley, a staunch and loyal unionist, had died two years previously (1).

The debris that cluttered Virginia Street reminded him of the morning's horrors. Johnny threw one leg over Red's neck and jumped down. He reached up and eased Serena off the sweaty animal. Johnny patted Red and hugged his neck. The animal's eyes grew big and he tossed his head up and down twice.

"Got him, Johnny?" A melodic voice sounded from behind him."

He stopped at the steps, turned, and watched John McKee descend the steps from the McKee house and approach Spurgeon's store. "No, didn't," he lied and helped Serena climb the steps. "He got away — over the Fox River. Ran down this young kid." He felt Serena's fingernails dig his biceps. "Ran him over so I figured better to save an innocent than catch a horse thief. How'd you do?"

"Up the hill we went, but could see nothing of them until we got to John Bedell's. There we fired a few shots and followed on through the prairie. Then we formed a line just east of John Beadman's. There was about 150 of the enemy across the hollow in the hazel brush, about one-fourth mile away. I fired a few shots at them in there and they soon left that shelter. We followed them, came to Ransom's house, halted awhile, pushed on to the Stafford house. Here a number of shots were fired while they were in front of Robert Gray's. These were the last shots exchanged. When we got back to Ransom's, we found one of the rebels had been shot in the jaw, the...(4)." While he talked, his hawk eyes examined the thin form adorned in a bloody shirt and mud covered leather britches.

"Your pa, the Colonel, okay?"

"Yeah, fine. He always worries 'bout me getting shot. We lost a couple, old man Sullivan and Preacher Harris — some wounded may die yet (4)."

"Gotta get the kid's shoulder fixed." Johnny dragged Serena up the steps. Inside the store he led her to one of the makeshift beds and told her to lie down. She frowned so he grinned and went to the box of dressings, grabbed a handful and then plucked two Union Army shirts, a small and a regular issue, from another box. He put one over her chest, slipped on the regular, and then fetched a pair of scissors from the table nearby. Three Union soldiers remained, their multiple splinter wounds attended to. No one paid him any heed so he reached under the small issue resting on Serena's chest and cut off his bloody shirt. It fell to the side. Serena stirred apprehensively. He winked with his right eyelid, searched the boxes against the far wall until he found the herbs. Gently, he removed the dressing. It seemed stuck. He teased it off. Bleeding started. Her narrowed eyes told him she still didn't trust him. After he gingerly applied a powder of dried spotted geranium roots, he put on a fresh soft mat from the inner bark of the witch hazel for inflammation and wound a long dressing around her chest, over the wounded shoulder, under the armpit and back around her chest.

"You're mashing my bumps into my lungs, jerk," she whimpered, only this time with a playful look in her large eyes, still green without the bright green shirt. "Go see if my pa, Mr. Hill, was one killed or wounded, please."

Johnny went to the front and checked the lists. He returned and stared at Serena, her face contorted. "He's wounded." He paused, considering whether to tell her he was the one with the splinter of an arm. "He was sent to Keokuk on the train out of Croton."

Serena stood, holding a shirt, and said, "I'm going to Keokuk."

"I'm going to St. Francisville. The ride to Keokuk won't stir up any bleeding with that wrap," he said and helped with the small shirt. He stepped back while she tucked the army issue in her britches. He giggled. "And your bumps don't show through the tight wrap." He took her arm and guided her for the door where he paused and whispered, "I'll drop you at cousin Jenkins farm on the way."

Having a girl, her arm wrapped around his waist, for the hours it took to reach the Jenkins farm, soothed Johnny's emotions, stirred by images of the dead bodies. Zeke sure screwed up my life he told himself. He's dead. Big price, he decided. Now Blake, Zeke's older brother, was a threat, an incurable, born mean skunk. Why didn't he die, he concluded. Nearing the Jenkins farm, Johnny shrugged off the debate and resolved to dump the pest behind him and go see Elizabeth.

He spied the two-story house and across the road, several head of fat cows grazing in the pasture next to the Eiler's small stone house, now the Jenkins school house. At age twenty-two, John William, Uncle Robert's oldest, managed the farm but the twins, Margaret and Catherine, born two years later, ran the household (5).

John and his three brothers, George Franklin, Robert Edwin, and James Amzi, worked the fields. The house seemed deserted, save for faint sounds from a kitchen window at the back of the house. Serena jumped down and duck-waddled for the door. Johnny, watching Serena's skinny form while he tied Red to the post, followed.

"You stare like an animal," she taunted and stopped short of the door.

"Smart mouth," he mumbled. At her side he said, "You

walk like a duck."

"Edge of the saddle, stupid," she said over her shoulder and pounded on the door.

Johnny made one of his too-quick frowns, the frightened face, and enjoyed Serena's shocked look.

The door opened. Catherine, one of the twins (5), recognized Serena, hugged her while smiling over her shoulder at Johnny, and led them into the kitchen. The five Jenkins's had finished dinner, James Amzi and a dark-skinned girl, tending to the dishes and pans, cousins John, George, and Robert arguing in between scoops of pie. They greeted Serena by name and waved to Johnny, except James Amzi who bolted out of his chair and put a bear hug on him. They listened in awe at the story Serena told after Johnny enthralled his cousins with an account of the battle at Athens.

"No need to go to Keokuk. I just came from there. I saw them load the wounded on a steamer heading for Canton. If you leave now you can catch it there," cousin John said.

Johnny looked at Serena and said, "I'll take you, but I have to go to St. Francisville first and see Elizabeth. I promised her."

"Don't bother, Johnny. She and Doc McGee are in Keokuk. You know her," cousin John said.

"If you intend to go to Canton with me, I want the twins to cut your hair so's that herd of wild and depraved soldiers will think you're my kid brother come with me to meet George."

"No way. I can tuck it under a floppy."

He argued, but with the twins reinforcing her refusal, gave up. They took a bedroll the twins fixed for her and a bag of food for a few days. Johnny borrowed a wagon and gelding, tied Red to the rear, and set out on the twenty-eight mile trek to Canton. To repeated questions, Johnny reassured Serena that if they traveled for three hours and slept outside Canton, they'd reach the steamer in the morning before it departed for Hannibal. A quarter mile past Gregory Road he pointed

to a large brick house standing on the hill overlooking the
Salt River Road, and told Serena that Judge Boulware, a
powerful slave owner, lived there (5).

Within the hour, clouds covered the moon and a drizzle
commenced. Johnny took his poncho and Serena held it over
their heads. The rain fell heavier so he steered alongside a
brook for a clump of trees below a small knoll thirty yards
off the road, some five miles from Canton, he estimated. He
unhitched the gelding and tied it and Red to a sapling next
to a big walnut tree. Johnny set the bedrolls under the
wagon, using the poncho as a shield in the direction of the
rain. Serena was mute. Leaning close he noted the shivers. It
crossed his mind, she had to be distraught about her father.

"Sorry, Serena. I shouldn't tease. I know you're worried
about your pa." He unwrapped the blanket from his shoulders and placed it in front of the poncho. "We must huddle
for heat, the chill from rain even if it's August. We'll put
your blanket over us." He noted the raised eyebrows. "Come
on, you're a kid. I'm safe as a brother."

"I have to piddle. I'm not doing it in the rain so you roll
on your stomach. No looking. Promise."

Johnny rolled over and buried his head in the blanket.
Who wants to stare at skin and bones, he mumbled to himself.

"EEEEEH!"

He snapped around to look at a shiny white butt supported two inches from the mud at the end of the wagon by two
arm stilts.

Serena scooted to dry ground and pulled up the leather
trousers with long white underpants. She crawled on the
blanket next to Johnny and turned her back to him. "You
said you wouldn't peek."

"You screamed."

"My feet slipped out from under me. You peeked. No boy
— no man has ever seen me that way."

"Sorry. I haven't hurt you. I got more serious things on

my mind than kid...than women, Serena." He rolled on his side, his back to hers. "I was wrong about you being skinny."

A wildcat's paw rolled him on his back. "That's the first nice thing you've said to me." She smiled. It almost looked cute in the dim light. He smiled too quickly, the unusual exchange causing him to forget.

Her breath blew on his face. She lowered her face closer, their noses almost touching. From the movements of the whites he knew she studied his face, the slow left side catching up with the right.

"Johnny, I'm sorry. Your face. I saw that before. What?"

"Aren't you sleepy?"

"No."

"I'll tell you about my family if you do the same. Least 'til we get sleepy." Johnny began by telling her that his father James came from Pennsylvania and his early death and his beating. When he finished telling how Dr. Payne patched him up and the Flacks took him in permanent to be a playmate for Ezra, she told him her grandfather, John A. Lapsley, came from Kentucky in 1836 and settled north of St. Francisville (2). Johnny told her he knew a David Nelson Lapsley who was off at Law School in Pennsylvania and wondered if he were her older bother.

"Grandpa had twelve children," she said and leaned back. "My ma, who was one of the first, stayed in Kentucky. When grandpa took ill in 1855 my father moved us to Missouri to help with the farm, and that's how I got to Missouri. David Nelson Lapsley is the twelfth, ma's youngest brother, my uncle. He was born in 1839 and so he's only seven years older." She reminded him that Grandpa Lapsley died two years ago (2).

"The year after I got beat I attended the school in St. Francisville instead of the Jenkins School. I went there five years. That's why we never met," he said.

Serena agreed and said a grandmother's maiden name

was McKee and some of those relatives followed her grandparents to Missouri. Bet Doc McKee is a relative, he offered.
His dad is some kind of uncle, she told him. The two dozed
off without saying goodnight, but Johnny smiled to himself
when she snuggled up close.

Brookside Death
Canton, August 6

Johnny couldn't remember when the rain stopped. All he knew was that the spot he picked, behind the big oak tree and partially hidden by the knob of ground that stood between them and the Salt River Road, seemed safe. From the occasional road sounds that penetrated his sleep, he knew the dirt surface would be a quagmire, its wheel ruts mini-streams. That and Serena's restless body, at times mashed against his back and other times almost draped on him when he was on his back, made for a long night. Leastwise, she didn't snore, he concluded. He eased up, pulled on his shoes and two trees away, behind a big bush, sprayed an outcropping of ivory white mushrooms. At the wagon, Serena was up, lacing her high leather shoes. He studied the shoes intently. She noticed his scrutiny.

"You don't like my shoes?"

He waited until she pulled her trousers down over her ankles and re-examined their appearance. "They're okay. Could pass for boys' shoes. Get your hat on and cover up all that hair." He reached down and pulled out the gunnysack with the food. He fished out some hard bread and a piece of beef jerky. "Lots of traffic on the road. Best we not build a fire. Probably tough anyhow, seein' how wet everything is."

She tucked her hair under the floppy and chewed on the bread. "Can we get the wagon along the muddy road?"

"Yeah. Slow goin' so we best move on so's not to miss the steamer." He saw her shifting from foot to foot while her eyes seemed to survey the woods around. "Back there twenty feet is a brook and some bushes. You can go over there. I'll walk down and check the road." He pointed away from the road and watched her disappear in the brush. Twenty feet from the road, the sounds of horses sloshing at a slow pace made him squat behind a cluster of thorn bushes. Three blue coats and a man in tattered farm clothes headed in the direction of Canton. The two up front in Union garb rode side by side and talked, their demeanor serious. He waited for them to disappear around the next bend, listened and, not hearing anything but the squawking of a crow zooming overhead, stepped to the road. The wheel ruts were full of water so he figured the gelding could move the wagon along, but the going would be slow. Horse noise and voices prompted his dash over the knob. Serena rolled up the blankets and poncho. She smiled, her mood the happiest he had witnessed so far.

"We'll fetch my pa and get you with your brother soon," she said. She wasn't so plain looking, yet still skinny, his analysis told him.

The snap of a branch guided his eyes straight ahead beyond a cluster of goldenrod. A wisp of brown caught his eye. Maybe a deer or bear, even a fox, he decided, though uncertain and hit with wariness because the bluejays suddenly squawked. He moved his eyes for his roll, bent over, fished through the mosquito netting and found the pistol he had taken from Serena. He straightened up. "Serena, I figure if I can't get with the First Regiment outa Canton and work with an army surgeon for a couple years of the war, I can get in one of them medical departments in St. Louis — a choice of one or two, I hear. And the thirteen dollars a month pay, if I save it, won't hurt. So we..." he spied a horse with its rider leaning over the horse's neck to miss the low branches, approaching from his right, from the direction of the brook. "Pull your hat down real low and think how boys move. Don't talk," he whispered, leaning close, pretending to help her tie a roll. Speaking louder, he continued as he picked up his roll and held it in front of his belly to hide the pistol, "Best we hook up old Puckett, Cap. The boys will be along any minute," Johnny said. Serena hunkered her shoulders and nodded. The man pulled up a sorrel and straightened in the saddle.

"You boys huntin'?" A couple of jagged teeth sat on each side of the spaces where some used to be. The three-or-four day growth of beard was coal black. But the shifty eyes made Johnny's palms wet.

"We joining up in Canton, we are," he answered and eased to Serena's side and whispered, "This ain't good. Don't talk, and don't look up. If things gets tough, remember the rifle under the wagon seat."

Johnny's skin tingled. He sensed every odor, a waft of wet leaves, a hint of the moss under the tree. The sun shot bright stabs through the overhead foliage. He studied the man who had nudged the sorrel closer to Serena. Johnny's pulse sped. Creaking of leather somewhere to his back filled his ears as if thunder. He sneaked his hand under the bedroll and wrapped it around the pistol handle. Like a hawk the rider leaned over the corner of the wagon and snatched the floppy off Serena's head.

His guttural sound joined her gasp. She grabbed her hair. Johnny smelled musty, wet horse from behind. His index finger moved to the trigger.

"Hey, Sherm. Look what we got here — a girlie," the rider, his face a picture of joy, one of a man who had just stumbled on a gold mine.

The breathing of a horse seemed in Johnny's ear. He cocked the hammer. The pistol had not cleared his belt before horrible, lightening pain rattled over the back of his head. Wet ground came up to meet his face.

Darkness gave way to a misty scene. His felt no pain, no wet, chilly ground, only peace when he gazed on Elizabeth. "When you come back I want you to get a big bucket for the shower, Johnny." He smiled real slow, turned in the shower stall and took in her warmth, her body warmth stronger with each inch closer. He wanted to tell her he would not be long at the war because everybody said it would be over in a few months. He would hurry home to let her wash his back every night, but his mouth would not move because it began to shiver with the rest of his body. Her face was so close and her mouth, its red, appetizing lips, half open, so close he could lick them with his tongue. He shivered hard. The lips turned black. They let out a scream, an eerie high pitched one as if from the depths of her belly. It made his head throb. A blood-curdling scream chased Elizabeth away. He opened the eye on the side that was not kissing moss. He saw a wagon wheel. He imagined he heard a sob. The smell of wet horse filled his nostrils. Johnny slowly turned his head and studied the gray shapes at ground view while his top hand felt the ground for the pistol. Mud, leaves, moss, and — a soft object, Serena's hat. The sight blasted his brain, momentarily masking the vice holding the back of his head. He eased on all fours. The earth spun and he fell on his back and stared at the circular motion of the green canopy above. With a gentle turn of his head he looked for the rider and his friend — maybe friends.

The twin trees that encompassed the area soon became single, so he used the wagon wheel to pull himself up, clinging with both hands when the earth rolled left, then right. It stopped swaying when he heard, "Please don't." Serena's pleading kicked in adrenalin. His vision cleared as fast as his brain. The voice came from the brook. He felt under the seat and removed the Springfield rifle and crept toward the brook. The rush of thoughts spawned by the view made heated blood race through his body. The rider at Serena's head had both knees on her upper arms stretched out to the side. The chest bandage was gone. He sang, "Lordy, lordy." A hulk of a man, his back to Johnny, sat on Serena, yanking at the belt to her trousers. Johnny quickly looked about for others. None. He peered back as the man pulled away Serena's belt. Simulating the charge of a bull, he had seen at Uncle Robert's farm, Johnny clutched the barrel of the rifle, sprang through the bushes and after three gigantic strides swung the rifle at the red head that angled his way. The stock of the rifle shuddered when it hit a side of the head. Blood sprayed and an eyeball popped out like a squeezed grape. The man fell over Serena's leg to her side, no sound. No movements. The rider, wide-eyed, lunged for Johnny's pistol to his left. He clutched it and rolled over, raised it. Johnny kicked. The pistol went skyward.

"Move and I'll blow you to pieces." Johnny jabbed the muzzle of the Springfield into the rider's groin. From his view at the man's feet he put on his mean face and saw the terror paralyze the man's greasy, strained face.

"Don't shoot. I got a wife and three kids back in Warsaw," he stammered.

Johnny stepped back and with a quick glance saw Serena on her feet, fixing the belt to her leather britches. "Put your hands on top your head. Serena, the pistol's in that azalea bush. Get it now." The rider flinched so Johnny pulled the hammer back and sighted the barrel at his groin. The man went limp on the ground and let out a pathetic whimper. Serena, the fine lines of her mud-smeared face beginning to streak from the silent tears, stood with the pistol. Without moving his eye from the gun sight, he snarled. "Pull the hammer back." He heard the metallic click. "Aim it at his left eyeball." He took a deep breath, finding pleasure in the total terror that consumed the body trembling on the wet ground. "He was going to rape you after..." he paused to cast a hurried glance at the other man, lifeless in the exact position as before. "After that animal had his pleasure. Shoot him or I'll blow him to kingdom come."

Shakes, then a distant hissing sound, and then sobs rolled out of Serena. Her arm with the pistol fell to her side. Johnny grabbed it and with the rifle aimed in his left hand and the pistol in his right he ordered the man to stand.

"Keep them hands on top your head. You move one finger and I move both trigger fingers. Now move back to the wagon." The man stumbled back to the wagon. "Get on your horse — easy, nice and slow like."

The man climbed up. Doc McKee had told Johnny many

times that people announced their thinking with their eyes. The man's terror had undergone transformation to an intense, eager look. Johnny read his mind and pointed both weapons at the man's chest.

"Slowly walk the horse to the road. Once there, turn north and walk him slow 'til you round that far bend. You do anything..."

Serena's footsteps moved Johnny's shoulders aside ever so slightly, and the rider lunged from the horse. Without looking, Johnny flexed both index fingers. One bullet gouged out a furrow alongside the rider's head. The other bullet struck him in the shoulder. His heavy body crashed Johnny to the ground, the stubble face against Johnny's scratched one. Blood spattered on the rider's lower face but his eyes glowered with hate. Johnny tried to swing the rifle around but the sinewy arm jammed it into the mud. Johnny groped for the pistol, fighting to get breath through the strangle hold on his neck. He bent his right knee up, his gasps moving nothing but his chin. He felt the knife. Fear surged through his being. The sky turned gray, sounds stopped. He strangled the knife handle and with the last ounce of air-starved muscle power he plunged the knife in the man's back. The vice remained around his throat. The rider twisted. And twisted. The man let go of the rifle and twisted his arm for his back. Red eyes got big, the vice loosened so Johnny gulped the hot, fetid air between their faces. The man's heavy body shook. Johnny pulled the knife out and drove it in the man's neck. He pushed up with both arms. Blood squirted from the gaping neck wound, hitting Johnny's face like a downpour. The man's eyeballs rolled back, nothing but white. With a heave of both arms the rider flew to Johnny's side, gasping, his arms and legs thrashing at the breeze that had come up. While Johnny watched the agonized breaths, he jerked up his shirt and wiped the blood out of his eyes, off his nose and lips. He hacked a mouthful of bloodstained spit toward the ground and saw it strike a shoe. He turned to Serena, her face a picture of fear. Yet her eyes stared at him, a stare of admiration, he concluded. She helped him stand, hugged him and then peeled the knife out of the hand that hung like a limp noodle at his side. He stared when she began slicing at her hair.

Gently, with both bloody hands, Johnny shook her shoulders. "It's all right. It's over," he said, slowly pulled her, dragged her back to the brook. The other man was getting stiff, still in the same position. He rolled him over and checked his pupils, felt his neck, and then tore his shirt open and listened with his left ear. He stood erect. Tears ran down his cheeks. "I just killed two men," he blurted.

"I never saw a man cry. I'm sorry. You were wonderful. If I had listened about the hair it wouldn't have happened. You said it would. You told me twice that if I didn't look and act like a boy some animal away from his woman would club you senseless, then have his pleasure with me. I did it to you. I want you to cut my hair short as yours. I want to see you smile." She took a deep breath. "I want you to like me. Be my friend. I want to take care of you. We was about to get...I was about to be raped, probably killed along with you. And like a hero, so fearless..."

"Just stop blabbering for a second," Johnny shot at her and failed to suppress a sob that surfaced. Suddenly, she threw herself at him and began sobbing. They held each other and cried together, the torrent of tears wetting his chest. Swaying back and forth on the wagon seat in the warmth of the morning sun, they slowly calmed, like a hush after a storm.

She pulled back, licked the tears off her lips. "Johnny, we got to talk open about the horror. It isn't healthy to be silent. Why do you cry so?"

Johnny tilted his head slowly up and down. "I lived with Quakers for four years 'til now. I ain't no Quaker but they're right. Killin' is bad. It makes one bad. I said I was goin' to war to patch up soldiers. I wasn't goin' to kill none. I just killed two strangers."

"For heaven sakes, they were going to rape me and then kill me for sure — and you."

In silence, they ate some dry corn mash, washed down by the cool brook water while they bumped for Canton. The throbbing in Johnny's head faded in the battle going on inside. He killed two men. He saved a girl — no, a woman — from a bad hurt. She was a talker, and skinny. She was a gentle person. He had a friend, could be as good a one as Sam, he figured.

"If we find your pa, we can take him to a church and tend to him before you take him home," Johnny said.

She squinted at him and asked, "Which church we going to visit?"

"Methodist — German Methodist, the one that is opposed to slavery. My mother's parents belong there."

"The one? Is there another, one that believes in slavery?"

"Yeah. About the time my pa died the church split over slavery into M.E. North and M.E. South (6)," Johnny said.

Johnny decided he would go to Regiment headquarters first to find George and see if Serena's father was let off in Canton or had to go to Hannibal. He also decided the morning's events had prepared him for real battles. I'm a growed up surgeon's assistant. I'll go with George to the big battles out east, and I'll get taught so's I get to medical school.

Chapter 5

Finding Serena's Pa
Canton, August 6

The wagon cleared a stand of cottonwood and offered a clear picture of Main Street, less than two blocks ahead. To the right Serena caught sight of the white dome of Christian College, one of the first co-educational colleges in the United States (1). More than 2500 citizens lived in Canton (2). The road seemed smoother now and was lined with houses. Johnny pulled over and spoke to a young looking soldier, "Private, where's Colonel Woodyard's headquarters?"

"Shucks, I ain't no private." The youthful eyes grew big scanning up and down the two anxious bodies on the wagon seat. He swung his arm beyond the mare and pointed to a cabin. "That be it."

Johnny thanked him and coaxed the lazy animal through a throng, a motley crowd of Union soldiers of all ages and attire, some beyond description, but all got the attention of the two on the small, old, rickety flatbed. Johnny reined up the mare but was greeted by a fat, sloppy dressed man in full Union dress.

"Hey, Johnny. Where you been?" The fat one pointed the yellow stem of a corncob pipe at Serena. "Rumor has it you are so good and busy you're training an assistant." The man moved beside the wagon, turned and yelled, "Colonel. The boy whiz come. He's got his own help with um." He bent to the side to look close under the straw hat, and before an answer came from the cabin, pushed it up with his pipe. Serena frowned. "Boy, you awful young lookin'." He hesi-

*Christian College administration building, Canton. The huge domed
structure as it exists today. Photo by the author.*

tated while he looked her over from head to toe. "Grown tall
quick, I reckon, but I'd wager you don't shave once a week."

"Cap's tuckered out," Johnny answered and waved at a
gray and black-headed man, his stiff posture, hat rather than
a cap, and the sword hanging at his side, hints that helped
Serena figure it was Woodyard. "Hi, Colonel," Johnny said.

Woodyard grinned, turned, and hollered over his shoulder, "Murph, bring a complete oufit, medium for Johnny."
He looked Serena up and down. "We gotta fatten you up,
boy." Yet, he stared, the puzzled look glued on Serena.

Johnny asked about the steamer with the wounded, and
the whereabouts of brother George.

"Bunch of Federals and a few rebs with wounds getting
better got off here. And one that's dying. The rest need the
services of an army surgeon and a hospital, ought to be at
Hannibal now. General Hurlbut's headquarters is there.

We're heading for Kirksville. Seems some of Green's troops are causing trouble (3)."

The fat one, obviously an assistant, handed Johnny a piece of paper, a list of those sent on to Hannibal on top, those pulled off at the bottom. He passed it to Serena. She searched the names while Woodyard said George had stayed in Palmyra to get better trained as a surgeon's assistant, so when the First Northeast Missouri Regiment from Clark County and the Second Northeast Missouri Regiment from Lewis County merged to make the Twenty-first Missouri Infantry, he would be able to go with them. Serena handed the papers back to Johnny. He paused, stared into her eyes and then gave the paper back to the fat one. He turned the mare around but Serena grabbed the reins and pulled.

"Stop. He's here." She frowned to fight back the tears. "He's the one dying — they took off the boat."

Johnny turned in the seat. "Hey, Murph. Where's the one dyin?"

"The reb?" Eyebrows above a round red nose raised. "Took him to a doctor on Main Street. Name's Hawkins (2). Only one could cut off the dead end of a stump."

Johnny's mouth dropped, his head turned ever so slightly, his eyes, narrowed to slits, locked on Serena's face.

"Thanks, Murph," he said and coaxed the mare onto Main Street.

Finally, she blurted, "I can explain."

"Just shut up," he mumbled through clenched teeth. "Look for the name Hawkins on one of these doors."

She felt the hot tears stream down her face. Johnny eased the mare along until they saw "DOCTOR HAWKINS" on a door beside the pharmacy (2). He pulled up the mare.

"You know what's wrong. You knew all along daddy has a bad wound. Didn't you, Johnny Jenkins?"

He squirmed in the seat, tied the reins to the wagon brake. "Not for certain. But I knew that he was the one with the hand shot off." He scowled. "And for certain I didn't think a

Lapsley would be a reb." He jumped down. "What else should I know?" He stopped when she let out a sob. "You got to cry. He's your pa." She wept softly, holding the straw hat over her face. "I know a couple good farmers with only one hand," he said. She peeked at Johnny from under the hat.

"I know what you mean, Johnny. He could still die 'cause lots of people die from amputation. That's what you want me to understand."

"I was the one who put the tourniquet..." He stopped because she sobbed. "Listen. After amputation, many die from infection. If high on the leg four out of five, Doc McKee tells me. If only the foot or arm, not one in five (4). So he can survive what they probably doin' at this minute. You can take him home if he don't get an infection — and nurse him to health. In a few months he'll learn to farm 'bout good as a two-armed man. He'll be free from the horrors of shootin' at friends and neighbors."

"If he lives," she said and followed Johnny through the door into a small dark room, the waiting room.

A man in black pants, with rolled up sleeves of a silk white shirt, covered by a black vest, looked at them over spectacles. "Yes?" he said impatiently.

Johnny had a subtle grin, with only his lower face. "Doctor Hawkins, I'm Johnny Jenkins. I'm assistant to Doctor Robert McKee of St. Francisville. I come to fetch the man you amputated, the one whose stump you revised. He's married to Doctor McKee's sister. "Cap here's a preacher's son. Goin' to help me take him back."

"Assistant?" The man shook his head. His eyes squinted.

"I figured the man would need surgery. In Athens I applied the tourniquet. His hand was already gone. An artery sprayed the road. I thought it was his radial because it was deeper than the ulnar artery should be..." Johnny paused.

Hawkins turned and held the curtain back so Johnny, and then Serena could enter. Pale and writhing, a form lay on a cot in the corner. Serena swallowed hard to fight nausea when she spied the bloody sheet with a grimy amputation kit and piece of an arm on the floor. The room began to spin but the sound that belonged to a harsh voice said, "I never saw the ulna, but the stick of a bone that pushed out of the fibrillating muscle had to be the radius." Johnny reached over and held her upright. Her legs felt rubbery.

"Okay. I believe you're an assistant or a medical student. You sure look young to me," the doctor said and kneeled beside the babbling patient. "I've done all I can, so if you want to take him go ahead, but I don't think his condition will allow survival, and especially if you take him on a twenty-five-mile trip."

Serena kept her head lowered and followed while Hawkins and Johnny carried her father to the flatbed. The doctor told Johnny he had two old blankets. She stroked her pa's forehead until Johnny returned with two blankets and a strange smile. They camped by the river two miles south of Canton in sight of the campfires from Riverside Park. For Serena the night proved difficult. Worry over her father and after administering laudanum four times, finally brought on a deep sleep.

Bizarre sounds mingled with muffled noises of people. Then her father's voice, incoherent messages, and a plaintive curse filled her ears. The early morning air was already heavy but the easterly breeze that whipped gentle waves against the Mississippi River shore cooled her face. Serena opened her eyes and recognized the ceiling of her bedroom, the splintered wagon bed. She leaned on both elbows and scanned the camp. A fire smoldered beneath a blackened pot. Gusts powered up flames and blew whiffs of hickory into her nostrils. The sun, well over the treetops, bounced off Johnny's knife, stuck in a log beside the fire. From left to right she looked. No Johnny.

Moans guided her gaze behind. The form of her father struggled against the cocoon, which had restrained his erratic movements during the night. Serena climbed from under the wagon, squatted behind the brush by the river and peed. At the fire she stuck a finger in the small kettle and licked the brown liquid. The taste told her it was a tea, made from Southern Maidenhair fern (5), one of Johnny's favorites for wounded soldiers. She poured the tepid liquid in a cup, aroused the delirious figure muttering gibberish from under a willow. Slowly, she spoke, uttering phrases they had used, the kind fathers and daughters latch onto, sort of as secret language. For an instant the bleary eyes opened wide, a hint of recognition, at least the slight retraction of the mouth suggested that, she thought. Half the liquid rolled down his scruffy salt and pepper-colored beard, but he kept most down. She repeated the procedure three times, the last better because all went down, his swallowing improved. She laid him back and noted wide eyes staring at her. "It's Serena, pa. I love you."

His eyes bleared but the wisp of a smile remained. Serena climbed under the wagon and pulled on her socks and boots. She folded up the blankets, putting her old leather britches and green shirt in one. Unfolding the other, she grabbed the two books, the mosquito netting, and began to roll them the way she saw Johnny do it. She stopped, struck by curiosity. Thumbing through Eberle's medical book, she searched for pictures of anatomy. None, not even of the human arm. How did he know that to calm Doc Hawkins? she mumbled, and put it beside the other, smaller book on the roll. "Gospels," the dirty golden letters said. Inside the cover, the name Weaver with the date December 24, 1802 produced a gentle nod. Her eyes froze on the face page. Just as a child sneaks freshly baked biscuits and looks around the kitchen, and finding no witnesses, sticks two in her pocket, she glanced from the message in small script, too perfect to be a boy's writing. Beyond the fire, small figures moved about the Federal camp at Riverview Park. Heat bathed her temples while her pulse quickened. With a slight shake to her hand she brought the words into focus.

Johnny-

Read my grandma's bible and remember me.
Husband's bad sick. I don't figure he'll make it
through another year. When you come back from
fighten be my husband.

love-
Elizabeth

Serena slapped the covers of the small book together and rolled it up with the other book and the netting. She secured the poncho around it, her mind filled with visions and thoughts about this older woman carrying on with Johnny. The whinny of a horse eased her head up. Out the corner of her eye she saw two horses approaching so she climbed from under the wagon, dragging the bedrolls with her. Both were secured under the seat of the flatbed when a deep voice called her name. She spun around and looked in the blue eyes of George Jenkins. Johnny dismounted and hung a pot over the fire, set the kettle of tea on the ground, and went over to her father, acting strange as if she weren't even present.

"Serena?" George tied the reins of his and Johnny's horses to the post sticking up from the front of the wagon and ambled toward her.

"Cap's the reb horse thief from Athens," Johnny said. He looked up from the fire, the lower half of his eyes, not hidden by his lowered brow, had a cool glare.

"Nice you remember me, George." She extended her hand but peered at his face. "I've seen you many times at the farm — with James Amzi and my little sister. They're pals."

George rolled his head and rubbed his chin. "No. It was at Jenkins schoolhouse — with that scoundrel Blake."

Her heart sank. To her left she watched Johnny down whatever grub was in the pot they brought. He didn't look at her, only walked around the wagon and took his roll from under the seat. He tied it behind the saddle on a horse that looked like Red and climbed up. Serena shuffled in the wet leaves stirred up by Red, who scraped the ground like a nervous bull. He and Johnny exchanged visual messages.

"Cap, I'm goin' with Colonel Woodyard to chase some of Green's men that are festering around Monticello and Kirksville." He pulled the blue cap down tight. "George is goin' to put some of that moldy bread we brought on your pa's stump. An Indian from Illinois said sometimes it draws infection out of amputation stumps. Use it and that other as a poultice."

"Johnny, I want to say..."

"You talk too much, Cap."

Serena sucked in the smoky air from the fire with the distant, cold tone that matched Johnny's glare. "George's going to the farm today. He'll take you and your pa to Alexandria." Johnny nudged the horse to George. He leaned over and patted George's shoulder, the older brother's face in a huge grin. "George, thanks for getting the Colonel to take me as his surgeon's assistant. See you when you catch up with us."

Not so much as a peek at her, Serena muttered under her breath, and stomped over to her father with laudanum. And why revert to calling her Cap? Why the hateful looks? She laid her pa's head on a rolled up coat and went to the fire. A cup was thrust at her. She looked in the warm eyes of George and took the cup. She sipped the gruel, chewing on the pieces of pork that hit her palate.

"We got along well, Johnny and I, 'til you come along. What you do?"

"He doesn't care you hid from him about your pa being a reb." George tipped his cup bottom up, grabbed a jug, and swished water in the cup, throwing it on the fire.

Serena did the same with her cup. The fire sizzled and the smoke made her cough. "He knew about that yesterday and wasn't perturbed. Come on. What?"

"Slater. Blake Slater. When he told me about catching you at Athens and the attack outside Canton the next morning, he talked with admiration the way you withstood all the terror and the worry about your pa. He said it didn't bother him your pa fought with the Confederates, because lots of families are torn apart — Moore's three sons are with the rebs," George said matter of fact, but his eyes spoke concern. Maybe doubts, she thought.

"So why all of a sudden does he act like I'm the one bashed his head?"

"Slater. I told Johnny I remembered seeing you and Blake friendly like behind the schoolhouse. And..."

"Had to be two years ago, 'cause you left school about then. I was thirteen. Doesn't appear to trouble you none, George." She searched his face.

"Blake is a bad guy. He's been in more trouble than a roused rattlesnake. But no fret from me. I don't care. Now Johnny — he's learned to control the scars on his face Blake put there. He hasn't learned to control the inside scars." George stomped out the rest of the fire, went over to the willow and, as if picking up a small animal, he hoisted her pa in his arms and placed him on the flatbed. He motioned for her to climb up. She hung the pot and small kettle on the hooks at the back of the wagon while he tied his mount to a tailgate post.

Serena climbed up and sat. When George sat next to her and grabbed the reins, she clutched his arm. He turned. "Blake's not a nice person. What you saw behind the schoolhouse was some of his trickery. It didn't work. Nothing happened 'cept I wolloped him good. I hate him," she lied, glancing at George. He seemed to take it in.

George flicked the reins and the mare suddenly acted alive. "I'll have you and your pa home by supper. We'll get Johnny's favorite doc — Doctor McKee..."

"I like — owe Johnny lots."

"Forget Johnny. He's got a burr under his saddle. He's never so much as held hands with a girl. He has this thing about being a doctor. Thinks people will like him then, overlook his problems."

"Boy, are you adrift in the current, George," Serena said under her breath. She started to ask him if he ever heard of some old woman named Flack but decided brothers were too close. If he had, he'd lie like Johnny, she figured. Serena closed her eyes and vowed she'd find Blake and tell him some juicy stories about the Jenkins boys.

Chapter 6

Battles at Clapp's Ford
and Memphis
Edina, August 16

An orange glow cast long shadows over the treetops on the hills surrounding Edina. Colonel Humphrey M. Woodyard led his bedraggled men toward the haze that hovered over the low-lying areas, a veil produced by the myriad cooking fires, a bluish-orange hue from the refracted orange glow. Born in Kentucky, Woodyard had moved to Lewis County where he practiced law. He served in the General assembly in 1849-1850 and due to his rabid speeches against slavery both Edward Bates and James Rollins labeled him a "radical" (1). By 1860 Woodyard owned 4,000 acres in Lewis County.

Through the lazy columns of smoke, the rifles, stacked in tripod fashion, appeared as wooden pyramids. The gray-white mist that drifted toward the cloudless sky dispensed a hint of hickory wood mixed with an odor of fresh horse droppings. Next to the source of the odor and huge horse flies was the temporary stable. Johnny tied the hospital supply wagon to a small tree, some type of fruit tree but unrecognizable without fruit. He looked past the corral of military mounts and searched for Moore's medical team. The panorama of blue coats, smoky haze, and rifles occupied his attention so that he missed the figure that approached until a voice stirred him to reality.

"Impressive, Jenkins," Woodyard's surgeon, Dr. L. Lusk, said, and stepped in between the view and Johnny. "Woodyard's Second Regiment and Moore's First Regiment finally have joined. With those," he pointed an arm splint at a huddle of blue-coated men wearing bright red capes, "Zouaves from Illinois, must be a thousand troops here."

Johnny turned his head, searching for George. "And I don't see brother George. I thought he was to be Aylward's helper."

"Aylward is back in Memphis with his patients. Moore's surgeon, Doctor Wilfred Wiley is here." Lusk stepped toward Wiley, an approaching gray-headed man, and shook the hand extended to him. "Wilfred, nice to see you again."

"I hear you took casualties at Clapp's Ford (2). Any I can help with?"

Waving the splint, Lusk motioned for Wiley to follow and went to the dray. "I was on my way to ask you if you have any of the new splints. I've been using boards from hard-tack boxes. Also, I need your advice about one of the wounded."

Johnny followed and listened as Wiley told Lusk they had left Athens, camped at Etna on the eighth, the only action occurring at Memphis. "We heard some of Green's men were prowling in the neighborhood. On the tenth we entered Memphis. Weren't no biggie, no wounded, but we did capture some of Green's scouts and put 'em in the local jail (1). The couple days there we chased some rebs, heard General Lyon got shot in the heart in the Battle of Wilson's Creek. We got here yesterday, the day to meet you. What delayed Woodyard?"

"We just missed Green in Monticello on the eighth, but found out he planned a raid on Kirksville. A company of Illinois "Zouaves" joined us and on the eleventh, all three hundred and fifty left Canton and marched all night hoping to get close to Green, find his whereabouts. Fortunately, a bright moon lit up the North Fabius when we approached Clapp's Ford, because the rebs under Porter had collected in tall slough grass with an equal number of men. When we fired on them, the surprised rebs fled, especially after we fired our cannon (2)," Lusk said.

"Cannon? Where'd Woodyard get a cannon?"

"The old piece used at La Grange for civic functions. I knelt over a wounded guy from Canton when I heard an officer yell, 'Boys, they've got cannon, too. Let's get out of this' (2)."

"How many casualties?" Wiley asked.

"Few. We found one dead confederate they left in their hasty departure. One union killed. We had three wounded. One reb we captured said he thought they had three or four wounded." Johnny watched Wiley examine one of the wounded.

"Moore heard about the skirmish and that Porter scurried for Kirksville to join Green." Lusk hesitated while Wiley removed the last of the bandage.

"Next day Woodyard sent some troops to Fairmont to find you guys. They just joined us here in Edina (2)."

Wiley straightened and while holding the man's arm in the air, spoke to Lusk, "Missile went straight through the flesh — between both forearm bones. Don't find any signs it broke either bone."

"We've been on the move. Didn't have time to amputate yet," Lusk said.

The man, perhaps early thirties, complained about needing his arm for farming so Wiley moved his head closer, at the same time feeling for a pulse at the wrist. "Good pulse and no signs of gangrene. What? After three days? Inflamed a might, though." He turned and faced Johnny. "Got some of those magic herbs Doctor Aylward told me about?" Johnny nodded. "Let's put some on the wound." He glanced at the soldier, whose eyes were big as saucers. "We don't have to amputate yet. If infection doesn't get worse, start to spread up the arm or produce gangrene, you might have an arm. May have trouble getting full use of the fingers."

Dr. Lusk frowned. "Risky, no? If we wait until signs it's spreading up his arm, we'll have to amputate higher, above the elbow."

With his good arm the man grabbed at Wiley. "I'll take that chance. Please," he pleaded.

Johnny handed Wiley the herbs and fresh bandages, and held the arm in the air during the application of a poultice followed by the bandage.

Wiley stood. "In the morning both regiments are leaving for Athens. Get you some of the equipment and tents supposed to come up the Des Moines Valley Railroad from Keokuk," he said and peering over the brim of the cup, added, "Couple days of training unless we get different orders from General Hurlbut."

Lusk smiled. "Likely have time to visit in St. Francisville, Johnny."

"What happened to brother George, Doctor Wiley?"

"He reported to Moore in Athens on the eighth, told us you stayed with Woodyard. Moore had him cross to Croton, catch the train for Keokuk and boat to Hannibal to plead with General Hurlbut about tents, much more calomel and laudanum. We've had more problems with disease in camp than battle casualties. I suspect Hurlbut grabbed him for the Illinois Sixteenth to help some professor from St. Louis. They use him because the Sixteenth doesn't have a regular army surgeon."

Johnny nodded for he knew the St. Louis professor had to be Dr. Rollins. Suddenly, with thoughts of St. Francisville and Elizabeth Johnny's mood grew happier. Added to her image, the thought of telling Dr. McKee about his medical experiences brought a deep sleep.

Skirmishes around Kirksville
September 2 in Bethel

Naked men splashed in the Fabius River near Bethel. Row after row of tents filled the rest of Johnny's view. He swatted a mosquito, and took the cup George Jenkins thrust in front of him. The turmoil of the past three days had his tongue in fetters. Heading back to Athens, Moore's and Woodyard's regiments scoured the country for bands of rebels, always showing their strength to intimidate the southern sympathizers. Any plans for a visit to St. Francisville succumbed to orders received to move hastily for Kirksville, the reason given that Green had Hurlbut surrounded (1). So close to her, so close and so far, he bemoaned as George sat next to him.

"You get the flux that hit Athens? Look sorta peaked, brother," George said.

"No. Just sad. I had plans to visit the Flacks when we got orders to make haste for Kirksville."

"Did you get the supplies, the ones Moore had me tell Hurlbut to ship?"

"Lots of calomel and laudanum, some uniforms for Woodyard's men. No tents." He forced a half smile. "How did you get up here? I heard you were assigned to a professor doctor with the Illinois Sixteenth. Bet that was Doctor Rollins."

"General Hurlbut arrived from Macon with Colonel Smith of the Illinois Sixteenth about the time I got to Hannibal (3)." George chuckled. "By the way, did you hear the story about the Speaker of the house?"

Johnny shrugged his shoulders. "Who's he?"

George put his thumbs in his belt. "Listen, because you need to understand General Hurlbut. They say he drinks a boot-full a day and is cantankerous. It seems on August tenth Colonel Smith took six companies of the Illinois

Sixteenth to the Hannibal-St. Joe Railroad at Hudson Station, and was soon joined by General Hurlbut, who being furious at the continual destruction of rail tracks and bridges, arrested many citizens (3)." George chuckled. "In Macon he had McAfee, the Speaker of the House of Representatives, who voted for secession, digging latrines, then took him to Palmyra where he ordered him to be tied to the top of the train engine. Luckily, a couple officers intervened. Didn't cool Hurlbut (4). He chastised Smith for not punishing people of Marion County for their various outrages and schemes. He wanted Smith to ferret out those shooting at the trains (3)." George studied Johnny's face and said, "Tell me how you came to be here in Bethel."

"Glad I'm not in Hurlbut's outfit," Johnny exclaimed but watched George's eyes shift up and down. "So after Moore and Woodyard joined at Edina on the sixteenth, they took us to Waterloo and then back to Athens on the 18th (1). With both regiments we had a thousand troops. I was about to ask for two days to visit the Flacks — I hear he's bad sick...but Moore heard Hurlbut was surrounded at Kirksville by two thousand rebels (1), so we lit out and got as far as Etna when word came that Hurlbut broke out and was heading here. So, here we are."

"Probably misinformation from a reb. We weren't surrounded. We heard there was skirmishing going on at Kirksville around the sixteenth to the nineteenth — between a company of the Iowa Third Infantry and one of Green's companies — so Hurlbut ordered us to move (3)."

Johnny interrupted, "We heard about that from some Iowa guys. A friend of theirs, a corporal from the Iowa Third, named Harvey Dix, died. They told us a squad from Adair County Home Guard under Dix and a company of the Sixteenth Illinois Infantry searching the countryside for Green, stopped for dinner at the house of a Unionist. Upon seeing the enemy, some of Captain Hagar's scouts approaching, Dix ran out of the house, backed himself into the chim-

ney corner, and fought 'til killed. Spotting confederate reinforcements, the rest fled. A picket stationed in the woods
while the companies ate, escaped and went to Kirksville for
help. They returned to the scene but the rebs had vanished
(4). Where were you?" Johnny asked.

George frowned. "With the Ninth. We, too, wanted to find
this elusive Green so we departed from Hannibal, loaded on
a train, and at Macon got off. On the twentieth, Hurlbut sent
hospital stores and sick on to Brookfield. He let me go with
his forces north through Atlanta, LaPlata, and on to a spot
just south of Kirksville. Confederate troops, two thousand,
were eight miles northeast of Kirksville at Bee's Branch.
Our troops took a position at Felb's bridge, near the southwest corner of Knox County on the Salt River (4)."

"I heard there was some killin'."

George stood and helped Johnny off his knees. "Hurlbut
went to Jackson's farm on Bee's branch to get some reb
ammunition. A fight broke out, one reb killed and old man
Jackson wounded — and we found fourteen rebs who had
been wounded during a previous skirmish, two bad, a chest
and a gut shot. Plus a gut shot man, Union guy, the rebs had
captured. Too tough for us. We sent him and two bad-off
rebs to the hospital in Keokuk, the old Estes House. But we
treated the ones without chest or gut shots, a couple amputations, most flesh wounds."

Johnny followed George to a row of tents and waited until
he appeared with a blanket, sat on it in front of the tent.
Johnny lay next to him and watched a hawk circle over the
river. The coarse army-issue shirt scratched his back and his
memory. He turned to George. "Think Cap's pa will make
it?"

"That moldy bread poultice was magic. By the time I left
he was alert." He looked over his shoulder at Johnny.
"Serena's a good nurse. Doc McKee was there and asked
about you. He's worried you might get hurt and not get in
medical school — look at Serena's pa. Going to have a job

of farming with one arm."

"I'm busy hepin' the troops..." Johnny rose on both elbows. "More with sickness than wounds. Seems wars are more about staying healthy. Unless I catch swamp fever or consumption like pa, I'll not have any problem. We medics aren't the ones getting pieces chopped off, not any injuries."

"I'm proud. But that should tell you something. No soldier's safe." George turned around, crossed his legs, and rubbed his stubble. "The First and Second Northeast Regiments don't have enough for each to make a regular army regiment, so the plan is for the two to make one and then go south next year to engage the rebs in Tennessee and Georgia. I'll be with them."

"I want to go. I'm no coward," Johnny said.

"Look, brother, you'll get plenty of opportunity to be a hero — and at some risk. Doctor Rollins told me about a young doctor from St. Louis, engaged. It seems the guy took a bad injury to the face when gray-coats attacked a building in Monroe City with cannon. Blind, permanently blind, so Doctor sent him on a riverboat to St. Louis. On the way, the guy jumped overboard. Couldn't swim. Committed suicide. Drowned."

Johnny sprung up and grabbed George by the shoulders. "I knew him. Saw his face, the horrible looking eyes." Sadness dropped his head to his chest. He blinked back tears and looked at George, feigning a curious look. "Who do I work with 'til sixty-two?"

"Me — the First Northeast Missouri."

Johnny looked about. "Hurlbut's troops have new uniforms and tents and regular rations. Colonel Moore's outfit? We got new uniforms, but we scavenge for diet, and we sleep in barns, under trees, where ever, 'cause no tents."

George told him General Hurlbut with some of the Third Iowa headed for Macon and then Brookfield while Moore's and Woodyard's forces were ordered by General Pope to make haste for Philadelphia. Scouts reported that Green was camped in the area (3).

Not finding Green at Philadelphia because he had escaped southwest toward Paris, Moore's and Woodyard's's forces made haste for Palmyra to get better equipped, and to chase Green's forces south of Hunnewell (3). They moved to Palmyra, where they picked up new 58-caliber Springfield rifles but no new clothes. Due to heavy rains they slept in Holtzclaw's warehouse at Palmyra, the first time in weeks Johnny had slept inside without the hum of mosquitoes trying to penetrate his netting. Rested, he realized a change. His step was forceful, his mood jovial. He watched George writing a letter.

"What's going to happen next? " Johnny asked.

"General Pope — you do know he's commander of all North Missouri forces — well, he took some of his own troops and Colonel Williams with his Second Kansas Infantry after Green because Hurlbut pulled back from Shelbina to Brookfield (1,3). Green's cut telegraph lines. Didn't you say they bombarded you with cannon at Athens?"

Johnny laughed, paused, and when the buzz stopped, and he felt a light feathery touch on his cheek he pulverized the mosquito that had made it into the building. "That's why I take Sappington's pills. Some skeeters are clever. Bombard us at Athens? Shucks, they bombarded Iowans across the Des Moines."

"Moore says it's a Colonel James W. Kneisley, same as at Athens but he's gotten good because they hit the Second Kansas so fiercely, Williams had to pull back his troops twenty-two miles west to Macon City (3)."

"We got orders?"

"Sleep well. We've been ordered to the Salt River. Pope thinks Green is still camped at Hunnewell."

Sleep came easy for Johnny, a tranquil feeling from being around George.

Upon arrival at Hunnewell they found that Green had moved to Florida (3). A forced march was to no avail. Somehow the clever Green had slipped by them at Florida. George told him it was because the drunk General Hurlbut was too hesitant, his behavior having exhausted General Pope's tolerance.

George threw a chicken leg at Johnny and waved a breast at him. "Pope told Williams to remove his regiment from Hunnewell. Boy, was he irate. He told Moore and Woodyard that Price was approaching Lexington and Green was about to join him." George threw the breastbone in the fire and giggled.

"Bet General Pope didn't laugh," Johnny said.

"Ha. Illinois and Iowa regiments are in pursuit, but today Moore and Woodyard got a letter from General Fremont telling them our regiments' three months enlistment is up and we are to head home (1)."

"We're going to Canton, like tomorrow?" Johnny's mind focused on Elizabeth, a smile trailed the heat the thought generated.

After the regiment rested and cleaned their equipment in La Grange, they moved on to Canton on September fifteenth where a grand entry greeted them. The streets of Canton were lined with a raucous crowd when Moore led the troops into town and marched up the hill to take quarters at Christian College. The party atmosphere was short-lived, for the next day, the sixteenth, they sent a squad of 300 horsemen to Monticello to counter rebels. They brought back six prisoners (1,2). At inspection on the nineteenth Moore congratulated his men and — with a more sober tone — told them that on September twelfth Green had crossed the Missouri at Glasgow in a captured steamboat called the "Sunshine" and on the eighteenth joined General Price at Lexington (2).

For Johnny the prospects of the next few months were not to his liking, no wounds from which to gain experience, only social diseases and injuries from the worst enemy of bored soldiers, whiskey. He watched for an opportunity to ask for leave to visit St. Francisville, but the surgeons always took the weekends, and George accompanied Moore, telling Johnny to stay in camp and gain valuable experience. Moore had stopped for four days, September twentieth to twenty-fourth, at Kahoka where, after learning about the battle of Lexington on September the nineteenth and the surrender of 3500 Union soldiers into the hands of General Price (1), he stepped up policing the northeast counties.

Events in and around northeast Missouri set the stage for winter and the war in '62. On October twenty-sixth Claiborne Jackson's Legislature met at the Masonic hall in Neosho, and on the twenty-eighth they passed an order of secession. On October thirty-first, the Southern Congress admitted Missouri to the Southern Confederacy.

November nineteen, Maj. General Henry W. Halleck took over the command of the Department of the Army of Missouri, replacing General John Fremont, a move that resulted from the death of Lyon at Wilson's Creek and the severe losses suffered at the hands of Price in the Battle of Lexington. Following on the heels of his appointment in charge of the district at Hannibal in October, General Ben M. Prentiss of Quincy assumed charge of the Army of North Missouri.

During October and November, Moore's regiment roamed throughout Schuyler, Scotland, and Clark Counties, intimidating the rebels and southern sympathizers (1). The effort eventually produced results, for after a one-and-a-half-hour fight in Lancaster in which they killed 13 rebels and frightened their supporters out of their britches, the secessionists sent Colonel Moore a letter that said, "We've had enough — secesh is no go (1)."

George had managed to get to the Jenkins farm for

Thanksgiving. Johnny volunteered to stay and render care to the troops stricken with a sudden outbreak of measles.

The second week of December a message scratched Johnny's itch to go to St. Francisville.

"Note for you, Johnny," the weasel-like kid from Luray said, and handed him a piece of paper.

> *Johnny:*
> *Mr. Flack died today. It would be nice if you could make it to the funeral. Elizabeth asked if I could get the message to you. She needs you.*
> > *Dr. R. S. McKee*
> > *December 9*

Note in hand, Johnny streaked for Moore's office at the corner of the first floor in the administration building of Christian College. Moore scrutinized the note and granted Johnny permission to go. Sleep came with difficulty in the basement of Christian College. Only troops occupied the building because the school officials cancelled the fall term when the war broke out. Johnny bolted up with his heart pounding against his chest, his clothes wet after a short night in bed. Johnny, now you have to take care of Elizabeth and Ezra, the form at his feet told him. He lunged at the figure and landed on his knapsack at the foot of the bed. All night one distorted scene from St. Francisville after another had broken into his sleep.

Eleven in the morning he rode down the main street of St. Francisville, his head having about jerked off more than once as he dozed in the saddle on the Salt River Road. The town was deserted but he spied a horse and buggy in front of the old stone Baptist Church. He peered inside and spotted Mr. Civer. After an emotional ten minutes, his former teacher told him the funeral procession had carried Flack to Wolf Cemetery. The gray day fit the event, he concluded, while Red eased along the familiar path to the cemetery gate. A crowd, most in black coats, seemed ghostly in the cool mist, created by the low clouds and the sudden warming trend. Johnny eased along the path that divided the grave markers and halfway — out of instinct — halted and side-stepped to his left. Eyes glued to the black forms, trying to pick out Elizabeth, his hand stopped its groping when it rested on a waist-high marker. He glanced: Jenkins. He knew it was uncle Robert's. A peek behind it brought a shiver when he recognized his father's. Suddenly, the dark forms began to trudge past his area until a short one moved to him.

"Johnny, my Johnny. I knew you would come."

A gentle hug warmed him. His eyes widened, no matter they made owl eyes for it was Elizabeth, her face awash in tears. He stroked her back with one hand and wiped her cheeks with the back of the other. "It's okay. You shouldn't cry. Mr. Flack can't suffer anymore." He heard the words and realized what four months of consoling wounded and dying men had taught him.

"I'm crying 'cause I miss you so much. You promised only one day, Johnny."

He felt the heat as she hung on tight. Obvious to him in spite of his rising pulse and warming face were the glances of the town folk shuffling for the gate. "I know."

"I need you to hold me. Please. Tonight, promise you'll come." She rose on tiptoes and put her mouth to his ear. "Stay the night." Her lips seared his cheek as she pulled away, turned, and left.

Johnny kneeled at his father's grave, and closed his eyes. The crunching of snow hit his ears. He bolted upright and removed the pistol from his belt.

"You wouldn't shoot a poor nigger boy, would you?"

"Sam. Don't ever sneak up on a soldier with so many battles under his belt."

They both laughed, jostled each other, and Johnny enjoyed the black face and the memories it produced until Sam, with eyes to the ground, began to shake his head back and forth. Years of sharing good and bad sank in.

"Tell me, Sam."

"I need your hep somethin' fierce, Johnny. They goin' to lynch my pa in the mornin'." The huge hulk heaved.

"Why? Where?"

"La Grange. Underground railroad got him outa Kentucky. He took a job at the pork plant, but some rebs come in town, saw him, and said they hangin' runaway slaves." Sam clutched both of Johnny's shoulders and locked on his eyes. "I know you can save him."

"Got a horse?"

A black finger aimed at the old birch to the right of the gate. "There, that's mine."

At the road, Johnny turned Red away from St. Francisville, his mind plotting the move in La Grange. But his heart grew heavier with each mile that carried him further from Elizabeth. Sam followed in silence.

The sun skidded off the ice at La Grange. Two blue coats rode stiff-backed into town on the river road. Johnny removed the Springfield and propped the butt on his thigh. He looked at Sam, smiled at the too-tight blue uniform, and nodded. Sam followed Johnny's action. They rode past the pork-rending plant, past the German enclave of stores. Buggies and single mounts surrounded a huge oak tree standing by the ferry landing. His heart went into overdrive, for a black man stood on a flatbed, an eight-knot rope around his neck stretched to the tree limb. He had a stained grayish-white shirt. A scarecrow of a man stood with a whip beside the mule hooked to the wagon. An elegant, white-haired man waved his arms, spewing invectives at the scrubby bunch of men in the front row.

"Don't say anything. Look mean and don't shoot. But if I shoot someone you shoot one of them trash in the front and make for your pa." He raised his rifle and squeezed the trigger. The discharge sounded like a cannon. He pushed Red's flanks with his heels and eased to the front. Two feet from the scarecrow, he lowered the rifle, shoved it in the man's crotch. "I'm a doc, but General Pope sent me to fetch this free man." He saw the sign in scarecrow's eyes, Doc McKee's lesson. He shoved hard. "If'n he flinches one more time I'm goin' to cure his clap." Nobody laughed. A man in the front row slid his hand onto a pistol handle. With his other hand, Johnny removed the pistol from his belt and aimed. "You got the clap too?"

A square-built man with a red beard jumped on the flatbed and cut the rope. Sam's father climbed on behind Sam and they eased over to Johnny.

"Look yonder," Sam said.

Johnny had already noticed the three blue coats, perched on powerful mounts. They eased through the crowd, their presence impervious to the stares. Johnny stuck his rifle in the scabbard. Sam did likewise. The lead man had sergeant's stripes and surveyed them, his stone face appearing colder the closer he came.

"You're no doc, son. You steal those blues?"

The two men behind stirred in their saddles. One eased a hand on his pistol holster. The other nudged his horse to Sam's side. The crowd back-peddled. The boom of cracking ice on the river filled the silent void.

Cautiously, Johnny pulled his Union cap to one side, made a grin with his mouth, and then a quick smile with the rest of his face. The sergeant frowned. Murmurs seeped from the crowd.

"Johnny, owl eyes," the man behind the sergeant sputtered. "Sarge, he's the one we come for."

The special insignia registered through the jumbled thoughts in Johnny's mind. "Merrill's horse. How long you been back there?"

"Since you poked that poor feller in the groin with yer rifle." The sergeant reached past his horse's head. He accepted Johnny's hand. "We were on our way to fetch you. General Hurlbut said you were in Canton. You obliged us some miles."

Before he could protest the other two had approached Sam's pa. One untied the roll behind his horse and handed it to the senior Huett, who promptly wrapped it around his shoulders.

"That's Sam's pa. Sam…."

The sergeant removed his floppy, broad-brimmed hat and wiped his forehead with his upper arm. Steam rose from his hair. He pointed his hat at old man Huett, peering from behind Sam. "Sir, you best come along where you'll be safe. Kind of work can you do?"

"Summers I work in the boiler room of side wheelers. I was loading hogs at that plant winters." He threw his head upriver in the direction of the pork plant.

The sergeant turned his eyes on Sam. "And you, boy?"

"I'm a magician with leather." Sam raised his leg out straight and pulled his pants leg up. "I made that prize boot. I make special shoes or boots and sleeves for the troops what lost parts of a limb." He nodded at Johnny. "Serena's pa has a leather sleeve with a hook. He's farmin' about as good as ever."

Johnny watched the sergeant's eyes soften the more Sam spoke. "All you are coming to Hannibal."

"I don't mind Hannibal," Johnny said. Then Elizabeth's words stung him. "'Course, Colonel Moore said I was supposed to spend the holidays with my step-mom, who just buried her husband." The rejoinder failed to evoke any hint from the sergeant as to the reason for Johnny's call to Hannibal.

Chapter 7

Hospitals in St. Louis
December 14

The short-cut hair had a suggestion of gray but the face of Dorothea Dix looked much younger, a vibrant aura emanating from her. Serena's aunt had told her about this ambitious and rigid woman. "She's demanding, but if you can do as she says you'll be better for it," her aunt had said. Dorothea Dix had come to St. Louis from Kansas, where she was well known for her role in women's causes (1). General Fremont had appointed her general supervisor of nurses for military hospitals because the citizens of St. Louis vilified the hospitals for their wretched care. Bad food, ragged blankets, and poor care by recovering soldiers trying to carry out nursing duties, was the critical litany of the citizens. The sad state of St. Louis hospitals had been broadcast by the crunch of wounded from Wilson's Creek.

Brought by railway cars from Pilot Knob over the Iron Mountain Railroad, 721 wounded soldiers flooded St. Louis, August twelfth to fourteenth and soon filled The New House of Refuge Hospital, located two miles south of town. The brick, five-story building, which the Government opened August 1, 1861, had huge rooms, but still proved inadequate for the shocking number of Union and Confederate wounded. The medical team sent a few wounded to the Marine Hospital, already nearly filled from victims of the numerous skirmishes in northeast and southeast Missouri. Wounded filled every ward at the City Hospital, at the Catholic Sisters of Charity, and almost every other available hospital.

The Western Sanitary Commission sprang from these degradations. General Fremont gave it his approval on September 5, 1861. James Yeatman, a banker, was president. Dr. William Greenleaf Eliot, founder of Washington University, sat on the commission as a director along with Carlos S. Greeley, George Partridge, and Dr. J. R. Johnson. Since the commission received no government money, the citizens raised money from private sources and bought blankets, clothes, food, and medicine for the hospitals (2).

Curious, Serena pondered. Her aunt told her to side with Miss Dix in her war with the doctors. The few Catholic sisters who served as nurses did precisely as the cold physicians demanded. Dorothea Dix stood up to their ignorance of good nursing and physician care that was bad for patients. While she waited for Dix's head to raise these stories raced across her brain.

"Your aunt says you have much experience, especially with patients who have lost a limb," Miss Dix said. The earnest face dissected Serena from toe to her hair, cut short by her aunt the previous night. That seemed to soften the corners of the small mouth. "You're a lot younger than I normally take on. You do as I say though and you'll make it," said Miss Dix. She rose and thumped the papers on the desk. "Inviolate rules, Miss Hill. No socializing with patients, nor doctors, only other female nurses. You will be a professional at all times, away from here as well. No bows, no make-up." She walked around Serena. "Hair like that. No helps, things that make your figure attractive, no butt aids, no breast helps, nothing."

While Serena found the comments about breast helps and butt aids curious, she decided her life on the farm had not exposed her to these sorts of things. "Miss Dix, I am only a farm girl but after helping my father regain his life after loss of an arm in this war, I know I can help many others."

Later during dinner at the Rollin's house Aunt Nancy quizzed Serena about her parents and the interview with

Miss Dix. Over dessert Nancy broached the subject that
Serena suspected a woman of her aunt's age had to discuss.
Serena told her that as the oldest daughter she had been the
son to her father and had little time, let alone interest, for
boys.

That lie played on her mind as she pulled up the covers.
On the way to the stage at Alexandria she had her pa stop in
St. Francisville, the purpose to extend her condolences at the
death of Mr. Flack. Well, not really. More a curiosity smol-
dering from the message in the Bible Elizabeth gave Johnny.
Initially surprised at the widow's youthful face and figure,
Serena soon decided Elizabeth looked rather sickly. She
smiled when she recalled telling Elizabeth about sleeping
under the wagon with Johnny and how he saved her life and
bound her wounds. Before Elizabeth could get her mouth
together Serena told her how tender Johnny was when he
wrapped the bandage over her breasts. Elizabeth just smiled
and told her Johnny came by after the funeral, stayed two
days and nights, promised to come back and run the store.
Her impish smile caused Serena's heart to jump. Serena
clutched the pillow and muttered, "I don't care. I love
Blake."

For one week Serena entered Good Samaritan Hospital,
the one Dix had organized for rehabilitation of amputees.
Nancy drove her to the front door and then took the buggy
to the Marine or whichever hospital the Commission directed her. Promptly at six in the evening, Nancy appeared at the
front door to drive Serena to the house on Locust. Only
Nancy's dialogue regarding the work of the Western
Sanitary Commission saved Serena's tattered emotions, the
abuse her emotions suffered all day at the sight of young
men without arm, leg, or both.

"I have Miss Dix's permission to speak to General
Halleck — you do know he has replaced General Fremont
as the commander of all Missouri forces. He would like to
have you fit three amputees with a special shoe or arm fit-

ting. You call them armlets?" Nancy asked.

Serena said, "Yes, ma'am. This Negro is very talented, gifted."

"Well, I suggest we pick three easy ones for the first. Let's be sure General Halleck is quite convinced."

A cold draft swept down the hall into the dining room, a resounding thump telling Serena the front door had allowed winter to invade the house. Nancy bolted from her chair and soon returned with a striking tall man in a blue uniform, a dark blue cape over his arm.

Serena pushed her hand toward Ogden, blushed when he shoved it to the side and hugged her. "You can't be sixteen!" he exclaimed. "Look like twenty-five to me, and the prettiest Lapsley I've ever seen!" She spotted his wink at Nancy, but still blushed.

"He's been gone from home too long. Out with the animal men, Serena," Nancy said, and planted a smooch on Ogden's cheek.

For two hours after Ogden devoured the remains of Nancy's corn bread and chicken dish, they talked about Serena's interest in amputees, her father's success, and her goals at the hospital.

"I've met this man," Ogden said. "Sam Huett's his name, a magician with leather. Young Jenkins introduced him to me."

Serena's heart skipped a beat, but her mind convinced her that he had to mean George. "I went to the Jenkins School with George, Uncle Rollins," she said, hoping to be corrected.

"I know him well," he replied. He glanced at Nancy. "He's the young medic that drove me to Camp Jackson. The one I worked with in Hannibal until he went north."

Serena pressed her lips tightly. "Is he okay?"

"Going with the Missouri Twenty-First."

"George drove my father back to the farm after his amputation," she said. She wiggled in place. "The kid Jenkins?"

"Johnny? The strange one they call owl eyes?"

"Yes, I know him. Strange Quaker, George's brother."

Ogden watched her — too closely. Serena looked at the plank floor, peered at Nancy.

"What is it, Serena?" Nancy asked.

"I owe my life to him. He saved me from some bad men." She waited for a response. Both stared, waited. "He has weird beliefs."

Ogden laughed. "I'll say. He talks like a Quaker, but threatens people with a rifle — George told me about that frightful morning."

"Johnny was raised by Quakers but I doubt he follows their teachings," Serena said.

"Doesn't he have a family to go to for Christmas?" Nancy asked.

"Only a stepmother up on the Des Moines River," Serena scooted her chair back. Serena excused herself, leaving Ogden and Nancy to catch up on their lives. Her head sank in the pillow when she thought, Poor Johnny, all alone at Christmas. Probably thinking of the night he slept with that Elizabeth woman, the not so old one.

The next morning Ogden drove her to Good Samaritan Hospital where they took measurements on three amputees, ones with lower legs missing, easiest type for Sam to fit with a false leg. After they visited Dorothea Dix and Ogden told her of the leather boots filled with wooden lower legs that a magician in Hannibal would make, Miss Dix seemed to act differently toward Serena. When Ogden left to visit the Headquarters of the Western Sanitary Commission, Miss Dix accompanied Serena to the amputee ward.

Dinner that night proved earth shattering. Serena lamented that while she had plenty of poor men with an arm or leg missing, most other Hospitals were jammed with sick soldiers, more of them Confederate. Nancy Rollins passed the succotash to Ogden.

"The Confederate troops are poorly dressed, most with

parts of a uniform or none, obviously not fed as well as the Union men," Nancy said. She swallowed a mouthful of beans and looked at Ogden. "With so many wounds of the arm and leg why aren't there more amputees?"

"Serena probably sees more men with part of a foot or the entire foot and some of the lower leg missing." He stopped, staring at Serena until she looked up. "Sorry, this isn't good conversation for one of Nancy's finest dishes."

"I see it all day long, eat lunch, talk to the wretched ones, so please continue."

"Of those that don't bleed to death or die before they get to a surgeon, too many die from infection after amputation, depending on the type."

"Type?" Nancy quizzed.

Ogden smiled at his wife. "Perhaps type is incorrect. Magnitude is more appropriate." He glanced at Serena, who seemed absorbed by his gestures. "Amputation of the foot carries only a six percent death rate, ankle twenty-five percent, and lower arm twenty percent. But above-the-knee amputation kills sixty percent and higher near the hip eighty-five percent, as does up near the shoulder."

"Helping those with part of a foot or hand, even below mid-leg or arm is a lot easier, ones Sam..." Serena paused and searched both faces. "He's a magician, makes great false limbs, beautiful boots and armlets with whole or parts of a foot and arm that make life tolerable, I suppose, for the men."

"I visited James Yeatman and gave him the medical report for the Union Army of Missouri, the disease totals for the five months, July through November (3)."

"Does Yeatman have any figures for the Confederate soldiers? I imagine that their numbers are much worse, but I doubt he has the time to hunt down their reports." Nancy said.

"Yeatman is only forty-three, a dynamo, a banker and philanthropist for years since coming to St. Louis in '42. A year ago he was named President of Merchants National Bank. As one of the founders I do not think he will neglect it," Ogden said.

Serena made a little cough and when the two looked at her, said, "Miss Dix told me his mother's second husband was a candidate for President of the United States on the Union ticket in eighteen sixty and that Yeatman is a strong Union man but wants peace badly (4)."

Ogden smiled at her. "When General Fremont named him head of the Commission in September he gave Yeatman a good supporting cast. They made that five-story building on the corner of Fifth and Chestnut, the City Hospital, Headquarters for the Western Sanitary Commission, and storage area for supplies the Commission donates to a half-dozen other hospitals."

Nancy waved a finger. "Probably eleven already. Mr. Yeatman gave Dr. Eliot the task of gathering southern numbers. Poor William Greenleaf serves on the Commission, works hard behind the scenes for the seminary that bears his name, still active as pastor of our church. I doubt he has the time it would take to collect their reports."

"That's assuming they have reports." Ogden suddenly fished in his coat pocket, smiling, his eyes inordinately dancing at Serena until he produced a rumpled brown notepaper. "How could I forget? Serena, when I went to see Yeatman, I met a friend of yours." He turned the paper toward the coal-oil lamp. "Blake Slater," he announced and stared, continuing after she nodded. "Says he went to school with you. He fought with your pa at the battle of Athens along with a dozen other Iowa Third Infantry men. He even volunteered how young Jenkins, who he thinks is a genius, saved your pa's life. And he said Jenkins's black friend is about as clever."

Serena feigned a sneeze in a hanky retrieved from a sleeve and forced a wisp of a grin, struggling to hide her disbelief — Blake, the Yankee. "Blake and I attended the Jenkins

School together. What brings him to St. Louis, to the Commission, Doctor Rollins?"

"Evidently his father runs the pork-rending plant at Sweet Home, so young Slater has the job of organizing pork supplies from that plant and the one in La Grange for the Union Army. He made Yeatman happy. Seems the plants will donate pork supplies to the Commission on a regular basis." Ogden studied Nancy for a spell. He stirred a log in the fireplace and turned. "He leapt for joy when I suggested you two should greet one another. I trust that meets with your approval?"

While Nancy smiled at her, she nodded assent in silence.

"Good, because I reserved a table at the Planters House for lunch tomorrow. Your friend knows where to bed down. Although The Prince of Wales stayed at the Barnum House, he spoke highly of Planters. It sits just north of the courthouse. Charles Dickens spoke highly of its magnificent cuisine and splendid bar. It has hosted Henry Clay, Daniel Webster, and Louis Kossuth (5)."

Nancy slipped out of her chair and, helping Serena from the table, said, "Come, we must find a suitable dress for the occasion."

With minor alterations Nancy had fixed a light blue short-sleeve dress with a tight bodice, a large bustle. Next she produced a shiny deep blue velvet jacket and made Serena twirl around slowly amidst her faint pleadings about the attire being too fancy for a girl. "You are a woman and a very attractive one," Nancy told her.

The quiet, dark bedroom sufficed to lead her through her anticipation of a romantic afternoon at the Planters House.

The four-story white building had an extra floor in the center turret as well as the two corners from where two huge flags waved in the brisk winter air blowing off the Mississippi river. Nervously, Serena followed Nancy and Ogden under the two-story entranceway into the lobby of the elegant Planters House.

Incredible, Serena's brain formed the thought with the sight of Blake, the memory of the boy behind the Jenkins schoolhouse replaced by the business-like man in the middle of the hotel lobby. The large purple bow tie and the white silk shirt seemed to highlight his twinkling eyes. He made a pass at kissing the hand she extended to him and the introduction of Nancy fleeted by. At the table her mesmerized state vanished when Nancy asked how, as a young man, he escaped military service.

"When they sent me with a couple rebs — gut-shot — to Keokuk I fooled the docs. I…"

"I didn't know we had a military hospital in Keokuk," Ogden said.

"They use a large building, called the Estes House, for wounded soldiers, not the hospital for the College of Physicians and Surgeons."

Ogden's intense scrutiny matched his comment. "If you mean the wounded we found at Kirksville, there were three and one was a Union, also gut-shot."

"Me — only I had a beard. The rebs surprised us, our Captain, named Dix, killed." He cast a hasty peek at Serena. "Iowa Third. I was shot in the belly and taken prisoner. Fortunately, General Hurlbut arrived later." He smiled at Nancy. "Luckily, the belly wound went through without hitting any gut, so I recovered at home and started the pork procurement business."

Serena labored to hide her disbelief. She studied Ogden. He seemed to enjoy the war story. And Blake continued with stories of his escapades as a Union soldier, the bigger the tale the more convincing he seemed, but not to her stomach. Serena nibbled, carefully taking in the reactions of both Rollins. Finally, Ogden took Nancy's hand and announced that they needed to pay their respects to friends across the room. He winked at Blake and suggested that he and Serena might want to catch up with old times alone. Blake ushered her to a corner of the lobby.

"You're a good sport, Serena, not tipping them that I am really a Confederate scout and procurement officer."

"Outrageous. More lies than I ever heard. Were you really the Yank shot and taken to Keokuk?"

"Good business men tell lies. And no, I was not the Yank, but I saw the whole thing. After that, I was with General Price at the Battle of Lexington. My, what a fine job we did to the blue bellies — three thousand prisoners. Green left with General Price and sent me to scout the northeast. Green has contacts in practically every town in northeast Missouri. Dressed as a business man I found where the enemy camped, their strength, and location of their supplies, making it easier for our patrols to acquire." He wiggled his eyebrows.

Serena shook her head vigorously. "Not scout. You're a spy. If they catch you they'll hang you."

Blake snatched her hand from her lap. She knew that was taboo, but enjoyed the sensation it created. "Agent for the pork plants has been fabulous. I've seen the fortresses at Hannibal and here at the Arsenal. Green, or I should say Colonel Porter, will be impressed."

With the approach of the Rollins from across the lobby, Serena withdrew her hand and quietly mumbled, "I worry so for you."

He interpreted her glances over his shoulder and, pulling her up, said, "This year I'll be with Porter in northeast Missouri. I want to see you more." His eyes burned into hers. "I intend to start a courtship."

Even the teasing rendered by Ogden didn't break her bubble. The departure for Locust Street and Blake's warm goodbye accompanied with a subtle rubbing of his thigh against her hip only served to perpetuate her dream.

At her bedroom door, Ogden's announcement clanged at her ears. "This Blake is quite attracted to you. Hope he stays awhile. I have tickets for the theater this weekend. Miss Julia Daly made her St. Louis debut Monday." He hesitated when

Serena admitted she did not know of Daly.

"Miss Daly has just returned from a brilliantly successful European tour, where she attracted crowded and energetic audiences each night of her appearances, the public testifying their approval by frequent recalls and enthusiastic encores of her original ballads (6)."

"Does she sing opera songs?" Serena knew she was about to reveal her ignorance of theater.

"Yankee songs and comic dances, things you young ones can enjoy. Good night."

After muttering good night to Ogden, she took the glass of warm milk from Nancy, opened the door to her room.

"Good night, Serena," Nancy said and then from her bedroom door threw a jab. "I know my dear brother-in-law, your father, fought with the Confederates at Athens."

Chapter 8

Columbia
December 19

They entered Columbia on the Paris-Columbia road and, traveling west toward downtown, they passed by Female Baptist College, chartered in 1857. A mile further in mid-downtown to their right loomed Christian College, chartered by the legislature in 1853, same as Christian College in Canton. Turning south onto Eighth Street, the sight of six magnificent columns announced the façade of the main university building. The clop-clop of horse hooves on the brick street faded, replaced by the muffled sound on the hard-packed clay road that led past spruce trees, scattered along the way. The impressive view stirred his memory, the day the troops fetched him and Sam from La Grange and delivered them to Union headquarters in Hannibal. General Hurlbut told Johnny he was assigned to Doctor Rollins who was scheduled to arrive from St. Louis. He said that General Prentiss stopped at Columbia last month on his way to set up district headquarters in Jefferson City. He decided to set up a regional commissary, a quartermaster's store, a prison, and a medical facility for his troops and Merrill's Troop in Columbia.

"The clinic is on the ground floor along with my quarters and the prison's on the top floor isn't it, Doctor?"

Ogden twisted in the saddle. "Yes, but you must stay with brother James. I built you up as a Quaker, wanted to ask him about his slaves." He hesitated until Johnny caught the gleam in his eye and grinned.

"I'm no Quaker, but I..."

Female Baptist College, Columbia. Shown as it is today.
Photo by the author.

With a long stretch, Ogden reached and grabbed Johnny's hand. "I knew you would say that. But you behave like one, George says raised by Quakers. You two will have a fine time. James wants to hear from the younger generation. Don't be shy, Johnny," Ogden said.

"I read the Hannibal Messenger article (1) that had your brother's letter, the one in February about staying in the Union. My teacher, Mister Civer, gave it to me, said it kept us in the Union. But I still don't understand. If he has slaves, he must be a friend of southern sympathizers," Johnny said quizzically.

A chuckle escaped from Ogden. "That February letter appeared in almost every paper in the state and was so logical. Brother James asked some poignant questions about the result should we secede; what becomes of the fugitive slave law? Have we any claim any longer on Northern states to restore our fugitive slaves? By this act will we not bring the Canadian Frontier, some eight hundred miles away, to our very doors, inviting the escape of all our slaves in the state and without any power to reclaim them? Won't division bring the necessity to have a standing army with heavy taxation and all degrees of constant collision with people of Illinois, Iowa, and Kansas? Will rights of the South be secured better out of the Union than in it (1)?"

Johnny listened intently to Ogden's recital and then said, "I remember the arguments. He also asked, 'What about our national debt? Who pays? What about free navigation of the Mississippi? What about division of the territories, the National capitol, the public buildings and properties, the U. S. Army and Navy (1)?' Mr. Civer told me that those arguments convinced most people, even those with slaves, to send representatives to the state convention who would vote for staying in the Union."

"Your teacher was correct. There are other factors. Ask James why he thinks the State Convention voted to stay in the Union."

"But with slaves he must be sympathetic to the South?"

"On the twenty-second of October, five hundred rebs under Captain Bob Sweeney, some young upstart from Renick, the town where Green crossed the North Missouri Railroad, cut telegraph lines, burned bridges, and tore up track before heading to Glasgow — well Sweeney marched into Columbia, camped at the fairgrounds, and then proceeded to raid brother's house. Took six horses, five head of mule, and a two-horse wagon with all the plow harnesses he could find (2)."

"I was wrong. I don't think the confederates like him," Johnny said.

"James was out of town, so the next day the rebs returned and took a large amount of corn — for their mounts and the rest of the company's (2). A week later, Sweeney's superiors, more political than the Captain, made him return the loot. The experience was very trying for Mrs. Rollins. She wrote him about the sad business. Her strong faith must help both because she closes her letters asking God to take care of him (3)."

"The war keeps many loved ones apart, causes much sadness," Johnny said, his mind conjuring up the image of Elizabeth standing in the doorway.

"Brother's job in Washington keeps him away from home, but worse with such war events. He has a son, James, a cadet at West Point in New York. Doesn't get to see him much (4)."

Ogden aimed a finger at the large, four-story building with its pretentious dome. On it rested several short columns supporting a small cupola that sent a tall weather vane skyward. After they passed a generous gazebo, Johnny spotted another large building southeast of the main one. Ogden guided them around the west side.

"That door leads to the area set aside for the army." He pointed to a door near the front on the west side, the entrance to the west wing. The first floor, its windows at ground level, sat partially below ground level.

"Does General Prentiss plan for you to be posted there? Am I to be the district surgeon's helper?" Johnny scrutinized the barren landscape around the building and pulled his coat collar tighter when a southwest gust howled along the side of the gray-white structure.

"I am to be stationed in St. Louis, beginning after Christmas. If I understood correctly, you are to set up this medical outpost, maybe train a helper to take your place, probably until spring, and then return to Hannibal."

"And you won't go back to be the surgeon for the Sixteenth Illinois or one of the Illinois regiments? I hear they lost surgeons and assistants."

"Of the Illinois infantry regiments, the Ninth has kept its original surgeon, David Bigger. The Sixteenth never had one, so I filled in, and my assistant, Captain David Wells, because he has chronic fever, possibly consumption, went home first part of the month to Macomb, Illinois."

Ogden steered them south on Providence. "You will help the surgeon I recruit from St. Louis to cover the Sixteenth. Charles Tompkins is surgeon and Wilbur Buck assistant for the Seventeenth Illinois Regiment (5).

Past Conley's property, a two-story brick house with a tall portico supported by two white columns appeared. Alongside the house a dark brown man appeared, greeted Ogden with a warm smile, and grabbed the bridle of each horse. Johnny watched Ogden dismount and quickly did the same. He removed his bedroll from behind the saddle.

The young man jumped to his side and snatched it. "I do that." He reached over and took Ogden's large, worn, black satchel from the saddle pommel. "Master James is waitin' fer ya, Doctor Rollins, Sir."

"Amos, this is Johnny Jenkins. He is going to be our guest for several weeks. He is a medical helper, a Quaker."

With the last comment, the man beamed, delight seeming to jump all over his being, his huge mouth fixed wide open. "Yes sir, we takes special care of him, Master Rollins. Yes, indeed." He tied the horses to the post and carried their bags to the back porch, then proceeded to lead the horses for the stable, mumbling barely audible words.

"What's that all about, his mumblin' that I'm one what's hepin' and more?" Johnny asked.

On the back porch Ogden turned Johnny and studied him momentarily. "Johnny, you have excellent qualities to be a doctor, and a fundamental knowledge and understanding of nature that a good doctor needs. With your medical experience and obvious talents I will happily help you get in medical school, if you make it through this war alive and without some injury that prevents you from being a doctor."

Johnny's heart leapt into his throat. Words stuck on his tongue. He cast his best — but slowly formed — smile at the man who put a hand on his shoulder.

"One important thing you must correct, must polish. Your speech. Notice how the darkies speak? Well, the uneducated whites, too. Finish words and do not say ain't or don't."

Johnny froze, the smile to mask his uneasiness at the critique. "Thank you. I know better. Mr. Civer has tried. I want to learn to be professional-like…"

"Good. So do not say mumblin', say mumbling. Say I am not. Watch the use of contractions and finish words. Practice the next several weeks. James is a fine speaker. Study him so when I see you Christmas you will be able to impress Mrs. Rollins and your friend Serena."

"Serena." His brain rattled the word around his skull until it rolled off his tongue. "Are they coming here for the holidays, Doctor?"

Ogden turned the doorknob, and as Johnny eased by said, "My, my. In all our serious conversations coming here, I forgot to tell you that Mrs. Rollins and I want you to spend four or five days with us. You can leave Red here and take the Columbia stage. Only costs four cents a mile. Our Christmas present to you."

"I — I don't…" Johnny shifted from foot to foot in the doorway. He wiped a hand across his mouth. "I do not know what to say. That is so exciting. Thank you. But Serena?"

A rich, smooth voice from behind him said, "Come in, welcome."

Ogden leaned toward Johnny. "Serena is living with us. Our niece, works as a nurse at Good Samaritan Hospital."

A strong grip on his biceps turned Johnny to face a tall man with a full beard and mustache. The deep-set eyes, shaded by somewhat thick eyebrows, dissected Johnny's features and grew warm, matching the grin visible in the bushy face. A long straight nose retreated to a forehead made abundant by the receding hairline. "Johnny Jenkins. You are very welcome. I have looked forward to your visit for some time." James Sydney Rollins shook his hand, dropped it, and hugged Ogden. "Brother, you look fit — proper in Union blue."

After a few minutes of cordial bantering, a graying black

James S. Rollins, Columbia.
Used by permission, State Historical Society of Missouri, Columbia.

man led Johnny to a spacious bedroom on the second floor, showed him the bed chamber, wash facilities, and informed him dinner would be served in one hour. The man closed the door behind him, leaving Johnny with feelings of awe at his quarters. "What a way to bivouac in Columbia," he chuckled. While washing hands and face in the white porcelain bowl, he pondered Dr. Rollins's revelations, his mention of Serena conjuring up anticipation, soon replaced by a creeping anxiety.

Dinner proved uncomfortable, although Mrs. Rollins made every effort to help him adjust to the fancy setting. When she handed him the platter with venison on one end and pheasant on the other, she smiled. "Just watch Ogden and do as he does," she whispered. By the time the meal, including a strange and tart dessert called apple potpie was served, his host had found out all about his upbringing, the Quakers, and his facial asymmetry.

That evening after the meal the two men and Johnny sat around the fire and Ogden told James of his experience at Camp Jackson in May, the Battle of Boonville in June, and his subsequent assignment to the Illinois Sixteenth in Hannibal, a change from consultant to an officer in the Union Army. When he told James about the attack at Monroe City and the shelling that blinded a young doctor he had taught in medical school, he excused himself and left the room.

"And what were you doing during this time?" James asked.

Johnny turned to face the barrage of questions he knew would be forthcoming. Hesitantly, he started with the Battle of Athens, one about which James confessed he knew nothing. When he related how he saved a man whose arm was shot off, James smiled and asked if the man was Serena's father. Johnny told his host how he and Serena found him and she — with his brother who had helped Dr. Rollins during the previous three months, took the one-armed man home — on the Des Moines River. He carefully skirted around the attack on Serena the morning before they entered Canton.

"Saving her father's life, finding him." James paused, made a funny grin, and added, "and saving her from rape and death, must make you two quite close."

Shock. Betrayed. And other indescribable arrows paralyzed Johnny. "I — I — I don' believe in killin'."

A hand rested on his shoulder. "Johnny does not believe in killing," Ogden, who had returned, enunciated slowly.

Johnny felt a gentle squeeze of his shoulder, a reassuring one, and recognized the speech lesson Ogden administered. He gave his patented upper face grin as Ogden returned to his chair. "I had not killed anything, not even a rabbit before

that dreadful day." He mimicked Ogden in a clipped enunci-
ation. "Serena is a kid. Haven't — have not seen her since."

Ogden related how brother George had told him about the
creek-side attack. In further explanation to James about
Serena, Ogden revealed the deep emotional replacement she
had become for the loss of their daughter to cholera years
previously. Johnny read the far away expression, the sad
countenance.

"So, you see why we would be delighted to have you
come to St. Louis for a few days at Christmas. Poor Serena
is shackled by Dorothea Dix's rigid rules (6). Though
mature, she must crave conversation with someone her age.
I have arranged for you to stay with Colonel Hitchcock next
door, a friend of the famous surgeon, Beaumont.
Hitchcock's place abuts the house of the widow Beaumont,
a true-blue Quaker. Oh, yes. That is why Amos made such a
fuss over you. All Negroes know the Quakers are responsible for extensive underground railroads."

Uncertain about Serena, about her mystery, her rebel
father, her flirtations with Blake Slater, Johnny merely
shrugged.

With James's quizzical look at one and then the other,
Ogden said, "Johnny takes life too serious, always reading,
asking question, learning as if intellectually starved."

"And what about the Bible. Do you read it, Johnny?"
James asked.

Caught off surprise by the query, he turned his head back
to Ogden. "I apologize," Johnny said when it dawned on
him that slight discomfort with Serena was a small price to
pay to nurture this powerful connection for medical school.
"I would love to come for a few days, if another soul would
not tax Mrs. Rollins too much."

"Quite to the contrary, your presence will be a joy for
Mrs. Rollins." Ogden threw his head toward James, slowly
twisted in his chair and grinned at him, a subtle, impish one.
"James asked you a very important question, Johnny. Your

hero — you've read everything he's written — well, Lincoln had read the Bible cover to cover by the time he was fourteen."

With that, Johnny stood, feigned a smile, hoping to mask his embarrassment. He looked at one frozen face and then the other. "I did not know that about our President. I have a Bible now. Elizabeth gave it to me when I left. Guess I better start reading it." He waved and ambled toward the stairs.

Both men said goodnight and, ascending the stairs, he heard Ogden add, "Every day. Read a chapter every day, Johnny."

Sleep came easily for Johnny, albeit the revelation about Lincoln and Ogden's suggestion — no it sounded more like one of his pointed lessons — made him restless. Finally he dozed off after he resolved to focus on the trip to St. Louis, an opportunity he had prayed for during the past three years.

The after-dinner topic the night before Ogden's departure for St. Louis reminded Johnny of the talks he and Mr. Civer carried on in St. Francisville. Hours helping Ogden organize the medical clinic at the University and several evening discussions that involved Congressman Rollins, especially when he carried on at length about the politics and behind doors compromises in Washington, emboldened Johnny. He felt at ease and responded readily to the invitation of these sophisticated men to quiz them until he understood.

"Mr. Rollins, I still don't understand your position as a unionist when you have slaves. Nor do I see how it is called coercion when the President takes measures to prevent states from secession," Johnny said.

"Johnny, the issue is states' rights," said Rollins. "This country is republican, a collection of states with people of different backgrounds, distinct geographic areas that mandate lifestyle and livelihood peculiar and foreign to states in other regions. Washington officials cannot know the importance and values basic to all the regions."

"Quakers believe that keeping another human in bondage is morally wrong," Johnny said, watching Ogden out of the corner of his eye.

"Slaves are our property. Even your hero — you have read all of Mr. Lincoln's speeches — he said he did not believe Almighty God ever intended the Negro to be the equal of the white man."

Johnny smiled. "Excuse me, Sir. Douglas said that at the Ottawa debate in 1858. Lincoln said he did not believe in social and political equality. But in another generation, if set free to obtain the same opportunities for education, they would catch up (7)."

James Rollins narrowed his eyes and leaned toward Johnny. "Nevertheless, each state has rights, part of the freedoms set down by our founding fathers. If the federal Government is allowed to dictate to the southern states on the matter of slavery, a worrisome precedent will occur. What next? In bad times will they take over key industries, or tell farmers what crops to grow?"

"Horrible, James," said Ogden. "A phony excuse, this states' rights issue. A person because of his skin color cannot enjoy life, liberty, and the pursuit of happiness."

"A small price to make certain the Union does not abrogate the freedom of states, of individuals in states," James said, throwing a finger at his brother.

"Freedom of only whites," Johnny blurted, and cowered in his chair under the chilly glare of James Sydney Rollins.

Ogden stopped the retort by standing and peering down at his younger brother. "Sin, murder, rape, anything to preserve states' rights, the freedom, whatever, without restrictions for the good of society."

"Yes, brother. Yes." James stood arms length from Ogden.

"A man with cholera gets on a boat that you and the Mrs. are taking to New Orleans. 'You must leave the Captain tells him.' 'But I must be in Natchez or lose my business. It's my right to travel where I please.'"

"Foolish. Not the same."

"Same logic. The man argues that because he has a disease you cannot restrict him from traveling, his God-given freedom. His rights cost many lives, same as states' rights for slavery costs murdered slaves and hundreds of dead soldiers — North and South."

James shook his head violently. "For you, that's a bad example. Cholera is a disease that is catching. It kills the innocent. Only due to the quarantine laws and legislation for better sewage disposal and water systems has the death rate dropped."

"Touche', brother. Slavery is a disease that kills the innocent, it grows, and because it hides behind the skirts of states' rights father fights son, brother kills brother. Before this is over millions of innocent, mostly white, will die."

Emotional electricity filled the room. The temperature rose, even though the fire had burned to a few glowing embers. Johnny listened to brothers poke, jab, tease, and cajole one another.

Johnny felt embarrassed, listening to the grown men argue so fiercely. "Excuse me, Sir. Help me understand how a state in which only 10 percent voted for Lincoln and Governor Jackson and state legislature made of mostly secessionists stayed in the Union." Johnny glanced at Ogden and continued, "I read your letter in the February Hannibal Messenger."

Ogden cleared his throat and when Johnny turned to him he said, "The editor of the Missouri Democrat on Locust Street (8), P. L. Foy, is a friend. He told me that in 1850, forty-seven percent of Missouri citizens were born in Missouri and thirty percent in Kentucky, Tennessee, Virginia, North Carolina, or Maryland, all southern states. Fourteen percent or around seventy-six thousand citizens came from foreign lands — three fifths of those from Germany. State population was almost six-hundred thousand (9)."

Johnny added the figures and asked, "What percent came from northern states?"

"Eight, around fifty thousand. But in the last decade enormous changes occurred. The population has doubled, foreign-born have increased to one hundred and eighty thousand, and the Missouri born dropped to forty-five percent, those from southern states decreased to twenty-four percent. The number from north states has doubled (9)."

James Rollins shook his head. "I am not convinced. On February 18 the election of candidates for the state convention sent unionists to the convention. Not by small margins, but by whopping numbers, almost every county by two to one and many by as much as three or four to one. Why, in Cape Girardeau nearly every vote went for the unionists and even in St. Genevieve the majority voted for unionists."

"The key is education and big city influence. I figure this way. In November the people voted for the man they knew best and not because of debates about issues like states' rights, slaves, or our relation to the Union," Ogden said.

"I was told only one in eight Missourians have slaves," Johnny offered (9).

"One in ten own a slave. And most are distributed along the rivers (9)," Ogden said, pointed a finger at his brother and added, "Just like you, James." He chuckled while he stuck a palm toward James and said to Johnny. "Here's the answer: Foy told me that in St. Louis in 1860, of a population of one hundred and sixty thousand people, fifty thousand were German and if you add up all the other foreign-born — Irish, French, Canadian, and so on — the total comes to ninety-six thousand. That is close to sixty percent being foreign in St. Louis (9)."

"Hannibal has a significant German population," Johnny inserted.

James stood, pulled on his coat lapels, and glanced from Ogden to Johnny. "Look. Seven eights of the people don't have slaves. They care more about the things my letter frightened them with, and the big cities posed a large problem for our secessionist general assembly."

Ogden nodded his agreement, pushed out of his chair, helped Johnny stand and said, "Remember when I first met you in Palmyra?"

"Yes sir — the battle of Monroe City in July."

"And you saw one of our state legislators, John Boulware, who had been meeting with the speaker of the secessionist general assembly, the former 21st General Assembly, John McAfee?" Johnny smiled and moved his head up and down, so Ogden said, "They were conditional secessionists."

James turned at the bottom of the stairs. "That meant they were not for secession if Lincoln didn't coerce the seceded states into rejoining — which he did, however."

Johnny felt uneasy, paused beside his host and said, "But the President didn't coerce. South Carolina fired on federal property first — Mr. Lincoln merely responded to their aggression." He smiled and headed up the stairs.

"Enough, Johnny. Have a good night's rest," Ogden said.

James waved and Johnny said goodnight to the men as they returned to the library.

Dressing for bed, he replayed the dialogue and concluded, I hope I wasn't too forward and offended Doctor Rollins, ruin my chances for med school. After he extinguished the candle, thoughts of his visit to St. Louis and the scrutiny of Dr. and Mrs. Rollins made his stomach churn.

Battle at Mt. Zion Church
December 26

General Ben Prentiss, a postmaster at Peoria before the war, had dark circles under his eyes, their gray-blue hue roaming up and down the figure of Captain Howland. Johnny had retreated to the edge of the group after he assured the General that the medical facility at the University, some twenty miles distant, was ready to handle sick and wounded. The depot at Sturgeon buzzed with a frenetic atmosphere, getting more agitated, so it seemed, ever since he had arrived.

Two hours before he was supposed to catch the 11:35 a.m. stage out of Columbia on the twenty-fourth, the telegram had arrived at the army facility in Columbia. General Prentiss announced his departure from Hannibal on that date and said Johnny must postpone his visit to Colonel Rollins in St. Louis and meet Prentiss and his troops at Sturgeon with medical support. So much for Christmas, he mused and sent a telegram to Dr. Rollins with the reason for his no-show in St. Louis. Then the excitement of demonstrating to this severe Illinois commander his proficiency at organizing medical support prompted him to organize the ambulance, a converted dray, similar to the way Dr. McKee had taught him and a support wagon laden with medical supplies, precisely according to the list Dr. Rollins had given him. Congressman Rollins and his wife embraced Johnny Christmas Day, even gave him a present, a light blue wool shirt.

But upon his arrival at Sturgeon early on the twenty-sixth, he met scouts who anxiously awaited the train carrying Prentiss from Hannibal. His stomach growled, not in protest, but with excitement when the scouts told him they had spotted a concentration of rebels at Hallsville, some twelve miles away. When Prentiss arrived with five companies of the Third Missouri Cavalry under Col. John B. Glover, the scouts immediately reported the whereabouts of the enemy. Prentiss sent for Howland, and waiting his appearance, had quizzed Johnny about the medical setup at Columbia and the support he had brought to Sturgeon.

A young doctor, named Schmidt, identified himself as Dr. Rollins's former student and recent appointee as surgeon for Col. Birge's sharpshooters. He introduced himself to Johnny. They listened to Prentiss direct Howland to scout around Hallsville for the strength and position of the enemy. Upon Howland's departure, Schmidt introduced Johnny to the surgery helpers for Birge's sharpshooters (10). The jumpy young doctor spent the twenty-seventh with Johnny, listening to him describe the prison and medical facilities in Columbia, a crude map eliminating the need to journey to the site. Johnny helped Dr. Schmidt with an early afternoon clinic, nineteen soldiers seeking help, most for catarrh, but one with bad lung inflammation, and two with rheumatism. By the time Johnny had familiarized Captain Schmidt with the supplies and surgical instruments in the medical wagon he brought from Columbia, darkness arrived and the scouting party under Captain Howland still had not returned.

Close to nine p.m., a distraught corporal from Howland's party rode into camp with a ragtag bunch of men, four with minor wounds. While Johnny and Captain Schmidt attended to the wounded, they heard the excited man relate events of the day to Prentiss.

"We reconnoitered cautiously on the way to Hallsville, and finding no enemy proceeded through town. Two miles past we came upon a force under Colonel Caleb Dorsey." After a gulp of air he continued. "We know it was his troops because in a scuffle we took nine prisoners. Soon it was obvious that it was a large force so we withdrew to come report, and when we did they shot Captain Howland's horse and wounded him. Private Gusman got shot, too (10)."

Preparations for immediate pursuit began and at two a.m.

on the twenty-eighth, five companies of cavalry under Glover and five companies of sharpshooters under Birge, a total of 470 men, started the twelve-mile trek to Hallsville.

When scouts informed Prentiss that a company of rebs under Captain Johnson had left Hallsville, heading southeast, he dispatched two companies of sharpshooters to pass at the rear and a company of cavalry to dismount and engage from the front, whereupon the rebs began to withdraw. Glover's men sent in heavy fire, killed five enemy and captured seven.

Johnny helped Schmidt bandage two of the rebels, who under questioning, told Prentiss the position and number of the main Confederate force, 900 men dug in five and a half miles southeast of Hallsville at Mt. Zion Church (10). In 1848 the congregation of the church, formally known as Mt. Moriah Church, had built the wooden structure on land donated by Thomas Flynt.

Prentiss ordered Glover's cavalry and two of Birge's companies, sharpshooters, to advance toward the church. Near the enemy encampment, one company of cavalry dismounted and advanced on foot while Birge's sharpshooters crept through a field on the right to engage the rebel left flank (10).

Vigorous shooting failed to dislodge the enemy, so Glover with the remaining available cavalry did double-time to aid the three hard-pressed companies: Captain Boyd's company of sharpshooters along with Company C of the Illinois Third Cavalry under Major Carrick had carried the advance to the middle of the enemy camp. The attack resulted in fierce hand-to-hand fighting. After thirty minutes, the rebels retreated, leaving ninety horses and over a hundred stacks of arms. Schmidt set up a temporary field hospital below the church. Medical helpers from Glover's and Birge's troops brought wounded, Confederate and Union, to Johnny who gave immediate care to those with bad bleeding and then helped Schmidt. Gunfire stopped at eleven a.m., signaling

Battle of Mt. Zion Church, December 28, 1861

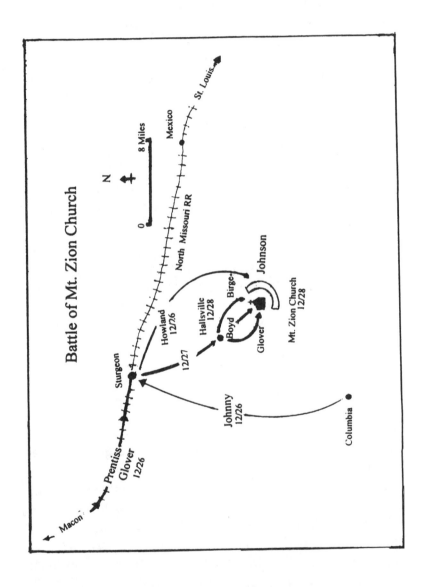

the end of the battle. Prentiss ordered the Confederate wounded to be placed in Mt. Zion Church and the Union wounded in wagons. They proceeded to Sturgeon, arriving at nine at night.

Covered with sweat and blood, Johnny accompanied Captain Schmidt when he gave the medical report to General Prentiss: Federal losses; 3 killed, 46 slightly wounded, 17 severely wounded. Confederate losses; 25 killed and 150 wounded (10).

Prentiss told Schmidt to take the slightly wounded to the facility in Columbia, a good way to test its efficiency.

"Sir, we need an experienced assistant to accompany the bad ones on the train to St. Louis," Schmidt said.

Prentiss searched Johnny's face. He rubbed the stubble on his chin. "Jenkins, I know you want to see the benefits of the fine work you did in Columbia, but I'm ordering you to St. Louis."

"Yes Sir. I've worked with Doctor Rollins lots, and he..."

Prentiss turned to his attaché. "Lieutenant, send a telegram to Colonel Rollins that we are transporting seventeen badly wounded under the watchful eye of Jenkins. Tell him that once they have been properly handed over to the care of surgeons at the hospital, Jenkins is ordered to take five days leave, the one he postponed before Christmas."

Johnny watched the Lieutenant enter the depot and grinned, a slow, controlled one. "Thank you, General."

Prentiss stood. He threw an arm, encompassing the troops collected around the depot. "Every soldier here had Christmas, five days sometime in December. Good rehab for the coming battles this spring."

Before the train with three cars serving as hospital cars departed, Johnny found time to wash the blood and sweat from his arms and face. His grimy uniform attested to the tragedy at Mt. Zion Church. Fatigue blanketed his body by the time the train passed through Warrenton. The wounded had their laudanum and two of Colonel Birge's medical helpers hovered over the ones who appeared near death. Johnny realized the implications in Prentiss's orders. He grabbed the Bible and removed the telegram that Rollins had sent Christmas day acknowledging the cancellation of his trip. He turned to the lantern, its light bobbing to and fro with each bump and jerk of the car over the track.

> *JOHNNY*
> *Sorry I had tickets for Nancy Me You*
> *and Serena to the theatre STOP*
> *I will change them for New Year's STOP*
> *Expect you then STOP*
> *You will stay next door with Colonel*
> *Hitchcock STOP*
>> *Merry Christmas*
>> *DR ROLLINS*

"Serena," he muttered, glancing about the crowded car to see if anyone heard. Feeling a surge of joy and locked on an image of a skinny girl in a green shirt, he smiled while he opened the Bible to replace the letter. Blinking, insistent, the handwriting on the first page of Grandma Weaver's Bible demanded attention. Johnny wiggled closer to the lamp:

> *Johnny-*
> *Read my*
> *grandma's bible and*
> *remember me.*
> *Husband's bad sick.*
> *I don't figure he'll*
> *make it through*
> *another year. When*
> *you come back from*
> *fighten be my husband.*
>> *love-*
>> *Elizabeth*

He bent his head to one side and squinted. It said the same thing. All these months, *Johnny, you stupid, funny face. She said that day I left for Athens I should read the message. Said it was her life. Oh, you clod,* he lamented. A smile crept across his face. *God, I think you just spoke to me. I will read the Bible — like I should have been doing — every day.*

By noon he and Ogden had transferred the care of the sev-enteen wounded from Mt. Zion to the surgical team at City Hospital. Dr. Hodgen had already amputated two legs and a third patient was on the way to the operating amphitheater. Chloroform, the gas that Ogden had said they used more and more out east, picked Johnny's curiosity. The two, the band-ages covering the stumps, slowly turned from yellow to yel-low-orange to pink to bright red, but the men dozed, even appeared to have a wisp of a smile on their faces. Curious, he surmised and wished the surgeons, if not in the field, at least at Hannibal and Palmyra, had the gas. The shrieking, writhing wretches getting an extremity chopped off under whiskey — in the field — or laudanum at Headquarters hos-pital, interrupted many a night's sleep with a ghostly visit.

Ogden appeared with a man Johnny's height but dressed in a dark business suit, a gray vest, and stiff shirt with a high collar that enhanced his military carriage. The man leaned forward, extended a hand to Johnny while Ogden told him that Colonel Hitchcock was his host for the three days. The man spoke warmly, although his eyes revealed an intense scrutiny. Handing Johnny a brown package, Ogden told Johnny that the new Union uniform came from Quarter-masters supply but the dark blue trousers were a Christmas present from him and Mrs. Rollins. When Johnny protested that the trip to St. Louis was quite a big gift, Ogden remind-ed him that the train trip, military ambulance business, was compliments of the Federal Government.

Hitchcock and Johnny left Ogden to help with the victims of Mt. Zion, his attention directed to one with a minie ball in his chest and two with gut shots, likely to die before nightfall. At the Colonel's house, Johnny bathed in a large iron bathtub, the hot water furnished by the graying man who seemed to turn fatherly once the two had entered the house. He tucked the blue shirt, Congressman Rollins's gift, in the trousers, Ogden's present, and grinned in the small mirror above the clothes chest. After Johnny refused a respite to sleep, Hitchcock escorted him to the adjacent house, the widow Beaumont's home. At the front steps, Hitchcock introduced him to the widow's daughter, Sarah, and little Lillie, Sarah's daughter. Hitchcock's enjoyment at greeting her was obvious to Johnny's keen senses.

Since leaving City Hospital to the time he received a firm hug from Deborah Beaumont, Johnny had listened as the Colonel informed Johnny about his personal history, his years in the military associated with the famous Dr. Beaumont, and his affection for the three generations of Beaumont women, hence his residence in St. Louis where he was blessed to have a successful business and stock brokerage firm. The oval faced, red-cheeked widow Beaumont, though short and somewhat matronly, a description Ogden had taught Johnny to use so as not to offend, acted spunky for her years. She told him of her Quaker background, focused on his face the while, and related her Quaker-like civic activities, as she called them.

"Ogden has taught you well, young man," she said.

Hitchcock informed him that the Rollins's and Serena would arrive home late and sent Johnny to bed early to get rest for the busy two days planned for his visit. Standing at the window in his flour-sack shorts, Johnny stared at the house next door. *I wonder if Doc Rollins knows Serena and her pa are Southern sympathizers — maybe die-hard Confederates — and Serena's boyfriend is a mean fightin — er...* He waved a hand at the house and grinned while he mumbled, *Sorry, a mean fighting rebel.* He sank into the feather mattress and pulled the thick comforter over his weary body. *Wait until I tell Doctor and his wife about the loyalties of Serena and her rebel boyfriend.*

The next day, Tuesday the thirtieth, began with breakfast, proudly served by the Colonel while he informed Johnny about the life of the Rollins's and the happiness Serena had brought into their home, the joys they had never experienced because their daughter died of cholera so young. "Ogden seems to talk about you as though you are the son he never had," Hitchcock told Johnny. As if to punctuate that comment, Ogden appeared, his buggy parked in front, to take Johnny on rounds and experience first-hand the hospitals where so many of the severely wounded he had cared for over the past months had come.

The buggy slowed at the corner of 8th and Gratiot. Ogden pointed with his whip. "That's McDowell Medical Building. Only it's a prison now." On Jefferson Avenue at the head of O'Fallon Street Ogden stopped the buggy. "That is Good Samaritan Hospital, Johnny. Built in '59. The government rented it while they built the Lawson and Jefferson Barracks."

"Wow," Johnny exclaimed and surveyed the three-story building, the basement walls stone but the rest brick. "First time I saw a real hospital, the one at Athens a store, and at Palmyra and Hannibal warehouses, University of Missouri building in Columbia."

Ogden pulled the buggy around back and tied the horse to a hitching post in front of the stable, the first brick stable Johnny had ever seen. From behind the buggy he took in the courtyard.

Ogden caught his quizzical look. "That two-story brick building with a veranda on each floor is quarters for full-time staff. There by the stable is a temporary wood-house." Next he pointed to a well in the center. "Water for cooking and drinking come from there. Two cisterns located here in the yard supply water for washing." As they strode to the rear entrance, he continued, "A tank under the roof in the

McDowell Medical Building.
Used by permission, State Historical Society of Missouri, Columbia.
During the civil war it served as a Union prison.

attic holds water for bathing (11)."

Johnny led the way up the few stairs and stopped on the screened porch that ran the length of the rear of the building. Ogden led him through a hallway to the front. He paused when they encountered a junction with a hall running to their left and right, the length of the structure. They turned right and entered a four-bed room in the center of the building. Rather than repulsion, a wave of joy swept his soul when a one-legged man yelled, "Hey, its owl eyes." He hobbled over and gave Johnny a hug. The emotion of such affection made tears well up in his eyes. He fought back the tears, to act cool, professional under Ogden's stare. After a short exchange of greetings Ogden pulled him back into the long corridor.

"The end room is a storage area. Against the front wall you see four small rooms, two nurses' rooms, officers' dinning room, and here by the front entrance is the floor office room." Ogden stopped in the hall that led to the front entrance. "The next room by the entrance hall is the medical officers' quarters and in the corner is a six-bed ward for patients (11)."

Johnny's question stuck in his mouth because a woman in a drab dress had appeared in his peripheral vision, in the door to a large room in the center. *Could it be Serena?* His mind rejected the thought when his gaze scanned the figure. Not skinny, the figure too attractive, even in the drab nurse uniform. He didn't remember Serena having a pretty face — under the wagon it was a kid face, a blank countenance.

"Hello, Johnny Jenkins," the smiling mouth uttered before the face looked over his shoulder toward the office, and returned to lock on his eyes. "You look grown up. A hero so many of these men talk of."

Heat rose up his face. He glanced at Ogden. He grinned from ear to ear. "You look different, Serena." With three steps he stood beside her in the doorway of the ward, again greeted by, "Owl eyes is here."

Ogden motioned to the office with his eyes. "Serena has work to do. You two can catch up at dinner tonight. Nancy wants to show off her cooking skills to Johnny. We'll see you then, Serena." At the nurses' station a gray-haired woman grabbed Serena by the arm and hurried her down the hall to the four-bed ward.

Descending the back steps, Johnny said, "High ceilings and large windows, Doctor Rollins." He hoped to divert the man's thoughts from the ones that had brought a peevish appearance to his countenance, thoughts of Serena's change from a skinny girl to an attractive woman.

"Three floors are the same as the one you just saw, fifteen-foot ceilings and eight-foot tall by three-feet-wide windows. Each floor holds nineteen beds. The attic has one open ward that normally holds thirty-two patients, only a seven-foot ceiling. When we use the basement and must squeeze in more patients the hospital can hold as many as one hundred and fifty (11)."

When the front door to the Rollins house opened, the Colonel stepped in first. The beige, frilly dress that Serena wore had a neck that reminded Johnny of Elizabeth when she left the top five buttons of her blouse unbuttoned. Her smile grew when he stared. The bustle created an aura of elegance for this horse thief, he mused, and followed her into the sitting room where Serena promptly introduced him to Mrs. Rollins. He was unsettled briefly by the prolonged hug — it seemed long and almost passionate. Yes, he surmised because when she drew back she wiped the corners of her eyes with a handkerchief.

She read his quizzical squint. "Ogden has talked of you so much I feel as though you are my son. Forgive me, Johnny."

Serena's mushy grin didn't ease the awkward situation. Fortunately, at that moment Ogden stormed in, a glass with red liquid in hand. He surveyed Johnny in the light blue shirt and dark blue trousers a touch short, revealing a lot of his polished boots. Hitchcock had polished them, instructing him the way career army men wear their most prized possession.

"Who wants libation to celebrate this wonderful evening?" Ogden sipped.

Nancy said she would join him. Serena requested tea, and when Johnny said he would like the same, Mrs. Rollins apologized, offering that she knew he was a Quaker.

Ogden returned with a tray, the tinkling of glass drawing Johnny's attention. After he handed the glass of tea to Johnny, he paused, his eyes piercing Johnny's. "Jesus drank wine, but I think it probably best to drink tea, if one can."

"I do not know any Quakers who do," Johnny said but felt uneasy because Ogden frowned. "Mr. Flack told me that Quakers' dress and language were more concerned with challenging men's pride than with achieving social equality (12), so I suppose they think the same way about alcoholic drinks, Doctor Rollins." That seemed to relieve the chill, hovering over the group.

"Quite likely, Johnny. And I suspect their involvement in social problems is part of their witness to the world as well," Ogden said, his frown melting.

"Yesterday afternoon Mrs. Beaumont told me about all her many activities. She is so energetic," Johnny offered.

Nancy rose from her chair, but before turning for the dining room addressed the group. "Mrs. Beaumont told me that the combination of inner experience and universal expectation was still the source of Quaker vitality in approaching new areas or issues. Her faith gives her energy, spark."

Once they were seated, Johnny asked Serena about her father. She told him about her father's recovery, the return of David Lapsley from Law School, and finished by relating her visit with Elizabeth Flack, concluding with a stare when she said Mrs. Flack told me you were nice enough to stay two nights after Mr. Flack's funeral. Her eyes shrieked at him.

Johnny squirmed in his seat, his curiosity to that point suddenly transformed to petulance. He picked up the dish of potatoes and plopped two small ones on his plate. Mrs. Rollins handed the butter dish to him, but didn't release it until he looked in her eyes. She had a motherly, encouraging look much like Elizabeth's when he squirmed under Mr. Flack's pressure. He turned his eyes on Serena's expectant gaze but before he could think of a way to answer the outrageous implication of her statement, Ogden blurted out that he thought that was not so, that he heard Sam had dragged him away to save old man Huett from a hanging.

"Too bad you couldn't make it before Christmas, Johnny," Mrs. Rollins shot in Serena's direction while the answer got just to the tip of his tongue. His mouth remained open when she added, "Blake, your friend from Sweet Home, wanted so much to see you, Johnny."

He tried, but failed to interrupt a low-pitched gasp. Nancy's smile danced, Ogden frowned, and Serena appeared as in a panic, written all over her face and in her body language.

"He's a business man, mustered out of the Iowa Third after his wound at Kirksville. Right nice young man," Ogden said.

Johnny's mind whirled with answers while he watched Serena, wringing her hands, shifting in the chair, perspiration evident on her forehead. *Thee must never judge, Johnny. Therefore thee must not ascribe evil to anyone, friend or enemy.* Flack's words thawed his frozen thoughts. "Serena went to school with Blake Slater. I never got to know him too well."

Serena's body seemed to slump, her eyes moist. Ogden had returned from stirring the fire at the far end of the dining room, and Mrs. Rollins went to get dessert, a freshly baked apple pie, Mrs. Beaumont's contribution to her young Quaker friend's visit, Nancy told him.

"Although we have won many minor skirmishes, much as Prentiss did at Hallsville, and kept Green on the run in northeast Missouri, they seem to be winning. General Price has led the attack in both major victories, Wilson's Creek and Lexington, for the Confederates." Ogden took a forkful of pie and waved it at Johnny. "So they won the first year. What do you think will happen in '62?"

"They won two battles but from the wounded I see they do not have the fighting equipment or supplies to realize the benefits of victory, to demolish the Union forces or control large areas in Missouri," Johnny said.

"And why is that?"

"Because as fast as they cut telegraph lines or destroy railway track, bridges, or equipment, we fix it. They may harass by their hit and run, but we control the tracks. The North's support for its forces grows by the month while reb soldiers wear tattered clothes, scavenge for food, and are in poorer health, so this coming year we'll finish off their army in Missouri." He noted the nod of Ogden, his approving gesture.

"Yes, and that we will do even after we have sent the Missouri Eighteenth, the Twenty-first, the Twenty-third, and others to help the Union forces outside Missouri."

Johnny appreciated the switch in topics, reticent to expose Serena, yet anxious to tell the Rollins's about the rascal Blake Slater. *Maybe I will find the right time during the remaining days,* he thought. The opportunity never appeared before he went to bed. He fell asleep vowing to inform at least Ogden about Blake's allegiance.

With no in-coming wounded during the absence of military events over the holidays, save Hallsville, and no scheduled operations on the last day of '61, Miss Dix gave Serena the afternoon off, Johnny figured from Ogden's arrangements, so they could all go to the theatre. Miss Daly's routine, her comedy, Yankee songs, and loose antics (13) brought out laughter from Serena at his side. The atmosphere bred shared time, laughing together, talking to each other, and enjoying each other's company as if they had gone to school together. When he demonstrated his amusement at one of Miss Daly's risqué remarks and unconsciously grabbed Serena's hand, he hastily removed it, but she put it back, leaned close to his ear.

"Thanks for not telling them about Blake or what you might think is between him and me." She wouldn't let go of his hand. "I just like you. Be my friend, Johnny."

Johnny gave her hand a firm squeeze and removed his hand. A strange sense, attraction blended with fright for this girl put his head in a swim. *Yet, she talks too much, a reb lover, lies about Elizabeth, maybe about her feelings for Blake but she sure is getting pretty.*

Seeming perched on a mountaintop, Johnny's mental view of the forces that tugged at his emotions assumed panoramic perspective on the stagecoach to Columbia New Year's Day. *I care nothing for Serena. She won't fool me, nor upset my plans. Dr. Rollins and his wife are my friends. By the end of this year the war will be over, and I will be in the med school Dr. Rollins chooses for me,* he told himself. But an image of Steed popped in his mind, fathering a morbid thought. *If I do not get hurt bad or killed.*

Overview 1862

As in Missouri, hostile activities in the eastern war zone came to a halt during the winter months. Not so for the Mississippi valley region south of Missouri where Brigadier-General Ulysses S. Grant started a campaign that would give him experience and a reputation as a fighting General. He captured an under-manned Fort Henry on February 6th, but shrewd tactics by the fort's commander allowed the majority of confederate men to escape to Fort Donelson twelve miles away (1). A confident Grant pursued and on February 15th Fort Donelson surrendered (1). Grant took General Buckner and 13,000 men prisoner. Nashville fell to the Union forces February 23 (1), followed in a few days by Columbus, Kentucky (1), leaving federal forces in virtual control of all of Kentucky and Tennessee.

At the battle of Shiloh church Grant's army of Western Tennessee was driven back on April 6 to Pittsburgh Landing, a costly ten miles for both sides. General Beauregard telegraphed the victory news to Confederate headquarters. His proclamation proved premature, for the next day, General Buell's Army, the 7th of the Ohio, joined Grant's forces in a surprise attack that sent the rebels in retreat (2). The number of men killed and wounded totaled 20,000 for both sides, a figure that foretold the huge scope the war would take.

Under a scheme of Robert E. Lee, Stonewall Jackson's Valley Campaign began in Virginia in late March as a diversionary tactic to keep McDowell's forces from joining McClellan in his campaign against Richmond (3,4). It continued into June, mainly as ineffectual skirmishes, and accomplished its purpose. But beginning the end of June "The Seven Days' Battles," June 25 to July 1, marked an intensification of the conflict in the east that would continue until the war's end. Thirty thousand men were killed or wounded during the week (5). Battles of Second Manassas

*on August 29 (4) and at Antietam (September 17) presaged
the Battle of Fredericksburg and Gettysburg and spelled
gloom for the Union (6).*

*Optimism over early victories along the Mississippi River
in Tennessee and surrounding region was short lived, for
Confederate forces regrouped and struck hard. The Union
would have to wait until 1863 and exert great effort at
Vicksburg to turn the tide back in their favor.*

*With Confederate forces wintering in northwestern
Arkansas, little fighting ensued west of the Mississippi River
until early spring. On March 7th at the battle of Pea Ridge,
Arkansas, General Earl Van Dorn with a force of 16,000
Confederate men attacked a Union force of 11,000 under
General Samuel Curtis who was entrenched on the
Arkansas-Missouri border (7). Due to naive miscalculations
by Van Dorn the smaller Union force routed the rebels.
Although each side suffered only 1300 casualties, Van
Dorn's troops scattered so far and wide it took two weeks to
reorganize them. Hostilities in Missouri remained quiet until
late spring.*

*The Confederate high command ordered Van Dorn's force
(7), reorganized after the fiasco at Pea Ridge, to take his
force across the Mississippi and join General Beauregard
and help stop the routing of southern forces. The scheme
worked but left General Price in Missouri to build an army.
His primary charge, however was to use Missouri as a
recruiting ground for troops to be sent east of the
Mississippi River. Hence activities in Missouri consisted of
skirmishes and bushwhacking. Coupled with clandestine
attacks by Quantrill, the south achieved another objective,
tying up a large Union force in Missouri (4). The Union
Command in St. Louis focused on control of the railroads
and attempted to obstruct rebels recruited in northern
Missouri from crossing the Missouri River. Thus northeast
Missouri became the bellwether for the entire federal campaign west of the Appalachian Mountains during the summer and fall of 1862.*

Chapter 9

Menace in Missouri
Winter 1862

The severity of winter precluded concerted activity by either army, and with Green's forces holed up in Arkansas, only bands of confederate soldiers foraged around northeast Missouri. Yet, the intensity of this menace prompted General Henry W. Halleck to issue numerous proclamations, directing most of these special orders at southern sympathizers who harassed Union troops and destroyed railroad bridges and equipment.

General Halleck had replaced General Fremont in November 1861 as commander of the Department of Missouri. He brought "order out of chaos left by Fremont (1)." Nicknamed "Old Brains" from his intelligence and experience, Halleck proved an effective administrator. After graduating near the top of his class at West Point, he had become bored, and while stationed in California, left the army to pursue a career in law and business. He rejoined the army with the outbreak of war.

On January 26, 1862, he issued a special order that forbade, among other things the display of secession flags in hands of women or on carriages in the vicinity of the military prison in McDowell's College, the carriages to be confiscated and the offending women arrested (2). And on February fourth, Halleck issued another order to railroad companies and to the professors and directors of the State University at Columbia, forbidding the funds of the institution to be used "to teach treason or to instruct traitors." Perhaps more discomforting to the citizens were the arrests and trials held to punish offenders of military orders. For example, on February twentieth Special Order No. 160 convened a military commission, which sat in Columbia, and tried Edmund J. Ellis, editor and proprietor of "The Boone County Standard," for publishing information for the enemy and encouraging resistance to the U.S. Government. The commission found Ellis guilty and banished him from Missouri during the remainder of the war (3).

The numerous punishments meted out by Union Headquarters in St. Louis had the desired effect, as shown by the action of the Assistant Adjutant General in St. Louis on February 20. He commuted the death sentence of several men who had been caught burning railroad bridges and destroying telegraph lines. "In consideration of the recent victories won by the Federal forces and of the rapidly increasing loyalty of the citizens of Missouri, who for a time forgot their duty to the flag and country, the sentences of John C. Tompkins, William J. Forshey, John Patton, Thomas M. Smith, Stephen Stott, George H. Cunningham, Richard B. Crowder, and George M. Pulliam, heretofore condemned to death are provisionally mitigated to close confinement in the military prison in Alton (2)."

The intensity of this drive to quell the activity of southern sympathizers can be seen in a letter Mary Rollins wrote on February 27, 1862, to her husband who was in Washington in legislative session:

> *My Dear Husband*
> *......Col. Merrill with whom I have become acquainted seems to be a very pleasant gentleman but a man of great firmness. He sent off this morning to military prison at Illinois....and will probably send more in a few days. Doctor Duncan, Mr. Tilley, John Samuel, Cash Newman, Doctor Victor and James Selby are those who left this morning. Cousin Warren is required to give bond in the sum of five thousand dollars or he will go with the next crowd....(4).*

General Halleck appointed General John Mayberry Schofield commander of the Army for Missouri. In March General Schofield divided the military district of Missouri, which comprised all but three southeastern counties, into five divisions and placed Colonel John M. Glover in command of the northeast division. Glover divided it into three military districts with General Ben M. Prentiss commander of the district with headquarters at Palmyra, Colonel Odon Guitar commander of the district with headquarters at Columbia, and Colonel Lewis Merrill with headquarters at Monroe City. In April General Halleck left for Corinth and Schofield assumed his command.

While the destruction of railroad property by southern sympathizers abated dramatically, bands of rebels, labeled guerillas by the Union command, resorted to Indian-style fighting. This hit-and-run tactic, also known as bushwhacking and perhaps more notorious on the Missouri-Kansas border, grew in intensity as spring approached in northeast Missouri. Near Monroe City on March 10 Captain Tom Stacy removed a Union man, James M. Preston, from his home and killed him. Bushwhacking episodes occurred near Colony and Novelty on March 25, and on April second Tom Stacy's band of bushwhackers killed two Union Militia men and a Union citizen near Shelbyville. At the same time, guerillas killed two or three Union men in western Marion County (5). In response to these depredations Glover sent five companies to Edina where he established headquarters to clear out the bushwhackers. The effort paid off, for he managed to break up all the bands of guerillas.

June fourth Schofield ordered Glover to southeast Missouri and replaced him with Colonel John McNeil, second Cavalry of the Missouri State Militia. After establishing headquarters for the district with a camp located one-half mile southeast of Palmyra at the residence of Colonel Culbertson, McNeil assigned Colonel Henry S. Lipscomb, of the Eleventh Missouri Militia, to command the post at

Macon City (5).

The battle-experienced Missouri Twenty-First Regiment under Colonel David Moore departed from St. Louis on March 21, leaving the northeast district with green troops, the newly recruited Missouri State Militia. On April 4, Moore's force joined Grant's Army at Pittsburgh, Tennessee, where Moore would be wounded, the injury requiring amputation of his right leg (6).

But the South did not intend to leave northeast Missouri in peace. Colonel Joseph Chrisman Porter, who lived in the vicinity of Whaley's Mill, had traveled with Green to Lexington in 1861 and then went south to join General Price in the fall. He participated in the battle of Pea Ridge and others, before being ordered to northeast Missouri, his mission to harass the Union forces, damage supply routes, raise an army and move it to Price in southeast Missouri. In late April Porter set up camp on the North Fabius River near Monticello in Lewis County and began recruiting (7). By May he had enlarged the network of contacts Green had used so that he had agents scattered throughout northeast Missouri. The agents, mostly older men, were not more than five miles apart and served as couriers, spreading information, and as guides to help move troops, in addition to their recruiting chores. And although Porter had recruited over 5000 men, he rarely had more than 1000 with him at any one time (8). Governor Gamble helped Porter's recruiting efforts when he ordered all eligible men of Missouri to join the Federal Forces.

Upon hearing of Porter's activities Schofield, in addition to implementing the draft, ordered all boats and other means of crossing the Missouri river, those not under the guard of Union troops, to be destroyed. He hoped this action would prevent recruits from moving southeast to join the main Confederate army.

St. Charles
May 1

"You didn't need to come on the ferry with me, Uncle Rollins," Serena said, but inside felt more at ease now that he had done so. She watched the ferry return across the Missouri River from St. Charles and head for the Olive street car terminal. Suddenly, her eye caught the stares of a tall, dark-haired man ten feet to their right. Dressed in a business suit, he shifted his gaze to the passengers climbing on the North Missouri Railroad. She turned her attention to Ogden, a commanding figure in his Union uniform.

"We discussed the attacks on trains and destruction of bridges that took place during winter months before I consented to let you go to Hannibal. Seems to be under control, but Nancy and…" He hesitated to point at a group of Union soldiers boarding the caboose. "Haven't heard of any murders, burned bridges lately, but I wanted to make certain the train had a military escort. You never know."

"I understand, but if I am ever to get to see my mom, now is the time. We have so few patients with battle wounds, just scads of sick soldiers." She squeezed his arm, headed for the coach, and turned when he yelled after her.

"Reservations are at the hotel in Palmyra tonight. Colonel Glover will have someone meet you at the depot. I received a telegram from a James Amzi, says he is coming with your mom to Palmyra to visit…."

"That would be James Amzi Jenkins. He and my sister are close friends (9). Thanks." She turned and mounted the steps.

Ogden approached the coach and with a huge smile said, "Better be sure to see Johnny, Serena."

She waved while casting a sheepish grin and entered the coach, taking a window seat in the middle of the car. After placing her small bag that contained an order for artificial limbs and some personal items on the seat, she grabbed the large suitcase, but struggled to shove it on the overhead rack.

"Allow me, Miss," a smooth, deep voice said.

Serena lowered the bag. A large, hairy hand grabbed it and thrust it onto the rack. She sat, scooted to the window, and then looked at the face of her helper. The same eyes, which had stared at her and Ogden moments before, prompted a squint.

The man held the back of the seat in front with one hand and hers with the other, suspending his body over the empty seat next to her. "May I join you as far as Renick, Ma'am?" He sat before she coughed out the answer. He shoved a hand at her. "I'm Mr. Arnet. I have a business in St. Louis. On my way to visit family. The farm is west of Renick." His smooth manners and pleasant voice dispelled her initial concerns.

She removed a hand that clutched the small bag on her lap and extended it to him, and offered her cool smile, the one Dorothea Dix taught her to use for patients and doctors at the hospital. "I am Serena Hill, a nurse at Good Samaritan Hospital."

"And the Union Colonel-I think the insignia indicated he's an army surgeon-your father?" His blue eyes seemed to twinkle with his warm smile.

"No, sir. That was Colonel Rollins, my uncle. I live with him and his wife." She decided to discourage further dialogue by removing the papers from her bag. She read the instructions, in the form of official orders. The list held the measurements for the manufacturing of six prostheses by Corporal Sam Huett of Hannibal. After she delivered this order, she was to escort to St. Louis a box with eight artificial limbs he had prepared from a list delivered six weeks previously. *Nice of Ogden to arrange me to be the courier so I can visit with mom and friends,* she rolled around her mind and grinned at the pages. Hair tingled on her neck. The man peered over her shoulder. She snapped her head at him.

"Sorry. I don't mean to peek but I couldn't help notice the

orders signed by one of our best generals." He turned partially to face her. "We are fortunate to have people like you
take care of our boys." He looked up from the papers. "And
how neat our Union troops get a new lease on life with
replacement limbs. I have been impressed the way citizens
of St. Louis have had such devotion to the Union."

"Five of these measurements are from confederate soldiers. At the hospital, doesn't matter the color of your uniform. Doctor Rollins says the boys in gray need help same
as those in blue." She searched the sincere face.

"Nice you can do that. If you had a brother killed by a
confederate soldier, do you think you could still do it?" He
twittered his eyebrows.

Perhaps it was the ease with which he chatted, or maybe
the fatherly mannerisms, for without reflecting on politics,
she answered, "My father fought for the confederate troops
at the battle of Athens. Lost an arm." She paused from his
quizzical look. "Nursing him back to health got me where I
am today."

"But you work for the Union. No loyalty for the South or
North?" He pushed back in his seat and stared at two blue
coats inching down the aisle. A third had stopped with his
back to the door in front.

"Sick and maimed are my loyalty."

"Does your family own Negroes?"

"No. But my father didn't like Lincoln, afraid the
Government might interfere in our life." She leaned forward
and put on her warm face at one of the Union soldiers, who
rested a hand on the back of the seat in front of them, and
seemed to wait to speak. "Hi, Private."

"Nurse Serena, isn't it?"

"Why, yes. I don't recognize you, Private."

"Mac. That's my buddy." He threw an arm toward the man
standing in front of the coach. "He was at the Samaritan.
Saw you there. Everything okay?" He turned a frown toward
the man beside her.

"This is Mr. Arnet, Private. Yes, the ride is peaceful."

"Greetings, Private," Arnet said.

The private touched the brim of his cap and ambled toward the back.

"Seems to be a lot of needless killing — young boys mostly-over this state's rights business. Guess both sides are guilty to same degree," Arnet said.

Serena broiled. All of her lonely cerebrations over the cause of the horrible scenes she witnessed at Good Samaritan Hospital suddenly reached a conclusion. "If you need a culprit, the single evil that has generated all the excuses from both sides, it seems to me that slavery gets the entire blame." She liked that, so she added, "No slaves, and the South couldn't cry coercion, and Washington power couldn't interfere with our state, Mr. Arnet. Yep, slavery, and nothing else has caused so much misery I have seen and so many deaths." She slumped back, felt warm all over. *Ogden would be proud of me,* she said to herself.

"You don't believe the Black Republicans would have run roughshod over us, coerced as you call it, even in the absence of slavery?"

The emotion in his previously calm voice sounded an alarm. "I'm too young to know all the politics. If slavery did not exist, what would they force on Missouri, on the Southern states?"

Silence, so she glanced at him. A faraway look appeared after a cloud seemed to pass over Arnet's face.

"Don't know offhand. They'd think of something, I suppose," he mumbled. His countenance remained frozen.

Serena stuffed the papers in her bag and shut her eyes, asking the image in her mind, "Doctor Rollins, what is the answer? Would there have been a war between the North and South if slavery didn't exist?"

Commotion erupted in the car ahead in the form of stamping feet, loud voices followed by a shot. The face of the private standing at the front of the coach disappeared, as did the glass pane of the door. Blood shot over the nearby seats. He crashed to the floor. A man in ragged farm clothes burst into the coach after the door fell off its hinges. He stood on the dead soldier and threatened the occupants of the coach with a shotgun.

A firm squeeze of her arm accompanied Arnet's soft admonishment, "Stay cool, no sound, don't move."

Serena looked out the corner of her eye. He seemed calm. He smiled at the man on the body and two others who moved around him. She fixed her peripheral vision on this calm creature. His eyes lit up.

One of the men, the one with a gray jacket, rested his gaze on Arnet. "Well, blow me down, Colonel. He lowered a squirrel rifle and approached their seat just as the man stepped from the body in front and pulled a middle-aged woman from a nearby seat.

"Looky this thing, boys," he said and ripped the front of her dress. "My," he shrieked. But no more words ushered from his open mouth. A vice grip around his neck only let out guttural sounds.

A familiar form grabbed his shotgun with the other hand, and the powerful figure pinned him against the doorsill. "We don't fight women. We behave like the Southern gentlemen we are."

"No. It can't be," Serena muttered when she recognized the figure.

"Captain Slater," Arnet bellowed and stood in the aisle.

No sooner had Blake's eyes turned on Arnet than he whipped a salute and a grin. "Colonel Poindexter. We came for you, not this business. Appears you recovered well from your wounding at Elk Horn (10)." He nodded his head at the dead body, then at the woman who had pulled the front of her torn dress together and hovered on the first seat.

"Blake Slater." The words flew from Serena's mouth.

Blake stared but briefly, broke into a magnificent grin, and after two giant strides, had her hand. "You are a welcome sight, Serena." He glanced at Arnet-Poindexter, who seemed curious. "Serena's my girl, Colonel." The Colonel nodded as if approving and left the car while the other rebels herded all the occupants, save Serena, out the back door. "You'll be safe. We came for Poindexter, and after we get him with his troops, my company will join Colonel Porter."

Serena looked past him at the still Union form resting in a pool of blood. Sadness bathed her body, dotted with muffled echoes of gunfire. "Why, Blake? That boy was just standing there."

"Jeb, the farmer, recognized him as the Yank what shot his brother last month near Shelbyville. I don't let my men kill needlessly. We take prisoners. Where you headed?"

"I am meeting my mom in Palmyra. Doctor Rollins arranged for me to deliver an order for wooden limbs and take some just made back to Samaritan." She watched the people outside start to re-board the coach.

"Serena, I am going to be in these parts the rest of this fight, so I will manage to sneak in town and visit. I will soon send you a very important letter. I hope you will take kindly to it." He grinned from ear to ear, a delicious countenance that stirred her being.

"I worry so about you. Please be careful," she said. Passengers climbed in seats around them, so she finished with a whisper. "I shall wait with great anticipation your next letter." She clutched his hand. He squeezed hers in turn and left the coach.

Before boarding the train for Hannibal at Hudson Station, Union officers quizzed the passengers. Serena's session started like a hostile encounter until she showed the Lieutenant her orders for the artificial limbs.

"I apologize, Miss Hill, but some of your fellow travelers said you acted mighty friendly with the leader of the rebs."

"I grew up with that man up in Clark County. He's a misguided boy-not some mean fighter. But…"

"Pardon me sayin' so, but your misguided boy ordered the four Union men taken to the woods by his bandits. Our troops found them murdered. Every one shot in the head."

"Can't be. He told me they just came to get Mr. Arnet, one they called Colonel." Confusion spiked with dread dulled her senses.

"Hey, blondie," the sergeant yelled toward his left, and when a tow-headed boy approached, he added, "You saw them rebs take the Union boys to the woods?"

"Yes, sir. They herded them like cows, and we heard the shots. That there Captain over there by the water tower said he found the grizzly scene in the woods-all murdered."

Convulsive sobs racked Serena's body. "This horrible conflict has turned boys into ruthless murderers." A thought surfaced. She wiped her eyes with a kerchief the sergeant put before her face. "Thank you, sergeant. That is not so. I have another friend I grew up with. He won't carry a gun and tends to the sick and wounded. He's my best friend," she lied, studying the craggy face that tilted to the right. "Johnny is a Quaker."

"Johnny owl eyes?" the sergeant exclaimed.

"You know him?"

"He treated me. This winter got me over a lung inflammation with some herb tea he give me."

That dialogue and images of that red-nosed face hastened Serena to Palmyra with excitement. When a trooper met her, carried her bag to a wagon, she asked if they might stop by at the hospital on the way to the hotel or by quarters to say hello to Private Jenkins. He told her "owl eyes" was with Colonel Glover up around Edina. The news produced a surprising glumness, soon washed away when she saw the Des Moines-Palmyra stage parked in front of the hotel. The smiling face of James Amzi and the warm hug from her mother greeted her in the hotel lobby.

Fit as she had ever seen her, Mrs. Hill warmed Serena with tales of her father, his resumption of farm duties, and

Des Moines Palmyra Mail Coach. The stage started in Des Moines, Iowa, stopped in Alexandria and traveled the Salt River Road to Palmyra. The mail coach may be seen in the museum in the state capitol building, Jefferson City. Photo by the author.

the trials he had getting her sisters, especially the next oldest, Mary Serena, to assume some of the duties Serena had managed at home. Images of the cozy clapboard house seemed real. During dinner James Amzi peppered her with questions. Following her recounting of the train attack at Renick, she asked him if he thought Blake Slater could have ordered his men to murder the Union soldiers on the train.

"Shucks, you don't ever know. I remember when he and you and neighbors came to our house the winter of '60 and then across the road for school pa set up in old man Eiler's house. He was sorta mean in them days, but killing is a lot of meanness. With his famous uncle being a southerner and holding many slaves, it don't surprise me he fights against the Union. All us Jenkins's don't care much for Abe (9). We don't care about slavery neither."

Serena watched the young boy, did quick arithmetic and figured him to be thirteen. "Posh, James. You all had a slave girl many years ago. You must have been five the days your father used the farm house as a hotel." She watched the somewhat frail boy, noticeably not as robust as his brothers, not even as muscular as his thin cousin Johnny (9).

"In the early '50s, bad farming years, we had as many as forty wagons parked by the barn, and that's why pa went to Alexandria and bought Lizzie, the Negro girl of seventeen, to ease the kitchen burdens. But she weren't really treated like a slave. I sneaked into the kitchen and she never failed to give me some of the cookies or cake she baked. She was my friend."

"My father, Blake Slater, and his dead brother fought for the south. Don't the Jenkins's stand up for one side? Except your cousin George is a strong Union soldier, fighting in Tennessee — and his kid brother a surgeon's helper here-abouts." Serena watched James pull a package from under the table and put it on her lap. "Aren't your closest neighbors to the south staunch southerners? (9)"

James pointed at the brown package. "That's honey from the hives on the back of our property. Yeah, the Cummins's are. All five of the boys went into the Southern army. But our neighbors a half mile further to the south, the Stanleys, they're rabid northerners. The old man, P. S. — they call him Ben — writes for the Alexandria Delta (9)."

"So why didn't you like Lincoln?"

"The most popular paper is the Keokuk Constitution, democrat paper owned and published by a man named Clagget. All of us at the farm read it religiously. He is fear-less and boldly denounces the Republican Party (9)."

"Mother, didn't you write me that James's brother George almost died this past winter?" Serena searched her mother's face.

"Yes. He and Mr. Butcher, Mrs. Stanley's father-he is quite elderly-both caught pneumonia. Dr. Payne made rounds to their houses daily. George pulled through, but old man Stanley died."

"It was nip and tuck, but George is back to his wild self," James said and paused to chuckle. "Last week he and broth-er Willie rode into Alexandria on horseback and had some spirits in Henshaw's tavern when talk of Porter being in northeast Missouri got everyone, James Gartrel, Gene Baxter, James Sullivan, Bob Lowery, talking. The more they talked, the more excited they became, which started the adventurous idea of joining Porter. They prevailed on George — they knew Willie had to run the farm. He raced home and started to pack until the twins spotted his feverish actions (9)."

Serena raised a hand. "Well, I know what they thought of that."

"Maggie said, 'You are not going.' And when George retorted, 'Yes I am.' She chanted, 'You are not going,' so fast over and over that he finally gave up the idea (9)."

Serena talked so late into the night that the army buggy transporting her to the harness shop in Hannibal the next morning had to return an hour later. Of course the news of her father and sisters, and seeing her mother occupied many of her thoughts. But the attitude of the Jenkins twins toward the war along with Johnny Jenkins's refusal to fight focused her thoughts on Blake. *I doubt he ordered those rebels to murder,* she reasoned. *He just acts tough like all young men. Oh, I hope he sends me that letter,* she concluded.

Chapter 10

Recruits and skirmishes
July 1862

In June General John H. McNeil of St. Louis superseded Glover as commander of the northeast division (1). McNeil, known for his temper as well as his red hair, seemed too accommodating when Doctor Rollins asked permission to take a faculty position at St. Louis Medical School. Ogden had argued, needlessly, that his part-time position for the school was important to the Union forces, for he had the task of lecturing on military medicine. The dean of St. Louis Medical School, Dr. Charles Alexander Pope (2), pointed out the lack of faculty that had hands-on experience with combat casualties and troop diseases. With the closing of McDowell Medical College in 1861, Pope's School, as some called it, was the only medical school in St. Louis during the Civil War. Pope, the leading surgeon after the death of Beaumont, had been elected as the eighth president of the American Medical Association, and commanded great respect enhanced by the fact that his wife's father, John O'Fallon, was the most prominent citizen of St. Louis (2). McNeil had no choice but to agree. And then he extracted a price.

"I want you to visit each of my district headquarters and educate the commanding generals and the medical officers," McNeil said.

Ogden knew that came as an order, one he felt unnecessary because the medical students he educated about military medicine would be ready-made army surgeons the day they graduated — well, at least assistant surgeons acquiring experiences to qualify them as surgeons. "General Schofield promised my traveling days were over if I would remain in the service after my term of enlistment expired," he protested.

McNeil shuffled papers. "I showed him these figures you gave me — twenty-five times as many sick as wounded and five times as many died of disease as wounds the first year (3)." McNeil glanced down the top page. "I told him how you thought with a little effort the toll from disease could be radically reduced."

Ogden squirmed at the thought of telling Nancy that he had to travel through the northeast, where rebels burned trains and murdered Union passengers. Many travelers simply disappeared. "Lots of younger surgeons can do just as well."

"General Schofield agreed with me that only you, the respect you command, could make people listen."

The green eyes bore through Ogden's cool front. If General Schofield is behind the order I'm trapped, he concluded. "Where do I go? When? How long should I plan to be gone?" He threw the questions rapid fire, a move to buy time.

"Each district headquarters, Palmyra, Monroe City, and Columbia. Leave tomorrow. Probably a day or two at each place with a day travel to each — may want to spend an extra day in Columbia and visit your brother." McNeil smiled, a chink in his tough armor that Ogden had waited to show.

Aha, he mused, an idea raced for expression, generated by his concerns for Nancy. The past week she had been preoccupied with Serena and the numerous letters from the phony reb, Blake. "Can't you get Serena's friend Johnny assigned to a hospital so he won't get hurt and maybe help Serena forget Blake?" she had suggested. *That's it,* he mumbled under his breath and scooted to the edge of his chair.

"Well General, I've sacrificed my personal and professional life for the army. But two weeks away will pose serious problems when I return. I have no..." He hesitated and glanced over his shoulder at a lieutenant and two clerks in the far corner. "I have no assistants to keep up with my hospital duties and the numerous tasks you and General Schofield give me."

McNeil's grin said he got the message. He stuffed the papers in a drawer and stood. "You have my permission to get an assistant."

"I appreciate that. I have in mind a young man I trained as a surgeon's assistant. He could help with the lectures, train young assistants, and do some of the menial hospital chores I carry out daily. He's stationed in Palmyra." Ogden rose and faced McNeil. "You'll need to give me an order that I can hand to General Prentiss."

"Done."

That night Ogden cushioned the news of his trip by telling Nancy that he had figured a way to get Johnny Jenkins transferred to St. Louis, a companion for Serena, and help for him, getting him home earlier every evening. Nancy seemed ecstatic. "I will bring Johnny home with me. Colonel Hitchcock will be happy to have a boarder," he said.

The St. Louis to Keokuk packet line brought back memories, not all soothing to Doctor Anthony Ogden Rollins (4). The breeze off the swirling waters of the grand old river cooled his brow. The chug-chug of the steam engines mingled with the swooshing of the huge paddle wheel. Ogden stood at the rail of the steamer on the Missouri side near the stern, the rhythmical sounds transporting his mind from the wane appearance of the sick and maimed at City Hospital. *Marvelous memories of last year in Hannibal with George Jenkins and the time I met the young Johnny owl eyes,* he muttered to a gull hawking for scraps from the boat. A bird's red head bobbing in the water suddenly whisked away the smile when he recognized Louisiana, the spot where the blind assistant, named Steed, had jumped overboard to commit suicide. He shook his upper body and walked to the opposite side to stare at the flatter Illinois shore. *I hope I find Johnny sound of body,* he thought. He felt the envelope in his coat pocket and removed it. A quick scrutiny of the order jabbed his enthusiasm because it ordered Prentiss to release Johnny for St. Louis when he had a satisfactory replacement. Ogden shoved the paper in the envelope and thrust a forefinger at the Illinois shore. "I will get his release, you hear?"

Thanks to the telegraph, a military carriage stood at the Hannibal wharf. He toted the old, black satchel, saluted a lieutenant with the other hand, and climbed up. Two other officers joined them and they started the seven-mile ride to Palmyra. Upon passing the Moses B. Bates mercantile building, a reminder of the founder of Hannibal, he smiled at the iron façade, a soothing memory. In Palmyra the lieutenant escorted him into General Prentiss's office. Cordial greetings and bantering preceded the exchange of information.

"From Camp Jackson to the last battle, the one you won at Mt. Zion, sixty encounters occurred during the first year in Missouri, over half south of the Missouri River (5)." Ogden paused to fish in his satchel. He held a paper and continued, "Mortality from encounters pale in light of the toll taken by disease. Twenty-five times as many men suffered from disease as from wounds and five times as many died (3)."

Prentiss pulled his chair next to Ogden. "Show me the ones with a big impact on troop performance."

"These figures are totals for the Department of Missouri from the beginning through the end of June this year. I have listed the most frequent diseases, ones that impact on our ability to fight." Ogden held the paper between them:

Disease	No. Sick	No. Deaths
Continual Fevers	2,054	201
Malarial Fevers	12,802	49
Diarrhea/Dysentery	13,535	63
Pulmonary affections	10,760	249
Rheumatism	2,029	3
Total All Diseases	66,690	943

Average strength = 19,560 (6)

Ogden pointed to the top row. "Continual fevers...." He glanced at the attentive face. "That includes typhoid fever and typhus (6)."

"Lots of lung problems," Prentiss said and pointed to the sheet. "Is that a lot of rheumatism — a little over two thousand cases?"

"Considering that most are under thirty, I'd say yes. But the total number with diseases, over sixty-six thousand, should tell you the major concern for your men this year — their health (6)," Ogden said.

"And the total deaths?"

"Close to one thousand (6). Perhaps not a lot in the big picture, but health of an army, the efficiency of the man in combat, is as important as the gun the soldier carries, let alone the great numbers sidelined from action." Ogden replaced the paper. "Consider the average strength of over nineteen thousand per month and the average of over five thousand sick each month — that means twenty-five percent of your men are sick."

"Precisely, good doctor. And now you will tell me what field commanders should do to improve health, prevent disease."

"First, make it an order that men take their quinine. That would have prevented almost thirteen thousand fevers, malarial. Next, I guess I would educate the troop leader, perhaps the company commanders, where to put the latrines — certainly not above or near the water source — and cooking and drinking water must not be contaminated."

Prentiss rubbed his hands together. "With a force of a few hundred that's a tough one."

"But it accounts for fevers from typhoid and likely most of the diarrhea and dysentery. Last item, food. Army manual says a pound of beef or pork a day, vegetables and fruit for each soldier (7). They scrounge for food, not as bad as the rebels, but the bread has so many weevils, big chunks have been known to walk out of camp." He grinned.

Not Prentiss. "I'll get after quartermaster. We can get all the pork, lots of beef from La Grange and from Sweet Home."

Upon leaving headquarters, Ogden walked across the street to Holtzclaw's warehouse and entered the medical clinic at the far end. A young surgical assistant from the Iowa Third told him "owl eyes" was in the back, changing dressings. He paused until Johnny had finished wrapping a man's leg stump and felt a surge of pride when Johnny told the man that a special boot with a built-in wooden leg would arrive in a week from Hannibal and he would be able to return to his farm near Kahoka.

"I'm surprised, with all those weeks of exposure to the congressman, that you have not switched to politics, Johnny," Ogden said, paused to search the quizzical face, continued, "Brother James says you began to argue like a politician, even argued about the decision your hero, Lincoln, made."

"Wasn't much," Johnny said.

Ogden hesitated until the fidgeting boy looked up. "Did you really tell James that Abe had another option when Fort Sumter was shelled?"

"Nothing."

"James liked it, liked your reasoning, laughed at the Quaker dilemma it gave you." Johnny just stared, squinting at him. "You told him that Abe should not have fought secession. Let the states, there were seven by then, form their own country, the Confederate States of America. And Missouri couldn't secede because Abe didn't coerce the rebel states to stay in the Union."

"Well, that's better than all the misery, killing of soldiers, murdering going on by bushwhackers, giving all the mean, devilish-minded men an excuse to rape, steal, and kill. Did you hear about the most heinous murder? By a Union soldier, Captain Lair."

"Heinous? My, my Johnny," Ogden teased with a peevish grin.

"The reb Captain Owen when captured was killed instantly. Lair used Schofield's harsh order that allowed such killing. The Union troops tied him to a barbed-wire fence after they found him hiding in the woods, beat him to death…" Johnny squinted so hard his eyes seemed to meet, lowered his head, and raised it, staring at Ogden with watery eyes. "They cut out his heart, returned to his farm, and handed it to his wife."

Ogden felt a surge of anger. He stammered. "I hear Owen had bushwhacked his share of Union troops and citizens."

"Precisely why war and killing are awful, Doctor Rollins. Soon peace-loving, decent farm boys become what they must do as soldiers." He ran slim fingers through his gnarled blonde hair. "Murderers — butchers — fiends."

"Good Quaker logic, Johnny. But what about slavery? Only this war could have stopped it. Quakers abhor that. They'd rather fight it through the underground railroad." Ogden wiggled a finger at the squirming youth.

"We — they would soon have all the slaves in the north, the Canadian border moved from eight hundred miles away to across the river just like your brother said in his famous letter in February a year ago."

"Come on, you think just like them. Interesting option for Abe, though. After a few years the Confederate States would be poorer than Mexico, so…" Ogden paused as a thought flashed across his brain. "So poor that Mexico would forcibly take back their Texas with ease."

"Doctor Rollins, it is good to see you again." Johnny thrust a hand at Ogden, his spontaneous response fathering a classic "owl eyes" expression.

"Did you miss me so much or is it Serena?" Ogden fished in his satchel.

"Thanks for the new Eberle. I've memorized it." When Ogden raised his eyebrows as he handed an envelope, Johnny added, "Well, I have read it a couple times, remember lots. Is Serena okay?"

"Read for yourself. I think she likes you more than that Blake feller. I haven't heard of any skirmishes to test your talents this year. Other than reading, what have you done with yourself?" He watched Johnny read the light blue sheet of paper he had taken from the envelope, a slow smile creeping over his face.

Johnny stuffed the paper in his pocket. "She is fine — seems happy." He studied Ogden's face. "She's always liked Blake. The Iowa First Cavalry saw a bit of action middle of January. The confederate, Captain John P. Caldwell from near my home, actually from Lewis County, had organized a company of recruits. On the way to join up with General Price in January he camped with Colonel J. P. Poindexter at Silver Springs in south Knox County. The Iowa detachment under Major Torrence attacked the camp and completely routed the rebsel. One was killed and Caldwell and a number of men taken prisoner (8)."

"I hear Green sent Porter to these parts in March to recruit for Price and destroy track (9). Any action there?"

"General Prentiss brought me here from Columbia." Johnny paused to search Ogden's face. "But only disease type action since arriving here. Well, I did go to Edina with Colonel Glover early May, but all we did was scare off rebel groups, no heavy fighting. I got to go with Colonel Lipscomb when he took out after Porter. It began on June seventeen when Porter with forty-three men captured Lipscomb's guys near New Market (9). He took equipment, paroled the prisoners, and from there he went to Marion County, eastern Knox County, and Lewis County, gathering recruits; many had signed on earlier but the inclement weather in winter and early spring had kept them home. Porter rested at Sulphur Springs in Knox County and then went north to Memphis. From there Porter gathered more recruits from Scotland and Schuyler Counties, some four hundred and fifty. Union troops caught up with him at Cherry Grove in north Schuyler County July first. This time Lipscomb with 450 State Militia, new recruits, routed the rebels, twelve killed and twenty-five wounded. One Union man died (1). Lipscomb couldn't follow because Porter scattered his force. Our scouts said he kept only seventy-five with him. Lipscomb's horses were in bad shape, many without shoes, so he took his exhausted horses and troops to Hudson Station (1)." Johnny tilted his head toward the light, revealing a fresh scar on his forehead. "Closest I came to the fight. I was leaning over a fallen man, when someone shot at me."

Ogden quizzed Johnny and, determining that few battle casualties occurred for his attention, he proceeded to tell Johnny about the diseases that afflicted the Missouri troops the past twelve months and then informed him of his suggestions to Prentiss. "You be careful. We've already lost six surgeons."

A grimace clouded over the grin. "I'll be careful. I want to hold you to your promise about med school."

"If you lose part of a limb or can't use a hand or arm, I won't be able to keep my promise." He mulled over the orders from McNeil and decided not to tell Johnny. "Are you ready to learn hospital medicine?"

"Ready."

"I mean would you be happy if transferred to St. Louis soon to work with me at a military hospital."

With the enthusiastic response, Ogden went back to headquarters, gave Prentiss the envelope with McNeil's order and waited for his reply. After considerable debate over when the transfer to St. Louis should occur, Ogden agreed that one-month's time for training Johnny's replacement was reasonable.

Ogden caught the train for Monroe City where he met

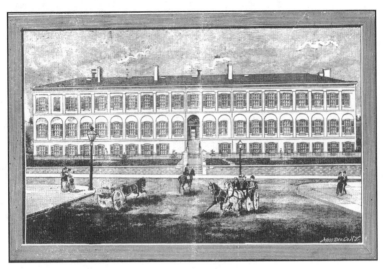

St. Louis City Hospital.
Used by permission, State Historical Society of Missouri, Columbia.

with General Merrill. After giving Merrill the same data and instructions, Ogden took a train for Hudson Station, also known as Macon, where he transferred to the North Missouri Railroad. At Sturgeon a carriage met him and transported him to headquarters in Columbia. Since brother James was in Washington, he went directly the University and met with General Odon Guitar and instructed him about the first year's casualties from disease and his recommendations for improvement.

On the stage for St. Louis Ogden's thoughts turned to Johnny. I must get him transferred to a St. Louis hospital. He closed his eyes and let his mind shuffle through images of the hospitals. An image of St. Louis City Hospital froze in his mind. He imagined Johnny walking up the long steps to the front entrance or sitting on the front wall at the end of the day, waiting for a ride to Colonel Hitchcock's house. He formed a grin and thought, *Perfect — for his safety and to get Serena away from Blake.*

Chapter 11

Battle at Memphis
July 1, 1862

The five-foot, ten-inch, slender Joe Porter, a charismatic leader who commanded great affection from his troops, had blue-gray eyes, a low musical voice and an agreeable look (1). He had with him a group of experienced field commanders, Poindexter, Franklin, and McCullough.

By staying constantly on the move, Porter avoided confrontation with the Union troops. After all, his mission was to recruit for Price's forces in Arkansas, not to squelch the Union forces. His scouts told him McNeil had brought a thousand troops to Palmyra to join the forces under Prentiss.

Blake Slater approached the mild-mannered Porter. He wiped his face with a red bandanna, the one Uncle John Boulware had given him. Spying the grime on the sweat-stained rag, he hesitated.

"Private Slater, you look a mess. The other scouts been here an hour," Porter said.

"Sorry, Colonel. I hung behind to see what the blue-bellies had in mind. Appears Lipscomb's men tired out their horses. I followed long enough to find out they gave up chasing us and retired to Hudson station."

"Good work, Slater" Porter said. He turned to his left and beckoned to a man nearby. When the man reached the group, Porter said, "Mudd, this is Blake Slater. He grew up in Clark County, knows these parts well. Take him over to your company. Be sure Captain Penny hears his report."

Joseph Mudd, from Lincoln County, was a medical student in St. Louis when the war broke out. He joined the

Missouri state guard in June of 1861, and after his term of duty expired he returned to his studies. But when fighting grew in intensity in 1862 he joined the command of Colonel Porter in June and was put in Penny's company. He first met Captain Sylvester B. Penny in August of 1861 on the march to Wilson's Creek.

After reporting to Penny, Blake searched for Walters. He spied Walters under a walnut tree and ambled over to him. He recounted for Walters his experiences since they separated at Cherry Grove. Walters patted his back when Blake told him he shot owl eyes. "I spied my old enemy, 'owl eyes.'" Blake gulped the humid air, the temperature he figured to be near ninety. "Got two shots off at him. I spied him tending to some guy what was gut-shot." He laughed. "I do believe I hit him in the head with the second 'cause he fell over the wiggling man. I know. I saw blood on his face and hands as I ran for my horse. Adios to one more nigger lover."

"How'd you find us? We expected you at Newark," Walters said.

"I was almost to Newark when I saw so many Yanks I figured you had left," Blake said as he shook the bandanna. "Some old guy, an agent near La Belle, told me you camped there on Thursday the tenth. Said you headed for Memphis. Who chased you out of Newark?"

"Didn't. We almost captured a Captain Lewis and his company of blue-bellies. He come upon us, that'd be the seventh, about three miles north of Newark. During the fightin' we separated Lewis from his horses, forcing him to retreat and fight. Under a white flag Colonel Porter offered Lewis unconditional surrender. He refused and holed up in a brick house we stayed in the night before (2,3). Some agents rode up and told Porter that McNeil was making all haste from Palmyra for the surrounded Lewis."

"Any of our troops killed?" Blake asked, removed his hat, wet the bandanna, and wiped his face.

"None of ours. Yanks had two killed," Walters said while

he got up, brushed off his britches. "Colonel sent his brother to Monticello, and we plan to take Memphis. Porter was told it's a strong Union town-with some supplies we could use."

Early morning on Saturday the twelfth, Blake, rested after a good night's sleep, listened intently to Porter's instructions for the capture of Memphis, telling his men to follow them in detail so that all exits from the town would be guarded and none of the Union-lovers could escape to alert McNeil's forces of their whereabouts. The plan (1) called for the troops to make four columns and at the signal three sections would make a dash to block the north, west, and east exits of the town. Blake and Walters joined Mudd. Captain Penny moved them with the rest of his company along the south road. Porter posted sentries at each exit and directed columns to advance to the courthouse. Mudd told Blake that silence was important to effect the surprise. Near town they posted a sentry, John Young, by the bridge. His job was to make sure no one went over the wooden bridge, the noise certain to sound an alarm (1).

The plan worked. Only when they began to round up the inhabitants of the town did the citizens realize the confederates were in the area. At the armory they confiscated a hundred muskets with cartridge boxes and ammunition along with some Federal uniforms (1). Walters took a blue shirt. Blake helped gather the male residents so that Porter could parole them.

While he watered Davis at the horse tank on the south side of the courthouse, Mudd arrived and described his experience with a woman after he and Captain Penny left the Smoot residence.

"She was the cussinust woman I ever saw. Feisty, she threw a stave at the Captain," Mudd said.

Blake listened with one ear and with the other heard Porter let a confessed man, a doctor, leave to care for his sick wife after he promised not to tell anyone of Porter's presence in Memphis for three days.

Walters out of breath ran up to the two. "They got that doctor, the butcher from the battle at Athens," he said.

"What's his name?" Mudd began to rub down his horse.

"Aylward. Seems after the battle he returned here and runs a hotel and store," Walters said.

Blake made a slash on Mudd's leg with the side of his hand. "Stacy told me he was going to find the guy and kill him, because some of our southern friends there said Aylward did a lot of unnecessary amputations on the confederate wounded at Athens (4). He's a scoundrel."

"Captain Stacy will even the score," Walters blurted.

Mudd shook his head vigorously. "Colonel Porter ain't that type. It won't happen. He doesn't truck with vengeance, murdering, and mean behavior."

"Aylward's frisky. I was with Captain Dawson (1) when we stopped at the doctor's house. He bolted out the door with a pistol and discharged it at us. He seemed very calm, but missed with both shots. In our confusion, we missed with a couple shots, while he emptied his gun and ran for the garden. There he took a bullet in the neck, forced him to surrender (1). If Porter weren't so insistent on treating the doctor properly as a prisoner, Stacy would sure 'nuf killed him."

At four in the afternoon, Porter led his force out of Memphis. The group of some 300 spent the night at Henry Downing's farm, eight miles west of town. Aware the Union forces were in pursuit, Porter sent Blake and half a dozen scouts to search around Schuyler County for Federal troops. The next evening reports placed McNeil in Memphis. From the information that he had, several officers with McNeil, Porter reasoned that it was a large force, sufficient to allow the general to send several small battalions across the countryside to locate him. Nearby Vassar Hill offered a perfect place to ambush the next company searching the area.

As anticipated, a force of blue coats pursued Porter on the

road to Pierce's Mill, called Vassar Hill by the confederates. Porter left a small band of men for bait at the bridge over the Fabius Creek, giving every appearance that they planned to tear it to pieces. When the Union's advance column — scouts said it was Major John Clopper's company — spotted them, the men were to act surprised and dash toward Vassar Hill as if in a panic.

Porter led his men, about 125 in number (1), two and a half to three miles past the bridge along a tree-lined road, across bottom land with few trees, to the opposite side; Dunn's command was on the way to join him. They entered the dense wooded bottom of the hill and secured their horses with a sentry, spreading in the thicket along the road and waited. Blake's pulse bounded when he heard the sound of hoof-beats, their crescendo sound telling him they approached rapidly. The bait, Porter's men, rode past them for their corral. A second thunder of horses grew louder, the thud of maybe twenty horses muffled by the soggy trail. Walters poked his rib. Quickly, Blake put his finger to his lips, looked at the wide-eyed man, and shook his head. Silence was necessary for them to succeed. The blue coats came on rapidly. Penny's company occupied the thicket at the end from which the Union troops, part of Merrill's Horse, came. As planned, they let them pass before commencing to fire. Of the twenty-one, Blake saw only three escape back down the road (5).

"Blake, I got that blonde one right between the eyes," Walters yelled. "Did you…?"

Rumbling thunder of muffled horse hoofs stopped his remark. A charge by some of the main body, threatened the men in the thicket. All in all, of the men with Major Clopper, likely each of the 400 participated in at least one of the seven charges. Major Rogers's Eleventh Militia came up to give support but had limited involvement (1). After the last charge, Blake helped place Captain Stacy in a wagon. A bullet hole below his left nipple told Blake he was not likely to survive (1). A small group of Porter's men eased down the road after forty-five minutes and found no enemy. With that discovery a group of men scoured the battlefield for equipment.

"Dr. Marshall, how many did we lose?" Porter leaned over his horse's head to stare at Stacy while the doctor and another man helped a man shot in the thigh, W. S. Griffith, on a horse. The pale-appearing man made no sounds but bent over, clinging to the horse's neck.

"Two, Colonel." The doctor threw his head toward the wagon. "Probably be three."

"And the Federals?" Porter inched his horse to the wagon and peered at the still form of Stacy.

"Eighty-three killed or wounded (1,2)," Marshall said.

When scouts reported that McNeil traveled with reinforcements for Clopper, Porter gathered his troops and headed for Newark, passing through Brashear and Novelty (2). Though younger than many men, Blake felt exhausted from the 65 miles covered in 24 hours. During the past two weeks it had rained almost continuously, leaving the roads and trails a soggy mess, the exertion by horses and men severe. At daybreak Sunday they rested near Whaley's Mill, three miles from Porter's home.Blake felt the creeping up his cheek and slapped, only to hear Walters giggle. Opening one eye he caught a glimpse of Walters's bearded grin, different some way. "Uncle Pres, you lost a couple teeth. How?"

"That Yank what shot Griffith, come on me whilst I was reloading. He tried to mash my head but only glanced the butt of his rifle off'n my mouth." He pulled his knife from its scabbard and proceeded to examine it. Walters brought it so close for inspection his eyes crossed. Then he spit on it and wiped the blade on his ragged shirt. "Yuk. Yankee blood. I slit his throat, only a dumb-lookin' kid."

Gray-blue smoke hung below the cottonwoods. Pleasant odors hit Blake's nostrils as he spied Porter disappearing into a far stand of maples. The wafting of hickory smoke turned his gaze to its source and the sound of crackling from a roaring fire, the origin of the blue veil bathing the lower branches of the trees.

"We got eggs and a couple chickens from an agent what has a farm hereabouts." Walters thrust a tin plate in front of Blake. "He give us that bread, too. Take it. I'll get mine." As soon as Blake grabbed the plate of victuals, Walters turned for the fire and soon returned with a plate heaping with eggs, bread, and half a chicken. He broke off the leg and handed it to Blake.

Blake swallowed a handful of egg and waved a greasy finger at Walters. "Where was Porter going?"

"His home is only 'bout three miles west. He won't stay long because he told Penny to get us ready to go later today, wants to keep Major Clopper and General McNeil on the run. We goin' to the vicinity of Florida and do some recruiting," Walters said.

A man at the fire reached into the pot and extracted a hunk of chicken. The bloody bandage on his upper arm tilted Blake's thoughts. "Think Captain Stacy made it?"

Walters gulped, took a swig of coffee and offered the cup to Blake. "Nah. Doc Marshall said he'd be dead in a day."

"What about Griffith? After we all swam the Fabius River, I saw two of his buddies put him in a wagon and head off on their own (1)."

Waving a chicken wing at a group huddled under a large red oak tree, Walters said, "That bearded guy with Penny and the captains said Stacy's brother would meet them in Sharpsburg and then sneak him toward Warren, where his parents can tend him."

"So you think he'll make it?"

Walters screwed up his nose and scrunched it to one side. "Tough bird. He'll survive, but won't fight no more."

Blake lay back to catch a few winks just when Porter returned. When scouts reported that agents said McNeil followed, having paused but briefly at Pierce's Mill to let

Major Clopper bury his dead, Porter organized the march to Florida, ending Blake's nap. He sent Blake and four scouts to lag behind and determine the whereabouts of the Federals by reconnoitering and checking with agents in a wide area of Marion County. "We'll meet you south of Florida on Tuesday," Porter said. Blake divided the scouts into three groups of two, sending one twosome south toward Philadelphia, another toward Newark, while he and a skinny kid who looked like he hadn't started to shave yet followed the Fabius River toward Palmyra. *If I don't find Serena there, I can at least send her this letter,* he reasoned. He felt in his britches pocket to make sure it was there.

From a thicket of dogbane Blake spied men leading horses across the ford that crosses the south fork of the Salt River. He grabbed a forearm of his young companion. Alf seemed to be dozing in his saddle; it was July twenty-second and they had just traveled 33 hours without sleep. After leaving Palmyra they had replaced their blue flour-sack shirts with gray ones. Slowly, he had led them through the covered bridge over the north fork of the salt, slowly so the horses barely made a sound on the wooden planks. Giving the signal for silence Blake nervously led them along the only street of the small village of Florida, their passing at five a. m. evidently not disturbing the sleeping occupants. Approaching the wooden bridge over the south fork of the Salt River, located a mile south of the north fork, Blake reined up when he spied dark forms of many men on the opposite shore, barely discernable in the early light. Soon Blake realized how lucky he was that he remembered to have them change back into their gray shirts because a voice from behind them said, "They're ours, reb." And when he turned to eye a gaunt face of a lean man on a bony sorrel, the sentry added, "You look about as bad as we feel after 33 hours. Slater, Colonel needs your report."

They forded the Salt River above the bridge and entered

the crowded encampment of men strung out along the narrow valley. Dispensing with formalities, although he threw the semblance of a salute, Blake told Porter that McNeil, on having no luck finding them, had moved on to Warren, located sixteen miles west of Palmyra and then returned to Palmyra. Blake grinned when he told Porter that an agent told him McNeil said, "He [Porter} runs like a deer and doubles back like a fox (1)."

Porter chuckled, paused while he sent Captain Hickerson, chief of the commissary, and four men to Florida for supplies. Blake told the Colonel how he and the kid ambled through Palmyra, bustling with Federals preparing to resume the chase after a brief rest and acquisition of fresh supplies. He smiled when he told Porter he even posted a letter to his girl in St. Louis. Of all the commanders, only Porter, always the warm, fatherly overseer, would not only approve but enjoy such personal actions. When he finished, the other four scouts took his place and began their reports. Blake searched for Walters, finding him asleep near a blackberry bush.

The groggy-eyed Walters had barely begun his account of their tiring journey from Whaley's Mill when a commotion from the direction of town stopped his tale. Captain Hickerson, the commanding guard with two of his three men, ran for the camp. Upon learning that a detachment of Major Caldwell's third Iowa Battalion had fired on Hickerson's band in town, hitting Hickerson's horse and taking Fowler of Stacy's company captive, Porter ordered a counterattack on the village. Using information from local agents he succeeded in forcing Caldwell to withdraw but not until twenty-three of Caldwell's fifty men were wounded or missing. Blake heard Mudd tell Porter that they found no dead Federals after they retreated for Paris, but two confederates had been killed-out of the 90-100 who fought (1).

Porter broke camp and continued in a southeasterly direction for twenty miles, camping near Santa Fe. After he allowed thirty hours of much needed rest, Porter resumed the march on the twenty-fourth. But two miles from camp a scout stopped the column and announced that the Federals were directly ahead; Caldwell's force of some one hundred men had caught up with him. Porter moved the column a third of a mile to the left and hid some of his force behind old, decaying logs, others behind an eighteen-inch embankment. Doing as Porter commanded, Blake flopped on his belly behind a log. Walters shoved next to him, Mudd on the other side. Musty smell of rotten log formed a whimsical smile soon erased by gunshots and whistles of missiles passing overhead. To his right Blake saw enemy appear from the foliage across the small meadow and charge, firing as they advanced. Porter shouted to get down but before he could do so, Kneisley was struck below the collarbone, the ball exiting through his shoulder (1). With that image Blake and the entire hidden Confederate line responded to Porter's next order. "FIRE." Virtually every advancing foe fell to the ground, the meadow dotted with writhing, groaning blue-coated figures.

Again, Porter had defeated the Iowan; two federals killed and thirteen wounded while Porter sustained no casualties, except for Kneisley. After scouring the battlefield, Porter continued south through Audrain County. He ordered a day's rest and then broke camp and went to Brown's Spring, nine miles north of Fulton. Here Captain Frost's and Cobb's companies reinforced him, giving a total of 260 men (1). No federal attack came, so he crossed Auxvasse Creek.

Porter sought to rest his weary troops who, in a span of 15 days, had marched 500 miles, captured one town, paroled 100 enemy, fought four battles, and captured lots of arms. Blake and the other scouts, however, made the respite short-lived. They reported that General Schofield had ordered Colonel W. F. Shaffer of "Merrill's Horse" to leave Columbia with 100 men on the twenty-sixth. Colonel Odon Guitar left Jefferson City on the twenty-seventh with 200 men and two artillery pieces. They occupied Sturgeon, soon joined by Major Clopper with 100 men. Blake saw Porter's anxiety when two scouts added that Major Caldwell with part of the Iowa Third and part of J. M. Glover's regiment left Mexico, the two columns heading for Mt. Zion Church.

The mid-day sun of July twenty-eighth scorched Blake when he looked for a place to rest after giving his report. He and the other exhausted rebels rested at Moore's Mill, seven miles east of Fulton. Blake scooted over until he found shade from a white oak. Not for long, because Penny roused the men, marched them five-hundred yards, and turned into the thick brush alongside the road, where they formed a line. No one told him, but he knew they waited to surprise some Yanks. After an hour of dreaming about Serena, the Federals came. Porter's line got off two volleys before Guitar's artillery commenced at the moment scouts reported that Lt. Colonel Shaffer's three hundred and a handful of men joined Guitar's four hundred. With these numbers fed him by his scouts, Porter realized his force of two hundred and forty needed an advantage.

"Forward. Charge." Porter had risen in the line. With the larger Union force the order seemed brave but bordered on the illogical.

Suddenly, Blake heard the yells of his comrades and joined the mass of men that ran headlong at the enemy. Severe fighting ensued, especially near the Federal artillery, and only when Shaffer's reinforcements hit the field did Porter's men begin a retreat that soon turned into a rout (1,6).

The battle had raged from noon to four in the afternoon. Porter's force scattered, many escaping along the Auxvasse Creek bottom, others over the creek. The Union forces lost 12 with 55 wounded. The rebels suffered 11 killed and 21 wounded, but in his official report (2) Guitar claimed that 52 confederate were killed and from 125 to 150 wounded.

With the death of Capt. Penny, Mudd and the rest of

Penny's company spoke with Porter before separating. He consented to their wishes to leave the regiment and attempt to join the Confederate army, the mission of the regiment at its inception (1). Porter with some of his scattered forces retreated toward Florida, crossing the North Missouri Railroad at Mexico on the thirtieth. He arrived at Paris with 400 men. Stragglers arrived until the force numbered 1000. Porter sent a detachment under Colonel Cyrus Franklin to Canton, leading the remaining troops to Monroe Station, where they crossed the Hannibal-St. Joseph Railroad. He camped at New Market. The next day he went north to Newark, where he captured a small U.S. force under Captain Lair.

Scouting reports said McNeil with a large force had left the troop train at Monroe Station and approached quickly, so Porter led his force north to western Lewis County to rendezvous with the battalion of Colonel Franklin after he captured Canton. With Franklin was Colonel Frisby H. McCullough. Altogether Porter's force numbered 2200. He called a conference of his officers, reminding them that their primary mission was to gather a large army, cross the Missouri River, and make it to Arkansas.

McCullough told him his scouting party found that all means for crossing the Missouri had been destroyed and the Feds patrolled the river as well. Blake, out of breath, listened intently, while Porter told of a scheme to feign a march north to Memphis. At this point Blake decided he needed to relay his findings.

"Colonel Porter. These men just came from Kirksville." He threw his head to a bunch of scraggly-appearing men. "They say Captain Tice Cain and his Schuyler County Company have taken the town for us." Porter nodded, his affable nature warming Blake. "Good work, Slater. Who was the Yank in charge?"

"Company A of the Fifth Regiment Militia, newly formed under Captain James A. Smith, held the place, but we heard

Colonel Gilstrap, in command at Macon, ordered him to leave. Must have thought Cain had a larger force."

"You just made our decision." Porter beamed at his officers. "If I figure correctly we'll have close to two thousand men at Kirksville."

"Colonel, if possible could we rest on the North Fabius? Flux about to wipe us out, some five hundred ailing bad. I understand only half of our two thousand have arms," Franklin said.

Porter caught McCullough's agreeing nod. Blake shifted from left to right foot and back as Porter massaged his neck but searched Blake's eyes. "Your home's around Keokuk. Yes, Slater?"

"Sweet Home, Sir."

"Go with Captain Owsley and see if you can get hold of medicine and other supplies. Union keeps lots at Athens. If the Des Moines River is low, they unload at Keokuk or Alexandria."

"My dad runs the pork plant at Sweet Home. We can get plenty of victuals." Blake went to pack his bedroll and ready Davis while Porter gave Owsley instructions. Excitement consumed Blake. *I will scout my own territory. Maybe Serena is home,* he recalled their brief meeting near Renick in May when Serena had said she planned to visit her parents in August. After he climbed on Davis, he patted the muscular neck and said, "Ole boy, I am already important. How Serena will love me!"

Chapter 12

Raid at Alexandria
Battle at Kirksville
August 1

Johnny tried hard to hide his grief. Since the battle at Memphis, which didn't seem so bad compared to his first experience at Athens, he felt lonely. In the dark of his room in Holtzclaw's warehouse he replayed the action of the rebels. He needed to make sense for the St. Louis Globe democrat two weeks after the dastardly event had "denounced the murder of Dr. William Aylward." His first battle experience, at Athens, had been with the older, gentle man.

Johnny had heard the Mayor of Memphis tell McNeil how a group of the rebels, against Colonel Porter's orders, had taken Dr. Aylward out from the camp at night and lynched him (1). Following Porter after the battle at Cherry Grove proved frustrating for the Union troops. Johnny grieved over the murder of Aylward, but McNeil swore vengeance, driving his men after a short rest at Stoddard's farm.

When they returned to Palmyra to take a brief rest and obtain fresh supplies and mounts, Johnny reasoned it was Ogden's intervention that prompted Prentiss to tell him that he could not go on with McNeil. Johnny told him he had suffered through the frustrating hide-and-seek all the way from Memphis and thought he should be allowed to be present when the Union forces caught up with Porter.

"You told me a bit ago that your family members were bad sick. Stay and help a week and then you can have leave for St. Francisville the end of July," Prentiss said. He had shown Prentiss a letter from Dr. McKee, a message now a month old. It described Ezra's failing health and Elizabeth's pleading for the doctor to convince Johnny to pay her a visit.

Guilt propelled Johnny along the Salt River Road. Recall of the message in the front of Grandma Weaver's Bible evoked a pitiful lament, only deepening his guilt.

Late on the thirty-first of July, Johnny eased Red along the familiar, but dark streets of St. Francisville. Right off of Main Street, he passed the Baptist Church, his gaze past it noting the dark cabin of the Flacks. Quietly, he eased Red to the back and dismounted. The backdoor stood ajar. The hoot of an owl made him jump. He peered inside. The bearskin hung open, revealing Ezra's bed. Empty. "Elizabeth," he whispered as he inched toward her bedroom. Nothing, so he raised the whisper two octaves and repeated the call. Nothing. The bedroom door stood wide open. He peeked in while rubbing his palms on his blue britches. A lump grew in his throat. Unmade, empty bed. He led Red over to Pastor Stone's house just north of the Baptist church. A light from a front window shone onto the yard. He knocked on the oak door and heard his rapid pulse over the soft footsteps. After greeting him, which pleased Johnny that the preacher would remember him, he sat Johnny on the chair next to his work table, offered him coffee, the intensity of his gaze and the hesitancy to his voice serving to heighten Johnny's anxiety.

"Both buried last week, Johnny. Ezra died with the same lung problem that took Mr. Flack's life. Elizabeth up and died next week. She had a cough for a long time. I thought she looked mighty pale the past several months. Doc McKee says she didn't die of consumption. Died of a broken heart. Yep, acted that way. When Ezra died she had nobody. Poor lonesome girl. And such a fine Christian."

His response and the following minutes remained buried in the recesses of Johnny's befuddled brain. He led Red to

Wolf cemetery, found Ezra's grave, parked between Mr. Flack's and Elizabeth's. Only a cricket heard the sobs. The midnight breeze dried his sweaty shirt, but not his face. A chill awakened Johnny. He looked for the moon but couldn't locate it through the dense foliage of the trees guarding the cemetery. He dusted off his britches, untied Red, and returned to the Flack cabin, where he washed his dirt-streaked face and hands in the familiar wooden bucket — at the table where Elizabeth had warmed his inner self so many times. He spun around hoping to see her. Instead the empty room asked for more tears. He stumbled onto the bed.

Street noise awakened him. Outside, he mounted Red, pointing the big animal for Dr. McKee's house, when a rider streaked for the river, shouting incomprehensible words. Johnny put on his blue cap and cut off the man at the edge of the town square. He didn't recognize the man.

The horse pulled up near Johnny. The early morning light revealed an older man, an agitated creature. "Soldier, you got any buddies near by?"

Johnny waited until the man turned from staring at the road behind him, the one that led to Alexandria. "I'm alone. What eats you?"

"Fifty rebs under a Captain Owsley rode into Alexandria at the crack of dawn (2). Ransacked the town. I heard one say they was coming this way. Get goods and then go to Athens and fetch the Union supplies," the man said.

Aware that a crowd gathered, more emerging from the shadows by the minute, Johnny searched for a familiar face. Before he could speak, a voice to his right said, "Welcome home, Johnny. Sorry about the Flacks."

Johnny smiled at Mr. Civer and spied Dr. McKee approaching. Greetings were short as several men huddled to analyze the report brought by the rider from Alexandria. He told them he figured fifty rebs filled a wagon with forty dollars worth of caps, powder, and lead from George Reed's store, seven guns and all the ammo out of Kenney's store as well as eight dollars worth of supplies from Coleman's. He told them they must have confiscated, in all, twenty guns, fifty thousand caps and powder along with supplies that filled two horse-drawn wagons (2).

Dr. McKee stood alongside Red and patted Johnny's leg. "You can't fight them alone and best not be caught. But you can make haste to Athens and alert the squad guarding the Union wares."

"But what will you all do?"

"We're going to pull two wagons of hay across the road and light them when they appear down the road." McKee aimed a finger toward Alexandria. "While it blazes we'll send off the tiny brass cannon we use to announce the arrival of river boats. May just make them think their detour here not worth the bother, 'specially since Athens has the big catch."

Johnny turned Red to go, but McKee grabbed the reins. "Sorry about Elizabeth. She loved you so much. I wish you could have gotten away when I wrote you the letter. Be careful." He let go of the reins.

Johnny wiped his eyes, kicked Red's flanks, and sped for Athens. Some five miles distant from St. Francisville on the Alexandria-Bloomfield road Johnny thought he heard the faint sound of cannon coming from behind him. He spurred Red on harder but his mind remained stuck on Elizabeth. I should have just left Palmyra. *Oh, Elizabeth, I hate war. It kills in many ways.*

An hour after his warning in Athens, Johnny watched the small band of Union soldiers prepare their defense. At that moment, a man in a business suit rode nonchalantly toward Spurgeon's store at the same time a company of Iowa Home Guard who had crossed the river from Croton came up the hill from Water Street. The morning sun shone brightly so that a hundred yards away Johnny recognized the businessman. Blake Slater slowly approached the store, his casual behavior detected by Johnny, who hid behind a bale of hay at the door of Spurgeon's. He pulled the Sergeant in charge of the Iowa Guard from his seat on the store steps and told him the businessman was a confederate soldier scouting their defenses.

The man stood, straightened, and strode to the middle of the street. "Ready rifles," he yelled.

From behind overturned wagons and bales of straw, black rifle barrels appeared. Blake stopped his mount ten feet away. He waved, producing a feeble grin.

The sergeant turned to the store and hollered, "Corporal Jensen, go over to Croton and tell Company B and C to come over now." He turned to another soldier who shuffled toward the two. "When I give the word, shoot this spy." He pulled a pistol and pointed it at Blake.

Faster than a leopard, Johnny sprang from behind the bale. "No. You mustn't." He noted the surprise that took over Blake's frightened face. "He was captured at Memphis, swore the oath." He eased over to the trembling figure perched on the horse as if cast in stone. "Get. You ain't no good to Serena dead. These four hundred men plan to ambush your comrades and reclaim the loot from Alexandria."

Blake wheeled the horse about and sped for the ridge.

"Whad ya do that fer?"

Johnny looked into the angry eyes of the sergeant. "Because he needed to live — he only saw twenty soldiers — but I told him we had four hundred hidden in ambush."

The sergeant screwed up his face, removed his cap, and scratched his head. "Well, I'll be hanged." He put his arm around Johnny and walked him to the McKee house. "That is real smart thinking."

Owsley's men never showed. Johnny gave thanks for that after he found out the ten men that came from Croton were local farmers, hadn't ever shot more than a rabbit, or pheasant. On August third, local scouts returned and announced that Owsley's band headed for Kirksville to join a large

Confederate force under Joe Porter. A telegram at Croton from McNeil Headquarters responded to the one sent by Athens with congratulations and added that General McNeil had left Palmyra on the twenty-ninth, intending to pass through Clinton, and catch Porter at Paris. Johnny figured when McNeil found Porter had left Paris for Kirksville, he would head there and force a fight. Anxious to catch up with his unit but wary of any Confederate scouts in the vicinity of Kirksville, Johnny took a familiar route, heading for Edina. The absence of traffic on any of the roads and the hush of the surrounding woods told him the countryside reeked of war. Cautiously, he eased Red west for Brashear, and fell upon a squad of men in blue coats.

"Hey, its owl eyes. We heard you went off to pluck a widow." The young man in a ragged blue coat ducked when Johnny aimed a finger at him.

He climbed down, and more to himself than the five men said, "She died with her son. I prayed at her grave, friend. Thee must learn manners."

The oldest-appearing soldier broke the silence. "We should have beaten Porter by now, but McNeil rested two days, said because we and our horses were worn out (3)."

A beanpole slouched on the ground behind him said, "I heard the character of the country and the fact Porter burned bridges and destroyed fords he crossed made us go slow (3)."

"Just as well," Johnny said and filled a tin cup with coffee from the pot hanging on a forked stick. "Scouts from the guard at Athens told me the rebs have amassed a huge force at Kirksville. Good we're rested."

"We'll go with you. Need to tell the General that Porter seems to be preparing for a real fight this time. We reasoned he'd make a stand on the Chariton River bottom, better place to put up a defense. But since he entered Kirksville on the third, he's ordered the people out of town, and has barricaded up houses for riflemen. Seems he's drawn his main line of defense along a rail fence just west of the central part of town." Only 658 lived there in 1860, not much of a place, extends only a few blocks each direction from the square (3).

They headed for the main force, and, spotting the medical team, Johnny thanked them and moved for Dr. Schmidt. The thoughts of a large encounter pushed Elizabeth deeper in his mind.

McNeil's main force reached the vicinity of Kirksville around ten in the morning. An advanced guard, detachments of the 2nd and 11th Missouri State Militia under Major Benjamin preceded the main column and artillery units. They occupied the northeast part of town, halting at Parcell's Place. Having learned that Porter deployed his troops in town, McNeil put his men on the north and east sides. Lt. Colonel Shaffer in charge of the right wing which was composed of Merrill's Horse under Major Clopper, a detachment of the 2nd and 11th Cavalry of the Missouri State Militia under Major Benjamin, and a section of the 3rd Indiana battalion under Lt. Armington. Major Caldwell, with his own troops, secured the left wing with the help of a detachment of the 1st Cavalry Missouri State Volunteers under Major Cox. A section of the steel battery of two-pound howitzers, Sergeant West in charge, and ten men of Company C, 2nd Missouri State Militia, acted as did the Indiana artillery units under Captain Barr of Merrill's Horse (3).

Schmidt directed Johnny to set up a temporary field hospital near Parcell's, telling him that they were short-handed because two helpers remained at Paris, stricken with measles. In order to determine the enemy's position, McNeil sent an officer, Lt. Cowdry, with a squad of eight men into town to draw fire. They approached the square, passed around it, and came out the corner. It appeared from Johnny's view that they came close, but due to the heavy fire, withdrew. Two died instantly, three were wounded, and five horses were killed.

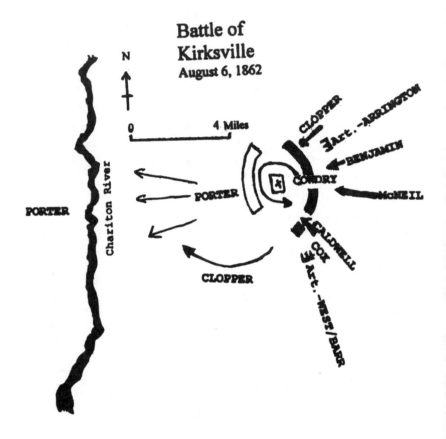

Battle of Kirksville
August 6, 1862

With the essential information he needed, McNeil began the fight. Five artillery pieces located near Cumberland Academy sent shots into cornfields, gardens, and trees. Infantry moved to the centerline of sheds and houses on the north and east sides.

A large number of Porter's men in cornfields fled. As the Feds moved toward the square, two wings met and then took the courthouse. Porter retreated, concentrating his main force west. The battle lasted three hours, until one p.m., but the Feds pursued rebels through the woods west of town, where they found many horses, a large quantity of arms, clothing, and camp equipment. McNeil ordered Major Clopper with a large body of Merrill's Horse to pursue the enemy as far as the Chariton River. Pursuit further certainly would have ended with capture of almost the entire Porter troop, but McNeil disagreed, emphasizing that hunger and fatigue put his men at too great a risk. Of his 1000 men available, McNeil had used only 500. He saved the others to guard supplies and support men on the firing line (3).

Three men carried McNeil to the field hospital, suffering a barrage of complaints from the General. A head wound, the reason for the Herculean oaths, proved slight, but Dr. Schmidt expressed grave concern about infection in the wound.

"Damn your concerns, Captain," McNeil blurted and grabbed the whiskey bottle dangling before his eyes. He gulped a mouthful of the brown liquid and looked around until his eyes fixed on Johnny. "Boy, you fix one of your famous poultices for this. I got this General's laudanum for a headache." He waved the bottle.

Within minutes Johnny had the poultice secured in place with a tight bandage. He stood, but McNeil jerked him in front of his face, downed another mouthful, and said, "Some day you'll ask for something from me. Make it big because I'd give you anything but my whiskey."

"I'm paid thirteen dollars a month to do my job, Sir."

"The hell you say." He turned to Schmidt. "Well. Let's have the damage report."

One of the helpers handed Schmidt a piece of reddish-stained paper. "We had 28 killed and sixty wounded. The enemy numbers are hard to verify but somewhere between one hundred and one fifty killed and maybe as many as four hundred wounded. I'm told over two hundred captured. Some have slight wounds (3)."

McNeil ordered surgeon Lyons and a town surgeon, Dr. Willard, as his assistant, to amputate and turn the care after surgery to Schmidt and Johnny. The Ivie Building on the northeast corner of the square served as the operating room. Amputated limbs hurtled out the building window, a size-able pile accumulating before men loaded the gruesome pile in a cart and buried the limbs (3). Johnny and Schmidt took care of the wounded Feds in the Cumberland Academy and Parcell's Place until they could be brought in town.

Depression bore down on Johnny. Elizabeth's death and the pile of limbs, most from young men, held no grain of sense. But the next day surpassed the horrors of the battle. The Union Army executed fifteen Confederate soldiers because they had violated their parole, and the following day, they executed Colonel Frisby H. McCullough because he had been a very successful recruiting officer in North Missouri. To Johnny the war had become a nightmare, a devil's curse. *Why, Mr. Flack?* he pondered on his bedroll, undisturbed by the buzz of a thousand bloodthirsty mosquitoes springing from the swampy bottoms of the Chariton River. *Must so many innocent die for the myth called state's rights, the clown of morally bankrupt slave owners? And of their aloof, sinful supporters?* The thought clanged across his cerebral cortex. He rolled on one side and watched the sentries gather at the fire to fetch a cup of coffee. I know your answer, Mr. Flack. I tried it with Blake at Athens. Perchance it will help him value life.

Chapter 13

Porter escapes
August 1862

For Blake the cornfield had served its purpose. He thought it offered good protection until the two men to his left fell with mortal wounds from a canister blast. Running for the woods, he checked the front of his pants and shirt. No blood, just lots of dirt from the blast. Blood mingled with dirt on his left sleeve and arm slowed his pace. Keeping his bedroll over his right shoulder he felt the arm from shoulder to hand. The survey elicited no pain. *Uncle Pres, where are you?* At the Chariton River he paused to catch his breath and search the bank to his right and to his left. No Walters. Sounds of gunshots and horses quickened his pulse. Walters can't swim, he remembered. Hordes of men in gray tattered clothes passed him, sprang from the bank and made for the opposite shore. Some seemed to wade. "Waiting for the stage, sonny?" an older man hollered and clamored toward the west bank. Of course, the August drought made the depth shallow enough at certain areas to be crossed without swimming. The heavy crashing sounds in the woods, produced by horses, forced the conclusion that Walters would have to find a place to wade. Fifty yards past the west shore, he huddled in some bulrushes with five other men. Only their heavy breathing disturbed the silence. He strained in the direction of muffled voices. Snapping of twigs to their left front prompted the two that had rifles to point them in that direction. A gray floppy hat appeared first, leading the figure on all fours. At the edge of the bulrushes the head raised.

"Uncle Pres," he whispered and smiled at the toothless grin.

"Shush," a gravel voice behind him demanded.

"Merrill's Horse. They stopped at the east shore," Walters said and continued on all fours toward the west.

Porter crossed the Chariton five miles west of Kirksville at Clem's Mill, pursued by a detachment of Merrill's Horse to the river's edge. Sensing the pressure from the feds, Porter disbanded his troops, keeping a small group with him. A large gang of Confederates headed straight for Macon, where on the eighth near Stockton a detachment of the Missouri 7th Cavalry caught up with them. Gen. Guitar did not command the attack because he had taken ill at Moore's Mill and remained in Jefferson City with several of his troops. Nevertheless, the Union forces scattered the rebels.

Porter made it to southern Audrain County on the ninth, still cognizant of pursuit by the feds. Scouts informed him of the encounter the day before at Macon, not too far south of his position at Walnut Creek. Quickly, he set an ambush along the creek, sending loud decoys along the road to Macon. The Feds under Colonel McFerran made haste for the distant noise. Porter sprang the trap. The complete and unexpected attack cost McFerran 100 men (1). The maneuver stalled the surprised Yanks, allowing Porter to escape cleanly, while McFerran blindly shelled the woods long after Porter's departure.

Joined by the survivors of the Macon attack and numerous stragglers sent to him by his many agents in the area, Porter brought them together on the east side of the Chariton.

Sadness registered in Porter's voice when he told the men that scouts had informed him that Guitar's force, after the encounter at Macon had headed west to meet Colonel Poindexter. Since Colonel Poindexter's return from Arkansas he had recruited 1500 men from Chariton, Randolph, and Monroe Counties (2).

Porter went around the ring of men. A bearded man with an immaculate uniform caught his eye. "You've been scouting west of here."

The man stepped to the center and addressed Porter. "Agents that away told me Guitar landed a large body of the 7th Missouri Cav. at Glasgow three days ago and gains on Poindexter (2)."

"I ain't got lots of specifics, Colonel." The red head with the green eyes removed his hat and looked at Porter and then Blake. "Information I got says some two thousand Yanks spread out from Kirskville and look for you." He wiggled his hat at Blake. "I personally seed one company of Merrill's Horse you'd like to hear 'bout, Slater. Owl eyes is with 'em, camped north of Paris."

Porter listened, pinching the tip of his nose. "Okay, listen up. Being pressed from all sides, we split, right now, into companies and scatter around the countryside. Use our agent informers to plan your moves. Captain Wills, you take Slater under your wing. Too many Yanks scattered along the railroad, so head east along the Salt River. That'll put you in Paris, Florida, and into Ralls County, all good southern folk to look after you."

A lanky man in tattered clothes stepped next to Blake and said, "I'm A. J. Austin from Goss. Been with Wills's company a long time. It's Captain Worden Wills, and he's 'bout as popular as Penny was."

Blake grabbed Walters and followed Austin. They headed southeast toward Paris with Wills and his company of forty. Traveling went slow along the back roads. Often they followed hog paths. August fifteenth they camped on the south bank of the Middle Fork of the Salt River, two miles past Woodland. Blake sipped strong coffee while an agent from Paris told them that Guitar caught up with Poindexter at Compton's Ferry on the Grand River in Carroll County on the eleventh. "Guitar soundly defeated him — a huge slaughter — so Poindexter fled north to Utica on the

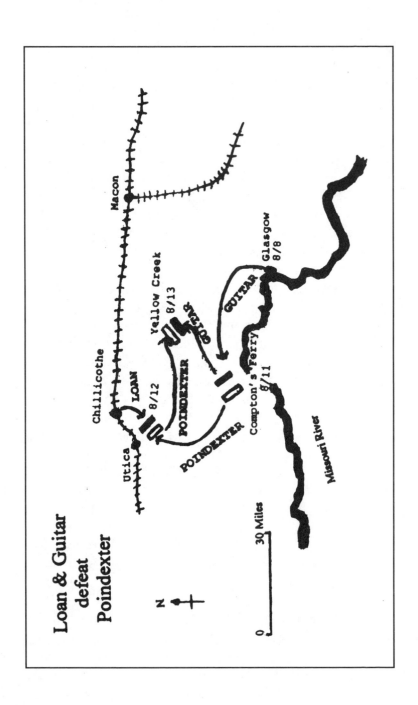

Hannibal-St. Joe railroad. There he ran into General B. F. Loan, who drove him back in the direction he came. On the thirteenth the pursuing Guitar caught him at Yellow Creek in Chariton County. His army destroyed, Poindexter broke it up. His troops are no more (2)."

"Dreadful," Walters said.

"Guitar's a gentleman. He didn't murder a bunch of our boys like McNeil did after Kirksville," the man said.

Most of the gang slept but the mouths of the four awake hung open, not Blake's. "We haven't been told. We saw them take a bunch of prisoners," he said.

"Next day after the battle, McNeil executed fifteen of our boys and then murdered Colonel McCullough. He wasn't even at Kirksville. Sick, but they found him on the way to his home second day and hung him 'cause he recruited so many rebs (1)."

"Murder, it is," Wills blurted, paused to look at each man, and waved a small brown book at the group. "This here book is a Bible being furnished to all Confederate troops. You need to read it, 'cause it tells of God's wishes. Our independence and successes are God's will. We are more Godly than the Yankees. We fight and have to shoot in our struggles, but we don't murder (3). Get some rest." He rolled over on his blanket.

Blake broke up the fire, and soon the camp turned into an eerie scene of gray figures scattered about in the dim moonlight. Heavy breathing played a sonata to Blake's visions of Serena, the delightful memories interrupted when a hand pressed his lips. Walters leaned close and whispered in his ear that his peein' problem got him up and he spied some figures in the far clearing across the Salt.

"I seed the moon a shinin' on weapons."

In a low tone Walters repeated the warning to the other four while Blake eased over and grabbed their rifles. Crawling from one sleeping body to the next they had warned half the camp when all bedlam broke out. Twenty

minutes of pandemonium and the attackers fled across the
river as Wills stirred up the fire. The blaze revealed one
Confederate and one in a blue uniform motionless in the
shadows. Two of Wills's men had arm wounds, but Walters
rolled over the grass tugging at his leg.

Blake ripped Walters's pants leg apart to mid-thigh while
Wills brought a torch, a burning log from the fire. Both
inspected the wound, a jagged hole below the knee. Blake
removed his bandanna and tightened it above the site of the
bleeding.

"You goin' to have that leg off or you'll die of blood poi-
soning, Walters," Wills said.

A pronouncement by a man at the edge of camp drowned
Walters's feeble protest. "We got us a live Yank here, boys."
He rolled the blonde-haired man on his back and raised his
rifle, resting the muzzle between closed eyes.

"No," Wills shrieked. "We're not murderers." He leaned
over the still form, shook both shoulders. The men gathered
around the groaning man, who rubbed the back of his head.
Two flaming logs held over the group lit up the face as the
eyes opened and then squinted, a twisted one, almost
grotesque in the light cast by the logs.

"Hey, Blake, come 'ere. It's owl eyes."

Blake sprang for the group and shoved next to Wills.

He pulled Wills's pistol and said, "Well, my favorite nigger lover. I'm doing to you what you did to Zeke."

Wills wrested the gun from his hand and straddled
Johnny. "No murdering." He peered down between his legs.
"Not more than fifteen minutes ago I awakened with cold
steel in my face. Some bushy-faced Yank cocked his pistol
and said, "Have a pleasant trip to hell, southern trash. This
young blond feller jerked him off me, hit him alongside the
head and said, 'Thee must not kill.' 'Bout then one of you
knocked him over the head."

They tied Johnny's hands behind his back while Wills,
Blake, and A. J. Austin, who acted as their medical helper,

argued over Walters's condition. A squat man appeared with Red and helped Johnny mount. The company began breaking camp while Wills informed Johnny that they planned to drop Walters, who needed an amputation, at the depot in Hunnewell so he could get to Hannibal and get the amputation he needed to save his life. And as repayment for his mercies to Wills he would be left with Walters if he promised to stay with Walters and tend to him.

The company proceeded east on a narrow wagon trail that coursed along the river, stopping every mile until scouts returned to say the road was clear. When the scouts next appeared, they reported that the main road to Paris lay a mile ahead, the junction only five miles from Paris. The small band dismounted and rested. Blake told Wills that marching the entire company through Paris posed too great a risk. He volunteered to take Walters and the prisoner straight north to the Shelbina station and meet the company east at Hunnewell. Wills sent the men toward Paris in groups of six to eight, telling Blake to wait to the last.

Davis seemed to sense Blake's excitement, for he pranced along the dirt road. The cool early morning air soothed Blake's brow, hot with fiendish ideas for the silhouetted figure riding immediately in front of him. Gray rays of dawn penetrated the dense foliage, making the task of watching owl eyes and Walters, weaving in the saddle of the horse leading the way, too trying. Around a sharp bend they passed a narrow wagon road and came upon a stand of birch trees. He figured them to be three or four hundred yards from the main road to Paris, so he yelled for Walters to turn left on a narrow, grassy trail, just wide enough to hold worn wagon-wheel tracks. Past the birch trees lining the trail that meandered across a clearing, richly adorned with buffalo grass, Blake surveyed the area.

"Stop here," he barked and dismounted. "Stay on, Uncle Pres. Get down, nigger lover," he snarled at Johnny. Blake felt the pounding of each heart thrust in his chest. He loved his plan the closer it came to execution. He untied Johnny's hands.

Walters lay on the horse's neck, his arms securing a tenuous perch. "Wills told you not to kill him."

Blake snarled, removed his pistol, cocked the hammer, and held it at waist level. He raised his rifle with one hand. Warm sweat collected on his back while the breeze that whispered through the silvery birch dried and cooled his forehead. The fright on Johnny's face brought a chuckle from deep inside. After the muzzle nudged Johnny's nose, he dropped it onto his left foot, and raised the pistol to Johnny's chest.

"This is a southern gentleman's, a Blake Slater's thanks to me for saving his life in Athens," Johnny said.

Bang!

Johnny shrieked. He fell onto his back, pulled up his left leg, groaning and rolling from side to side. Blake inched forward, the pistol still pointed at Johnny's chest. He stared at the left boot, most of the foot part missing, the frayed leather end, blackened from gunpowder, turned red. He bent over the moaning figure, loved the agony, the twisted, drawn ugly face, and spied pieces of flesh dangling from the boot end.

"I ain't gonna kill you. The Bible says thou shalt not kill." He giggled while he backed away three paces, glanced at Walters, and added, "'Sides Serena would be mad. Get up, cry baby."

Johnny struggled to a sitting position, removed the kerchief from his neck, wrapped it around the left leg above his boot and used his hunting knife to twist it tight. Blake smiled when Johnny studied the remains of his boot, even marveled at his cool as he twisted the kerchief until the blood ceased to flow from the boot end.

"I said get up, ninny." He paused while Johnny struggled to his knees and then stood on the right leg, fell, and then fought his way to his knees again. He looked up. Blake pulled a bluish envelope from under his shirt and waved it.

"Serena will really feel sorry for more than your ugly puss now. I got this last week. She and I are engaged. Gonna get married Christmas. Now put your hands up."

Blake stuffed the letter inside his shirt, his mind dancing with anticipation. Johnny slowly raised his hands.

Bang!

The blonde head jerked back, followed by the rest of the tense form. Johnny screamed, grabbing his right arm at the elbow with his left hand. Blake climbed on his horse and smiled at Walters, who sat upright, his mouth hanging open. He guided his horse beside the bent form on the grass, the right arm in the clutches of the left, a hole in the middle of the forearm spurting bright red blood.

Blake replaced the pistol in his belt, bent over, and picked up Johnny's hat with the rifle muzzle. "Pray to your Quaker God to send you some nigger to save your life." He turned, snatched a blue jacket from Johnny's bedroll, dropped the roll on the ground and grabbed Red's reins. Blake hummed "Dixie" as he led Red and Walters' horse down the wagon trail for the road.

The fast pulse pounded at his temples, his eyesight seeming five times more acute than normal. A dry mouth led him to remove his drinking bottle and swig three mouthfuls. He replaced it and muttered, "John Newton Boulware, you needn't worry. I did it for you. One Johnny Jenkins will never be a doctor — if he lives."

After they turned east on the wide road that led to Paris Walters began to sway in the saddle, forcing Blake to ride beside him to be sure he stayed in the saddle. From his position hugging the animal's neck, Walters carried on about Blake's behavior and finally said, "You are the meanest man I've ever known. Why? And after he saved your life — Wills's, too."

The Yank hat fit well but Johnny's jacket was too small so Blake put one arm in and let it hang off a shoulder. "I saved his. I ain't mean. Important people do those things — control others' destinies. That's why slave owners are important — they control the niggers. Heck, Uncle Pres, the poor darkies would starve if free."

Finally, they reached Shelbina, where Blake eased Walters off his horse onto the depot platform. He opened Walters's bedroll and covered him with the blanket. Inside the depot he found a midget of a man sweeping the creaky, splintered floor. The worn boards announced Blake's presence, so the man whipped around and, seeing the uniform, smiled.

"How much to St. Louis?"

"Four cents a mile. Twenty-three miles to Hudson. That'll be ninety–two cents to connect you with the North Missouri Railroad. From Hudson to St. Louis on the North Missouri is hundred and sixty-nine miles, seven dollars and seventy-six cents more."

"Four cents times that mileage amounts to only six seventy six, you cheatin' midget."

"That includes a dollar for the ferry at St. Charles and the railcar to Union Station."

Blake followed him to the counter and gave him ten dollars. He motioned for the man to follow outside. They stopped at Walters. "The ticket is for this wounded soldier. The extra is for you to see that he gets on the next train."

The man put the money in his pants with glee and showed Blake where he could write a note. While he wrote, the man extolled the wonders of the Union troops and the manner in which they had squelched the traitorous rebels. Ignoring the man's idiocy, he sealed the note in an envelope and printed, "Serena Hill, Good Samaritan Hospital," on the front. Blake stuffed fifteen dollars in Walters's shirt pocket and gave him the envelope. He blinked back tears during their farewell because he was important and those men never reveal their emotions.

Four more hours passed before Blake caught up with

Wills west of Hunnewell. Pride engulfed his being when he told him Johnny tried to escape, was only wounded, not killed, and that Walters on his way to St. Louis rather than the nearest hospital because the trainmaster told him the track at Ely had been torn up by southerners. *Blake, putting on Johnny's hat and jacket, was brilliant. Uncle Pres, Serena will see that you get the best care and love my offer to be engaged for marriage.* Blake hummed "Swannee" so loudly that Capt. Wills slowed until he was alongside.

"You should be happy. Clever man you are, Blake."

"Wars are good. I love the excitement. Gives a man a chance to be tough — powerful."

Wills leaned on the pommel. "Just don't get shot or caught."

Chapter 14

Good Samaritan Hospital
September 10, 1862

Dorothea Dix's scrutiny, ever since she had snatched Blake's note from Walters and read it out loud to Serena and Walters, never ceased. Serena yearned for an opportunity to inquire about Blake and quiz Walters about the seriousness of his request to become engaged. Walters certainly didn't alarm Miss Dix, so why hover so closely? The simple man, his toothless smile a curiosity, was a good bet never to bother to polish tales, make them anything but the stark truth. Finally, Dix was nowhere to be seen. Walters, her third amputee of the morning, rubbed the fuzz on top of his head and jabbered away at Serena, about his new friends, some even Yankees, and the delicious meals, the clean sheets and soft bed.

"Well, it does not matter if you are Union or Confederate soldier here. Our job is to get you well, recovered enough to return home, and sleep under your own roof," Serena said.

"Been a long time since I did that — 'til here."

The last amputee left the room with an older nurse, Serena's opening. She began to take measurements of Walters's good foot and lower leg. Next she measured the length of his stump. "I send these to Sam Huett in Hannibal and he'll make you a boot with the wooden leg built in." She put a hand on Walters's shoulder and stared into his eyes. "Sam is Johnny Jenkins's best friend, a Negro and wonderful boot-smith. Doctor Rollins told me that when you were awakening from the chloroform you kept pleading for owl eyes. You must tell me."

"Can't. Blake'd kill me."

"You must. You owe it to Sam, to me, to Doctor Rollins, who did your amputation. Doctor is Johnny's friend and going to get him in med school."

She watched the pale face turn whiter, the eyes distant, then fleeting. The story seemed to take forever. Her insistence that Walters repeat precisely what Blake said and Johnny's condition, created a lead weight in her chest. Her mind raced while she extracted from Walters every detail of the location of the clearing north of Paris, or was it west? Walters seemed confused. "Now that I know, you must tell Doctor Rollins. He will think better of you because you tried to stop Blake."

For two days Serena had scoured the countryside north of Paris, examining a dozen clearings, locating farmhouses nearby and inquiring about a wounded soldier. Local farmers seemed cool, distant. She understood when a scrawny farm girl told her everyone was frightened because General Lewis Merrill had executed 10 of Porter's men at Macon. Folks said he did it because the prisoners had been captured previously and paroled, so Merrill had a firing squad shoot the parole breakers. No news about Johnny. But September the thirteenth proved lucky. In Paris at a grocery store that sat across the street from a large white building, a sign dangling on the street side post stating, William J. Howell, Attorney, the clerk seemed patient but not forthcoming with her unending questions, his continual gawking at her chest and butt a bit unsettling, though. Fortunately, a light drizzle wetted the dusty main street. Desperation gripped Serena. She returned to the gawker's store and pretended to look at samples of cloth until two mangy-appearing men departed. She couldn't help catching the excitement of their voices when they told the clerk that the day before the twelfth Porter raided Palmyra with four hundred men because McNeil had his men up in Shelbyville and Hunnewell looking for Porter. They said Porter captured several Union soldiers and released fifty Confederate soldiers from prison, then beat a fast track up to Lewis County.

"Is there another road someone might take to get here from Hudson Station, a back road, if they rode east along the Salt River for a spell?" The man acted cool, his roaming eyes settling on the counter top.

"There's a nice road runs straight west toward Hudson and about four miles out of town a narrow dirt road joins it. That'd take you to Woodland, couple miles from the Salt."

A frail woman with thick glasses appeared from the back room. "You the nurse from St. Louis been looking fer a wounded Yank?"

Serena's waning hope leapt. "Yes, have you seen or heard anything?"

"No, nothing. If that woundin' happened three weeks ago the man's dead or gone to his friends, I'd figger," the woman said.

Ambling for the door, Serena rolled her head from side to side, a gesture to bolster her premonition that told her Johnny still lived, still needed her. But where? When her head rolled to the left, her eye caught bottles of chemicals on the shelf behind the end of the counter. Her brain flashed an operating room shelf. Leaning over the counter, her anticipation grew. "Anybody ever buy that permanganate stuff?" She pointed to the brown bottles.

The woman wiped her hands on a stained apron and walked behind the counter to stare at the bottles. "Not many."

"Mrs. Howell's nigger bought some in the past couple weeks," the man said, and stole a glance over the counter at Serena's backside.

Serena grinned and walked back to stand in front of him. She glared while he made a map showing the way to Howell's farm. The dull woman seemed to come alive when Serena bet that the permanganate was being used for gunshot wounds. The woman took Serena's two dollars and drove her in a rickety buggy, the wobbly left rear wheel making the chore difficult for the shaggy-appearing mule. Each mile made Serena's hopes sink lower, her experience with amputees telling her that only a miracle would keep Johnny alive so long without a surgeon amputating the dead, infected tissue. The fine mist of rainwater rolled off her head, larger drops from overhanging foliage hitting her shoulders. A sniffle told her the water running down her cheeks came from the wells behind her eyes, the salty taste confirming it. Silence, except for the buggy wheels splashing an occasional puddle.

Almost five miles west of Paris they turned north onto a narrow dirt road. A quarter mile further, under dense foliage of elm and maple trees, the woman turned the buggy right. Through a thicket of birch trees they traveled a short distance on a grassy road with worn wheel-ruts that threatened to shake asunder the rickety vehicle. Passing through a clearing with tall buffalo grass, they went two hundred yards through a dense thicket of poplar trees and emerged in a clearing occupied by a large two-story house. Serena followed the woman up the porch steps. The screen door opened. A dark brown face set off by speckled gray hair belonged to a large Negro in a pink flour-sack dress. She held the front door, filling the opening as if guarding the gate to a castle. She said nothing.

"I'm Serena Hill, a nurse from St. Louis. I heard you might have seen a blonde-haired man, wounded three weeks ago. I believe he was shot in the clearing at the bend in the road." She pointed over her left shoulder down the road, acting as though she knew precisely which bend, which clearing.

The hulk of a woman stepped back, motioned for Serena to enter as she announced, "A visitor, Mrs. Howell."

A lean, auburn-haired woman about Serena's height strode into the room. She wore a blue dress, buttoned to the top to hold the white lace collar up to her neck. She had smooth ivory-white skin, not even a tan to her arms. Two shy, but obviously curious, children, the boy probably six and the girl five, peeked around a doorway.

"I am Mrs. Howell. I heard. Please come sit. You have made a long trip — I'm afraid for nothing."

Serena's heart sank. It thumped her chest. "When did he die?"

"I'll get some tea and biscuits," the woman said, rose and threw her head toward the Negro. "Cindy will tell you." At the door she paused to scrutinize Serena and added, "Others call her Aunt Cindy."

The round, brown face frowned. "We was coming from Paris 'bout noon the seventeenth when we seed this figure dragging a leg, crawling with use of one arm, the other tucked in his shirt. Best we could tell was two days after the a-tack. Whee, what a mess. We cleaned him up, got some broth down him and he come about. Said he was a Yankee soldier shot by a neighbor from up around Canton. First thing he asked fer was if we found his bedroll. When I told him we got it he asked for the Bible. Said he reads it every day." Aunt Cindy paused while Mrs. Howell handed Serena a cup of tea and set a plate of biscuits and a jar with honey to her left.

"We treat Confederate or Union same in this house. My husband, William James Howell, has his law practice in Paris these days," Mrs. Howell said. "We've had Southern troops here twice. They were right decent. And lately we tended General McNeil, the Union Commander from Hannibal. He was ill and I nursed him several days. He was kind, but some of the foreign men got all liquored up, not so nice (1)."

Serena put the teacup down. "Please, tell me. What happened? How he died." A chill filled the room, soon warmed by Aunt Cindy.

"Shucks, he ain't dead yet," Cindy said.

Mrs. Howell rested her hand on Serena's arm. "Be

patient, child. There's time. You must hear to understand."
She sipped from a teacup, magnificently decorated with
dainty roses, and indicated that Serena should help herself to
a biscuit. "He had a hole in his arm right here." She used an
index finger to point to the middle of her forearm. "Didn't
seem the bones broken, but mighty painful, unable to move
it. Some angry red 'round the hole."

"He was putting what he calls a poultice on the hole, even
had me get some moldy bread and put it with the poultice,
mostly the green-blue part of the bread," Aunt Cindy said.

"I cried when I first saw the left foot. Poor boy. I knew it
would be trouble. We had a devil of a time cutting the boot
off." Mrs. Howell poised the cup, searching Serena's face
over the brim. "He didn't peep but I could tell it hurt fierce.
With it off we cleaned all the old blood and mud by soaking
it in warm water. Seems he's some sort of doctor helper and
knows lots."

"He told me he learned a whole bunch from a shaman, a
Negro lady what lives on the Des Moines River," Aunt
Cindy said, pride written on her grinning face.

Serena's impatience overtook her. "The foot."

Mrs. Howell beckoned to the browned-haired girl looking
around the doorway. "This is Bennie. Tom's her brother. I'm
Mr. Howell's third wife. His mother is sister of Moses D.
Bates, the one who founded Hannibal. Mr. Howell had five
children by his other wives. Three older daughters are out in
the field. I lock them upstairs when the soldiers come by.
You'll meet them at dinner. She pulled the reticent girl to her
side, hoisted her dress up to her knees, and removed a shoe.
"This part was gone." With a finger she drew a line between
the second and third toes halfway back to the ankle and then
made a slash motion to the side. "Gone. But the two remaining toes, dangling funny, were black and smelled bad. The
flesh back to the ankle was red."

"We put him in one of the slave quarters, the nicest one.
We had twenty-six darkies before the war, but all the young

men run off since the war started, and some of the younger women, too. A few of the older ones are still here. Cindy's husband Jake drives Mr. Howell's carriage for him and does personal chores. Anyhow, we fed that poor boy. He seemed to grow stronger, the arm looked better, the foot worse. He announced he needed to amputate." She stopped to study Serena's face. "We told him all the docs were in one army or the other. Two from these parts been killed. I can't tell it. You tell her, Cindy. You were there."

Mrs. Howell went to the door, taking the little girl away while Aunt Cindy continued. "He said he was a Quaker, didn't cuss or drink whiskey but wanted some for his chore. I sharpened the biggest knife and took it with a jug of corn whiskey and bandages to the cabin. He drank a lot of the jug, tightened a rope around his ankle and told me if he passed out I should loosen it for a moment and retighten it every ten minutes. He sat on the floor, said 'cause if I faint, can't fall.' I couldn't stop cryin'. He took two passes at the foot, right at the middle where the angry, live flesh seemed to jump with each of his'n heartbeat. With the second pass, I shut my eyes — so frightful. Then I heard this blood-curdling scream. It shook that old cabin. I looked. Johnny was unconscious on his back, the knife still in his left hand. The bright red end of his foot just past the ankle stared at me." Aunt Cindy wiped her eyes with the apron. "That bad part of the foot with them two black toes, lay nearby, quiverin' like it was mad."

Serena slid her chair next to Cindy's and put her arm around her waist. "You are so brave. Then what?"

"I wents over and sat beside Johnny, put his head on my lap and sung Negro spirituals like I did to my babies. Shortly, he opened one eye. The other didn't want to open. He said he hadn't figured angels had black faces." Aunt Cindy sobbed.

Mrs. Howell returned and picked up the rest. "He read his Bible every day, got along well, even hobbled around on a crutch we fashioned. Then after a week, even though he was putting some herbs on the raw end and some permanganate we bought for him in town, the infection got real bad. He turned delirious three days ago. That's why we reason he's dying."

"I reads to him from his Bible every morning. He takes a teaspoon of broth is all, calls for his woman." Aunt Cindy eyed her. "He has a heap of love for this woman. If we could find her I think he would fight harder, maybe live. Before he lost his senses he told me he couldn't be a doctor with one arm that didn't work and half a foot. So without the woman he loves he'd soon be dead."

Serena stared, hesitating for fear of the answer. "Elizabeth. That the name he calls out?"

Aunt Cindy shook her head. "Nope. That's the name in front of his Bible. A strange girl's name, maybe not said right in his stupor. Cap. He begs for Cap."

Serena's heart jumped into her mouth, her head swam, she seemed to float above the chair. "What'd he say about this Cap?"

"Lots. Seems she's skinny, wears green shirts. Oh, how he loves her."

Delight could not be subdued, her behavior beginning to catch the attention of the two women. Aunt Cindy leaned over and seemed to search Serena's body. "This morning, mind you he's unconscious, started blabbing and talking to Cap. He told her something bout not marryin' an older woman, that she weren't no kid no more. He giggled and gestured with his good arm, his eyes flickered when he said, 'You sure have filled out, Cap. I'm goin' to get you under my wagon and pray for a rainstorm.' He snorted and slept."

Heat melted Serena's anxiety. She stood, followed by Aunt Cindy, who led her around to the back where fifty feet from the house stood a row of log cabins (1). At the door of a small 10-by-10 foot-size cabin, Aunt Cindy stopped. "He ain't recognized me for five days. Won't look at me, squeeze my hand, nothing but sip broth put to his lips."

Serena stepped onto the earthen floor of the dark cabin. Aunt Cindy stirred the embers in what she called "the immense fireplace, it taking two men to put on the back log that is renewed twice a week and always holds a fire (1)." A sob penetrated Serena's lips when she moved beside one of the two high beds, its fat feather mattress resting two feet from the hard packed dirt floor. The room had no closet, so clothes were kept in boxes under the beds (1). Curtains around the bed were drawn back, revealing the thin figure, mumbling and rolling left and right, the agitation shoving covers to the floor. Serena looked at the left foot, wrapped in a loose bandage but stained yellow. Johnny's right arm lay stiffly at his side.

The image blurred. She wiped her eyes with an edge of the cotton cover. "Johnny, it's Serena."

The eyelids fluttered, revealing dull blue eyes sunken in dark sockets. Serena turned and focused on the one wide-open eye. A ray of hope spurred Serena to action. She rose. "Please tell that nice store lady she may go. And I need your help. I saw some herbs in the store in Paris. I need spotted geranium, that's for inflammation or if they don't have that, try stone beech — it does the same thing. If they have spreading dogbane, bring some. It keeps the kidneys going." She reached in her satchel, the one Dr. Rollins had fixed for her and handed Aunt Cindy ten dollars. "This is more than enough. And one more, please. Go to the hotel, remove my bag. It's brown, has my personal things. I've paid the clerk for today. I'll need to stay here — that bed." She pointed to the other bed.

Aunt Cindy giggled and raised her eyelids, so Serena added, "No problem. I have a boyfriend. Wants to be engaged. Besides I've taken care of, bathed so many men past months, it's nothing."

Aunt Cindy tucked the money down her dress and left. Serena ran to the door and hollered after her, "If they happen to have ginseng get lots. Tea made from it gives great vigor to patients." Serena turned back and surveyed the room, contemplated the arduous task.

For two weeks, except for washing behind the cabin or visits to the one-hole privy, Serena bathed Johnny, washed him from head to toe, gave him hourly sips of broth and herbal soups. She put warm rags on his arm and massaged it, turning it more and more as the stiffness left. Aunt Cindy brought the broth and every meal for Serena. For a week Serena watched Johnny grab at invisible objects and talk to the darkness. She managed a smile when one of the ghosts he teased was called Cap. After eight days, the stink from his foot left, the redness lessened. Was it the moldy bread or the bark from the spotted alder she put over the end of the half-foot three times a day? Fevers, the high ones, always at night, brought out sweats and gibberish, some nights leaving little time for sleep.

The eighth morning followed a night of interrupted sleep, brief catnaps. Serena went to the washstand beside the cabin, removed her top, and doused her face and upper body, the cold water having the desired effect. She bounced into the cabin, bent over her bag in the corner and retrieved a beige linsey-woolsey blouse.

"Serena, that you?"

She walked over and sat on the edge of the bed. His continual stare told her he would live. She buttoned the blouse and smiled. The questions came to her in rapid succession, salted with his conclusion about not being a doctor, thanks to a useless arm and part of a foot.

In a matter of days Serena had Johnny convinced that with hard work he could have a useful arm and with a Sam Huett special boot he could walk, perhaps with only a slight limp. During the intense exercise sessions Serena thrilled at the dialogue with the shy, usually reserved Quaker, his behavior a striking change from the experiences when they rescued her father, and noticeably different from the stiff, formal holiday time they shared. They read from his Bible every morning and after each reading Johnny held her hand and thanked the Lord for sending Serena to him, for saving his life, to bless the Howell's and especially Cindy. Serena made detailed measurements of the amputated foot and gave them to Mrs. Howell, who sent them to Sam via telegram when Uncle Jake made a trip to Paris for kitchen supplies.

The cool October evening air soothed Serena's anxiety when she watched Johnny hobble on his half foot. They passed the long row of log cabins for the servants and next to them the log smoke house where every winter the meat of fifty or more hogs was stored. Fifty feet away they stopped in front of the large old rambling white frame house, part of it originally of logs covered over with weather boarding. The structure sat in a long deep yard in which grew nearly forty varieties of roses. Two great pippen apple trees stood on each side of the gate. On the west side of the yard a vegetable garden lay, in which grew strawberries, raspberries, currants, gooseberries, rhubarb, asparagus, the best of vegetables, and all sorts of medicinal herbs. Surrounding hills and streams made it an ideal playground for children (1).

Two days before, when she told Mrs. Howell that Johnny was doing well, and they would depart as soon as they could arrange transportation to Shelbina, Mrs. Howell said she would tell Mr. Howell. Now, the night before their departure, she watched Johnny limp up the stairs to the porch. He seemed to bear more weight on the partial foot. The door opened and a lean man in dark suit and high-collar shirt stepped toward them.

"I am William Howell. I have been anxious to meet you, Serena." He took the extended hand and squeezed it, peering at Johnny, who eased up the last step. "And I have heard about this brave young man." He went over and when Johnny raised a stiff right arm, he grasped the upper arm and smiled. William James Howell, born in Louisville, Kentucky on May 14, 1813, married Winifred Bates, sister of Moses D. Bates, the founder of Hannibal, and studied law under Uriel Wright in Palmyra before settling in Paris. "Before age" he was elected circuit clerk of Monroe County. Elected to the legislature in 1844, he remained a staunch Unionist, even though he had many slaves, all part of four families brought from Kentucky (2).

"I am so delighted to meet you, Sir," Serena said and studied the small gray eyes, a pleasant countenance, and concluded he resembled pictures she had seen of Robert E. Lee (1).

Howell held the door so Johnny could enter. The room was awash with attractive young women. Serena caught Johnny's appreciative eye, deciding he was indeed well. The three older daughters came up one by one, first Agnes, then Mollie and Julia. They greeted him. He seemed uneasy until little Bennie ran up, and when he bent over to her, she planted a kiss on his cheek. Mrs. Howell grinned her approval and all found seats around the huge oak dining table. From the head, Mr. Howell said the blessing. The turkey and stuffing prepared by two older slave women set the stage for a series of songs from the older girls, Agnes and Mollie, but Julia was a wonderful musician and could play the piano by ear, all the popular songs born in the war, including variations (1).

While the servants passed the dessert Mrs. Howell said, "Did you tell Johnny about the Confederate raid on Palmyra the day before you came here — two weeks ago, Serena?"

"Yes, Mrs. Howell. How Colonel Porter released Confederate prisoners and captured Union soldiers all in a two-hour time. And how angry General McNeil became, vowed vengeance. Johnny treated a wound on General McNeil's head and was delighted to hear he still commanded. I told him you said he visited here," Serena said.

Mr. Howell said, "Johnny, it seems that Porter's men murdered a citizen of Palmyra during that raid. The man,

Andrew Allsman, for months had furnished the Union army with the names of southern sympathizers in Palmyra." He withdrew a piece of newspaper from his coat pocket and handed it to Serena.

Quickly, she perused it:

> *To Joseph C. Porter.*
>
> *Sir: Andrew Allsman, an aged citizen of Palmyra and a non-combatant, having been carried away from his home by a band of persons unlawfully arraigned against the peace and good order of the State of Missouri, and which band was under your control, this is to notify you that, unless Andrew Allsman is returned unharmed to his family within ten days from date, ten men, who have belonged to your band, and unlawfully sworn by you to carry arms against the government of the United States, and who are now in custody, will be shot as a meet reward for their crimes, amongst which is the illegal restraining of said Allsman of his liberty, and if not returned, of presumptively aiding in his murder. Your prompt attention to this will save much suffering. Yours, etc.*
>
> *W. R. STRACHAN,*
> *Provost Marshall General Northeast District of Missouri, By order of Brigadier General commanding McNeil's column (3).*

Johnny grew an intense look. "Mrs. Howell, General McNeil can be a wild animal."

"He acted the perfect gentleman when he stayed here," she said.

Mr. Howell cleared his throat. "You are correct, though, Johnny. But what do you think of his retaliation demands?"

"I don't believe in war." He squinted at Serena.

"Johnny was raised by Quakers. Doesn't believe in killing

— except maybe a mad dog if need be." She beamed at Johnny as tension melted from his face.

"Quakers don't believe in slavery." Howell glanced around the table. "I have been in Philadelphia and New York, other big cities. The factory owners treat their workers, many poor and ignorant, worse than our Negroes-they treat the immigrants worse than me or my neighbors treat our slaves. The Yankee slavery makes them richer than me and my southern friends."

"I never been to a big city, except St. Louis. I don't like any..." Johnny paused, sipped milk. Serena recognized his dilemma, his respect for his host. He pursed his lips at Howell. "I don't think I could enjoy getting ahead from some others' ignorance, skin color, or because they were foreign. I only got things by my own sweat." He beamed at Howell. "Until your wife took me in and saved my life. How can I repay you, Sir?"

A warm smile replaced Howell's stern demeanor. "You already did that by taking care of wounded boys, whether rebels or Federals."

Johnny surprised Serena with a gentle hug before he climbed in bed. She flopped in bed, pulled the curtain, and watched the flickers of faint orange from the fire dance ghostly figures on the thin white curtain.

"Johnny, that was considerate of you."

"What was?"

"I know you wanted to tell Mr. Howell that the difference between his well-treated slaves and the poor, abused foreigners working in northern factories is freedom." She rolled over and drew the curtain back to stare at the silhouette in the far bed.

"I suspect he knows that. He treats slaves well. This here cabin is nicer than the one in which I grew up. Yet many have fled to uncertainty, maybe harder times so they can be free."

Serena rolled back, letting the curtain close. "You did

good on your foot. Goodnight." The events of the evening moved over for concerns about Blake. *Was he one of the many captured? I must get to Palmyra and find out,* she told herself.

Chapter 15

Palmyra Massacre
October 18

Foreboding, perhaps better described as a wake, Johnny thought, as he stepped off the train. All the way from Shelbina Serena acted morose, the blabbermouth almost mute. Yet her eyes were open, staring blankly at the passing countryside. Sam popped out of the silent crowd of Union soldiers loitering around the Palmyra station. He, too, acted sullen. Johnny blinked in the bright mid-day sun and waved to Serena, who rode a buggy to the National Hotel. She didn't seem concerned, perhaps didn't notice his brief farewell. A shrill sound broke the solitude. The train blew steam and its wheels ground forward.

"Sam," Johnny crushed his hand. "Did our President die? What ails everyone?"

"Big execution. You knew about McNeil's threat?" After Johnny nodded he added, "He executed ten southern men this morning at the fairgrounds (1). Barbarous, the citizens call it. Yeah, and many of McNeil's men are shocked." Sam pulled a pair of shiny brown boots from a sack. He explained how a thick sole, he called it the last, had a wooden forefoot built into it, making up the toe of the left boot.

Johnny helped Sam pull the boot over a piece of sheep-skin he put on the raw end of the half-foot. "Was Blake one?"

"No, but most probably deserved it as traitors, murderers. Some strange things, Johnny. McNeil told his Adjutant, a mean man, to pick five from the Palmyra prison and five from the Hannibal prison and execute them as an example to stop the bushwhacking."

"Strange things, you said."

Sam pushed on his boot, said, "A guy named William Humphrey was on the list until his wife pleaded his case to McNeil, so he told Strachan to release Humphrey, shoot only nine." He helped Johnny stand, froze him in his stare. "Strachan added a man named Hiram Smith, making ten."

Johnny walked, short steps, up and down. "Shouldn't have done it — should have sent them to prison." Using Sam for a crutch, he took more unsure steps.

"They drove to the fairgrounds in three wagons with the men sitting on their coffins. The firing squad shot them kneeling beside their coffins. A botched ordeal, killed only three outright (2)." Sam's head hit his chest. Johnny eased back and forth alone, his gait doing better than his emotions.

Schmidt joined Sam and Johnny, watching the unsteady steps. "Much pain?"

"Nope."

"Unsteady gait. Let me see your foot," Schmidt said.

Johnny sat, removed the boot and the piece of sheepskin stuck to the amputated end. The bright red, unhealed surface covered a long area, the size of a thumb on the very end. "Clean. No infection."

Schmidt's eyes glared, his mouth hung open while he inspected the remnant of a foot. "Good job. With Sam's special boot you'll walk normal — with some change in your gait." He eased the foot to the floor. "Who did the slick work?"

"I did it," Johnny said and described how he methodically prepared for his own amputation and then executed it. "I did it exactly the way I saw you do hundreds," he said.

"And your recovery?" Schmidt bit his lower lip when Johnny winked at Sam.

"A big mamma slave took care of me and then I ordered a nurse from Good Samaritan Hospital to come for my rehab."

Sam laughed. "When he and the nurse got off the train I give him his new foot-boot."

"So why the long face?" Schmidt nodded as Johnny put the sheepskin over the end, held it in place with a heavy stocking and pulled on the boot. Johnny extended his hand toward Schmidt and slowly went through supination and pronation of the forearm, extension and flexion at the wrist, and the same with fingers and thumb. He stood and with small steps walked to the next table and returned. "I'm sad — upset that our troops murdered those innocent southern men yesterday." He caught eye language passing between Sam and Schmidt.

"Miraculous recovery," Schmidt said, and took Johnny's arm. "Come, you've forgotten what a southern gentleman did to you. Just because you escaped death, a cripple, doesn't make the guy less a crook."

Schmidt slowed so Johnny could catch up. Sam helped him into a buggy. Neither spoke. Schmidt drove slowly north. At the corner behind the courthouse they paused to stare at the prison where the ten executed men had been held. They turned right, went a block and then north on Main Street, past the courthouse. Union soldiers hung around every corner, but they saw few citizens. Three blocks north of the courthouse, Schmidt pulled up to the hitching post in front of the second house from the northwest corner of Jackson and Main (3).

Johnny pointed to the two-story white structure, his suspicions mounting. "Who lives here?" Sam helped him step down from the buggy.

"Mrs. Allsman, Johnny. The widow Allsman." When they reached the top of the stairs the door opened and a thickset man with a yellowish beard opened the door. He smiled at Schmidt and then scrutinized Johnny, his glance whisking past Sam.

"Woodruff, this is the surgeon's helper I've talked about so much. He was anxious to meet you." His not-so-sly wink

Jail at Palmyra, as it stands today.
Used by permission, State Historical Society of Missouri, Columbia.

at Sam did not escape Johnny's visual field.

"Doctor, how kind of you." He held the door so the three could enter the house. When Johnny paused, the man extended a hand. "I'm Woodruff Lee, married to Mrs. Allsman's oldest daughter, Sarrah (3)."

Johnny shook his hand and followed Schmidt into the sitting room, where Lee introduced him to Mrs. Allsman, to Sarrah seated to her left, and to Henrietta seated on a piano bench. He sensed a mood that, though obtunded, differed noticeably from outside. He struggled to speak.

"Johnny was raised Quaker. I thought if he knew what you all suffered he might understand today's necessity," Schmidt said and went over and sat next to Henrietta.

Lee pulled two chairs across from Sarrah and the widow. He pranced between. "Pop Allsman was loyal, patriotic, a Christian man 62 years old, too old to be of any threat to the

Rebels (3). Doc Schmidt ministered to us when we suffered those days, not knowing if Pop was dead or alive."

Henrietta stared blankly at the floor. Sarrah put her arm around her mother. "I know Quakers don't hold no truck with this business. But it weren't no massacre as they call it. All of us elected men to the convention in '61, men who said they would vote to hold Missouri with the Union," Sarrah said and stared at Johnny. "But these men, like Porter and his murderers, ambush soldiers loyal to our country. They broke in our jail that holds men who have tried to destroy the country by killing Federal boys."

When she hesitated, Mrs. Allsman said, "It don't help our sadness seeing men shot, but how else can the Union men, the enforcers of the people's wishes, stop these bandits. Mr. Allsman's crime was that he pointed out the people who hid the criminals, encouraged them, did anything to destroy our country."

"Johnny knows they have murdered others." Schmidt turned and looked at him. "Remember last winter when the reb Stacy dragged people who supported the Union out of their homes — Mr. Preston, a man near Shelbyville along with two Militia men, and guerillas murdered three Union men in April, dragged them from their homes here in Marion County."

"Does everyone who loses an election get to take up arms and resort to murder?" Henrietta waved a hand holding a hankie.

Johnny paused while Sarrah rose and disappeared down the hall. After he offered his condolences, the best he had learned in his months helping soldiers with their grief, he tried Mr. Flack's way. "I guess one has to kill a mad dog now and then…"

"And Porter's a mad dog, not the angel his supporters want us to believe," Lee said.

"Mr. Flack, the Quaker that raised me, told me that many a man who didn't believe in killing but carried a gun ended up killing." He hesitated when Sarrah entered with a tray of pastries and set them on the table in front of Mrs. Allsman, the interlude letting a scene pop into his brain, Doctor Aylward tending the wounded rebels at Athens. "Porter's men killed a mighty fine doctor friend of mine, just as Mr. Allsman. If you're the boss of people fighting the law by murder, I guess you're trapped like the man that doesn't plan on killing but does — just as guilty as those who plan to kill." Johnny felt his words stab his being.

"Sam knows the cruelty of these people who want to wage war against their own country," Schmidt said. "I think we need a monument at Pierce's Mill for the massacre of those Union troops who were ambushed trying to keep this country from being ruined."

Johnny finished the pastry and rose when Sarrah helped Mrs. Allsman stand. At the door Lee patted Johnny's shoulder and said, "All wars are ugly. Call it massacre, murder, execution, or killing. It's horrible. Those who started this, the politicos who announced their intention to stick with the traitors down south, have killed a lot of good young men, gray and blue boys. Lots of civilian folk suffered."

Johnny felt the after-effects of a restless night while he rode on the huge gray behind Sam. At Strachan's house on Olive Street (4), a block from the jail, a private told Johnny that Strachan had his mustering-out papers in the courthouse office. The two-block ride passed along deserted streets, an ominous silence hovering at each corner. Sam held the horse at the front walk and Johnny slowly climbed the few steps. Partially obliterated letters spelled John McAfee. Johnny leaned close to the door and made out faint words, 'Speaker of the 21st General Assembly.' He mused at the faded words, the faded importance. Down the hall he spied a Union soldier, a bizarre scene. The man comforted a young girl, maybe ten, sitting on the steps to the door that had

Strachan house, Palmyra. Shown as it stands today.
Photo by the author.

Strachan's name. Soon the door flew open and a beautiful woman, but disheveled in appearance, bolted out, grabbed the girl, and ran for the door (5).

"Mrs. Humphrey, let me..." The sergeant stopped after three strides toward the fleeing woman. The bellowing from Strachan's office applied brakes.

The man held Johnny's arm and shoved him into the office. Strachan, a wild look to his sweaty brow, wiggled a finger at Johnny. "Johnny owl eyes. I am proud to be the one to muster you out — that is if I can't convince you that..." He stopped, his mouth agape, for Johnny had been alerted to his game and had sat and removed his boot and the sheepskin, the red end of his half foot threatening the unsettled Strachan.

He rolled up a sleeve, and with obvious effort thrust a stiff arm at the frowning man. Without success he tried to make a fist. Strachan shoved an envelope across the desk. When Johnny snatched it with his left hand, Strachan pounded his fist on it, smirked, and waved a paper.

"Sign this, owl eyes."

Johnny scanned the paper, snapped his head at the grinning man. "I can't. You didn't give me my separation pay."

"You're not too…"

The rattle of the door against the coat rack stopped him. Johnny felt a body press from behind. "General Strachan, General McNeil wants you for the hanging at his place now."

Perturbed, Strachan opened the desk drawer, threw a brown envelope at Johnny, and moved the paper closer. Johnny peeked in the envelope, saw the money, and signed the paper without counting the green bills. He followed Strachan and an officer the Adjutant General called Captain Reid (4).

Johnny hobbled down the steps as the two men hurried south on Main Street. Sam guided his gray over the lawn and helped Johnny climb up.

"They got the noose around Blake's neck. Serena's pleaded her case — and others tried. Hurry."

At Reed Street, the site of General McNeil's residence (4), a large crowd composed of citizens and Union soldiers pressed close to a platform. Johnny's heart skipped a beat when he spied Blake with the noose around his neck. Hurriedly, he searched for Serena. Sam jabbed an elbow in his ribs and pointed.

"Over there — to the left by the two men in dark suits," Sam whispered.

Johnny saw Serena, distraught, wiping her eyes with a hanky. She leaned against the leg of an older man sitting stiffly on a black mount. He recognized the beardless face, the heavy eyebrows hiding the intense gray eyes. John Newton Boulware. He turned to Sam and with a low voice told Sam he recognized the beardless man, but asked the name of the thin bearded man next to Boulware.

"John McAfee, speaker of the house for the secessionist general assembly," Schmidt volunteered from his left.

"How is it he is free?" Johnny recognized the man who climbed the steps to the gallows, General McNeil.

"November last, Gamble stated that to be sworn in office all the elected officials in Palmyra had to take the oath (6). Judge McAfee swore loyalty to the Union. I think he still had to post a bond. I don't know about his friend."

McNeil read the charges against Blake. A breeze rustled the yellow-orange leaves of the trees standing along the side of the brick house. Johnny could hear Sam's heavy breathing, his own heart beating.

Johnny figured it must be the reaction of papers, citizens, and his own men that drove McNeil to step to the edge of the platform, wave a roll of papers, and yell, "Is there anyone here who wishes to protest the execution of this murderer?"

The crowd in front of the platform pushed back, making a path, further back until a lone figure stood in the center of the lawn, the grass a trampled brown. Murmurs rolled around the gathering like a giant wave. McNeil leaned over, shaded his eyes. Johnny's heart sounds — lub-dup, lub-dup, lub-dup, roared in his ears. Sweat ran off his palms, from under his new brown civilian floppy down his forehead into his eyes. The platform and its terror blurred. Johnny Jenkins removed his hat, took two steps closer, wiped his eyes with the back of a hand. He raised his head to McNeil, and, fast as he could, threw a smile. The crowd, those that could see his face, made a cacophony of discordant noises.

McNeil stiffened, "What — that you, Johnny owl eyes? I thought you was dead."

"Quite alive, Sir. I ask that you not murder this young man." Johnny's muscles twitched. He meant to say execute.

"Last execution," McNeil hesitated and seemed to survey the crowd. "Yesterday a young man substituted for a condemned man (4). You want to take Slater's place?"

A rumble spread through the crowd. Johnny's legs felt rubbery. He replaced his hat and, turning, waved to the people for silence.

"Well?" McNeil demanded.

"When I tended your head wound at Kirksville you promised I could have any favor I asked as long as I didn't ask for your whiskey." He paused. Every soul stood still, the trees stood still, Johnny's heart stood still. McNeil screwed his face into prune shape. Johnny continued, "My favor — release Blake Slater, parole him, and send him home to his mom. She's already lost one son in this war. 'Sides, he's not guilty of murder. I am quite alive, Sir." Trembles shook sweat off Johnny.

McNeil paced back and forth at the front of the platform. Finally, he stopped in front of Johnny, beckoned him with an index finger until Johnny stood against the platform, looking up the flaring nostrils of a raging bull. McNeil's face was red, his eyes protruded. He threw his arms to the heavens, looked up at the clouds and screamed, "You miserable Quakers are nothing but trouble. Get outa my sight, owl eyes." He swept a hand, the index finger a demanding pointer, toward the back. "Get, before I break my promise."

Johnny turned and, with maximum effort nonchalantly inched for the edge of the crowd. He heard McNeil bellow to cut the pathetic reb loose, parole him, and send him home to his mommy. Sam met Johnny at the crowd's edge, put an arm around him, and ushered him through the crowd amidst numerous claps on his back and a chorus that chanted, Johnny, Johnny. He paused and stared at the platform. Serena and Blake were in each other's arms.

At Schmidt's wagon a pair of horses blocked their way. Johnny looked first at Boulware and then McAfee. They grinned.

McAfee leaned on the pommel of his saddle. "Brave act. You and the Quakers have shown us that life, regardless of skin color or politics, is the most precious thing this grand country must preserve."

Before Johnny had a chance to thank him, Boulware dismounted and grabbed Johnny's hand. His eyes were flooded. "Son — neighbor, I'm an old man, and I learned a lot today from a young man I have misjudged and mistreated. Do forgive me." He climbed on the jumpy horse, saying, "Easy, Buck." In the saddle he peered down at Johnny. "When you get home — when this war is over come visit me. And if you need help through medical school, let me know."

Numb with rubbery legs, Johnny smiled with the lower half of his face and nodded. The men left. At Holtzclaw's Johnny retrieved his newly purchased satchel, one similar to Ogden's. He stuffed the brown envelope on top of the second pair of boots, shiny brown boots with wooden toe prosthesis in the left one. Grandma Weaver's Bible warranted a kiss, and a tear. He and Sam recounted the morning's events on the short train ride to Hannibal. He left the depot, situated at the southwest corner of Main and Centre Streets, after suffering an off-the-ground bear hug. On the way to the ticket office for the St. Louis and Keokuk Packet Line, located at the corner of Levee and Bird Streets, he read the telegram given to him by the stationmaster:

> *Johnny*
> *Will meet you at wharf STOP Colonel H*
> *has your room ready STOP I have med school*
> *place ready STOP Mrs. R has great feast ready*
> *STOP*
> > *Ogden Rollins*

The St. Louis-Keokuk Packet steamboat sat at the dock an hour while they loaded much grain, leather goods, and timber. In the passengers' cabin Johnny found a seat in a corner. No one occupied any of the seats in that row or the three rows in front of it. He slouched down in the seat. Fatigue from emotional battles of the day sent him into pleasant flashbacks. He felt the gentle rocking of the huge rear-wheel steamboat and heard its mighty engines thunder to their task. The rolling Mississippi generated a whimsical smile. He peeked over the windowsill and watched the distant Illinois shore march by, its red walnuts, yellow and orange elms, and red-brown maples offering a new picture every mile.

"Is this seat taken?" The voice came from a body that crushed him against the side.

He shoved the floppy back and rolled his head to the right. The view bolted him straight up on the hard bench. "Serena. You…"

"Say, Serena, my favorite nurse, I am so pleased to see you."

The eyes, talking, coaxing, warm — the lips, full, pink, luscious. He made two attempts at speaking. Finally, he touched her arm. "I am more than pleased, I am… but Blake?"

Serena leaned close, her warmth blanketing him. She shoved against his shoulder, her eyes sending messages reminiscent of those Elizabeth had given. "I sent him home to his mommy. Blake thinks life is all about being important. Well, he's important to his mother. What you did…" She lowered her head briefly, raised it, the watery eyes, the smile that spoke of love. "When I climbed the platform and hugged Blake, it was out of happiness for him, that he would live, freed by the one I love. The hug said goodbye forever and sent me looking for the bravest, nicest man I have ever known."

Johnny grew warm. His soul burned. "Ogden sent me a telegram. I stay at Hitchcock's while I go to med school."

The wet, hot smooch on his cheek loosened the animal. He turned to meet her lips, but she pulled back, smiling, yet inviting.

"Later. I got a telegram. Dix is angry, so I will be Doctor Rollins's private nurse."

"And us?"

Serena grabbed Johnny's wet hand, held it to her lips and kissed it passionately.

He held her chin, turned her face. "What is that?"

"I must continue your rehab." She scooted close again, her face consumed with a huge smile. She squeezed his hand. "I'm taking you home Johnny."

THE END

Postscript

After Whaley's Mill, where in late October Porter disbanded his troops and crossed the Missouri River, the war in northeast Missouri essentially ended. Destruction of one hundred miles of North Missouri Railroad track ended 1862. This act by ruffians presaged the meanness and evil that would persist, the rape and pillage of countryside and the murder of innocent citizens, by thugs who saw an opportunity to act out vile urges, for some vengeance from wrongs they and their loved ones suffered, and for many the chance to demonstrate the baseness of their being, for they attacked southerners as well as northerners.

Not long into 1863, March, General Price suffered a definitive defeat at the battle of Westport. Union troops chased him south into Arkansas. His army disbanded, completing the legitimate encounters in all of Missouri.

The effect of the struggle for eighteen months on the future of the fictional characters is left to the reader. Blake Slater, Serena Hill and her amputee father, Sam Huett and his parents, Ogden and Nancy Rollins, and Johnny Jenkins, all certainly would have interfaced with the one or more of the non-fictional characters.

Many places identified in the preceding chapters can be visited today. Others have taken pieces of their history into oblivion with them. The Arsenal, Jefferson Barracks, and Bellefontaine Cemetery, where the Beaumonts are interred, stand witness to those days. Lindell Grove, the site of Camp Jackson, shortly after 1861 was converted into a park and now is occupied by buildings. Structures nearer the waterfront have long given way to transformation of St. Louis as a business capitol of the Midwest, its arch signifying its position yet as the gateway to the west.

Jefferson landing has been preserved and the Union Hotel, the Maus home, and the warehouse-hotel which contains an exhibit of civil war relics and pictures give the visitor a sense of life when Jefferson City served as the railhead for goods coming down the Missouri River. The state capitol building that burned to the ground has been replaced by a magnificent domed building, a museum on the ground floor containing Civil War memorabilia. Time and the growth of trees block a view of the Governor's mansion and the capitol building, but these are readily accessible for tours.

Upon entering Boonville from I-70 a huge marker tells the visitor about the establishment of the river town and the two battles. Thespian Hall, the theater that housed wounded after the battle, stands today on Main Street and around the corner one can visit the jail with attached jailer's residence, restored as it was when General Lyon faced the town's acting Mayor. Unfortunately, the marker for the first battle of the Civil War in Missouri was washed away by the disastrous flood of 1993. However one can follow the road east that ends near the site where the battle took place.

Hannibal, too, has lost most structures of the Civil War days. A marker denoting the location of Bird's claim sits on the high school lawn and Moses Bates's first store is remembered by the area designated by the wording on the huge wall, near the spot of his mercantile.

The third Palmyra courthouse is a structure built in 1900 when the one of Civil War days was razed. A large marker on the lawn serves as a marker, a memorial for the ten men "massacred" October 18, 1862. The yellow Gardner House, two blocks south, has been renovated and serves as a museum and quarters for a historical society. Strachan's house is well preserved as is the old jail where the "massacre" prisoners were housed.

Alexandria, washed away by the flood of 1993, barely

survives, and in St. Francisville one can identify Fort Pike by a simple marker. The yellow Baptist Church appears as it did in 1861 and Wolf Cemetery, the resting place of the Weavers, the Jenkins', the Alexanders, and the McKees, is preserved.

On the way to Wayland one recognizes the Jenkins farm and across route 136 about two hundred yards west, a few stones of the Jenkins school are strewn beneath a cluster of trees. Revere is a quiet burg and no vestiges of Sweet Home can be found.

Athens is a ghost town, now undergoing remarkable and exciting restoration. The old mill on the river's edge is reduced to the lower rock foundation, but on the bluff the Benning-Thome house, the cannonball damage from the battle carefully preserved, is a small but tidy museum. The McKee house and several others have been rebuilt as they were during the battle days. One can walk the empty streets of this state park, facing the ridge where Green had Kneisley fire over all but the Benning house and strike Croton across the De Moines in Iowa. With cemetery ridge, now dotted by tombstones, to the east and the woods to the west one can feel the excitement when Moore yelled to ready bayonets.

Dr. Joseph McDowell returned to St. Louis at war's end, re-established McDowell Medical College. He died in 1874. Colonel Joseph Porter was severely wounded in the battle at Hartsville, Missouri, and died of his wounds February 18, 1863. Joseph Mudd finished medical school and practiced medicine in Maryland.

General McNeil was haunted the rest of his life for his order in the Palmyra massacre but William Strachan died a lonesome man.

John McAfee was arrested in December 1864 and set free on $10,000 bond. He died in 1884 in Quincy. John Newton Boulware and his son Willis fled to Sangamon County, Illinois, after the battle of Athens, staying at long-time friend Thomas Wooldridge's. After the war John Newton returned to Canton and was elected to the legislature in 1873. His son Willis, who had stayed in Sangamon County, Illinois, with his father during the war, married the daughter of their friend-distant relative William Wooldridge in 1864. He returned to Canton, and was a prominent judge and lawyer.

Sources and Notes

Introduction

1. Shades of Blue and Gray, by Herman Hattaway (San Diego, New York , London: Harcourt Brace and Company, 1998). Hattaway further emphasized the cost and the importance of the war in Missouri (pg.151) "It was important to the Union war effort to retain control in Missouri because if the Confederates got that state they would enjoy easy access into Kansas or, more crucial, Illinois (pg.152)." "The impact of rebel raids and guerillas caused tremendous dispersion of Federal forces...Including the garrison at Washington and troops deployed by both sides in Missouri and Arkansas, 190,000 Union soldiers, more than one-third of those in the field, were defending territory and communications against 42,000 Confederates."
2. Battle Cry of Freedom, by James M. McPherson (New York: Ballantine Books, 1988).
3. Missouri: Mother of the West, Vol. II, by Walter Williams and Floyd Calvin Shoemaker (Chicago, New York: The American Historical Society, Inc., 1930).
4. Quincy Herald, March 11, 1881, obituary.
5. History of Monroe and Shelby Counties Missouri (St. Louis: National Historical Companies, 1884).
6. Bates-Gash, by L. Hazel Bates (Quincy, Ill.: Kibler's Point-of-Sale Printing Company, 1971).
7. Jenkins Family Book, by Robert E. Jenkins (Boston: New England Historic Genealogical Society, 1904).
8. Missouri Democracy: A History of the Party and Its Representative Members-Past and Present, Vol. I, by Wm. Rufus Jackson (Chicago-St. Louis-Indianapolis: S. J. Clarke Publishing Co. Inc, 1935).

9. War of the Rebellion, Series I, Vol. II, by BVT. Lieut. Col. Robert N. Scott, Third U.S. Artillery (Washington: Government Printing Office, 1880).

Prologue

Overview 1861

1. War of the Rebellion, Series I, Vol. II, by BVT. Lieut. Col. Robert N. Scott, Third U.S. Artillery (Washington: Government Printing Office, 1880).
2. War of the Rebellion, Series I, Vol. V, by BVT. Lieut. Col. Robert N. Scott, Third U. S. Artillery (Washington: Government Printing Office, 1881).
3. The Time Chart of the Civil War, by James K. Arnold and Rebecca Wiener, Editorial Consultants (St. Paul, Minnesota: MBI Publishing Company, 2001). This pictorial book offers excellent time charts to give an overview of the war during struggles in northeast Missouri.
4. Battle Cry of Freedom, by James M. McPherson (New York: Ballantine Books, 1988).
5. The Civil War in Missouri Day by Day 1861-1865, by Carolyn M. Bartels (Independence, Missouri: Two Trails Publishing, 1992).
6. War of the Rebellion, Series 1, Vol. III, by BVT. Lieut. Col. Robert N. Scott, Third U.S. Artillery (Washington: Government Printing Office, 1881).
7. St. Louis Missouri Republican, May 10, 1861.
8. Missouri Democracy: A History of the Party and Its Representative Members-Past and Present, Vol. I, by William Rufus Jackson (Chicago-St. Louis-Indianapolis: S. J. Clarke Publishing Co., 1935). "Perhaps no more effective public speaker has ever raised his voice in Missouri than Rollins. Of magnifi-

cent intellectual attainments, splendid physique, superb dress, imperturbable good nature, fluent in speech and graceful in gesture, he was a born orator." These words were used to describe James Sydney Rollins.

9. Beaumont, America's First Physiologist, by Rodney B. Nelson, III, M. D., FACP (Geneva, Ill: Grant House Press, 1990). Col. Ethan Allen Hitchcock resigned from the Army in 1855 and moved to St. Louis, living on one side of the duplex. In 1862 he was offered a commission as Maj. General to supersede General U. S. Grant at Fort Donelson. He declined.

10. St. Louis Missouri Republican, May 11, 1861.

11. The Union Cause in St. Louis in 1861, by Robert J. Rombauer (St. Louis: Press of Nixon-Jones Printing Co., 1909).

12. Jenkins Family Book, by Robert E. Jenkins (Boston: New England Historic Genealogical Society, 1904). James H. Jenkins died in 1853 and his widow, Mary Long Jenkins, married David Eiler in 1855. His oldest child, George W. Jenkins, born in 1843, in real life did not participate in the war. He went with the family to California when they joined a caravan that departed Clark County in 1859, not in 1857 as described here.

13. Missouri State Gazetteer and Business Directory 1860, by James Sutherland and Henry N. McEvoy (St. Louis: Sutherland and McEvoy Publishers and Compilers, 1860).

14. The Presbytery of Kansas City and Its Predecessors 1821-1901, by John B. Hill (Kansas City, MO: The Burd and Fletcher Printing Co., 1901).

15. Washington University in St. Louis, by Ralph E. Morrow (Missouri Historical Society Press, St. Louis, 1996).

16. St. Louis Missouri Republican, May 13, 1861.

17. This is Our Saint Louis, by Harry M. Hagen (St. Louis: Knight Publishing Company, 1970).

18. Encyclopedia of the History of Missouri, Vol. II, by Howard L. Conrad (New York, Louisville, St. Louis: The Southern History Company, 1901).

Chapter 1

1. History of Lewis, Clark, Knox and Scotland Counties, Missouri (Marceline, MO: Walsworth Publishing Company, 1887).
2. History of Marion County 1884, by R.I. Holcombe (The Marion County Historical Society, Hannibal, Missouri, 1979).
3. The Quincy Herald-Whig, Sunday, December 29, 1935.
4. Missouri State Gazetteer and Business Directory 1860, by James Sutherland and Henry N. McEvoy (St. Louis: Sutherland and McEvoy Publishers and Compilers, 1860).
5. Encyclopedia of Missouri Courthouses, by Marian M. Ohman (Columbia: University of Missouri, Columbia Extension Division, 1981).
6. War of the Rebellion: Official Records of the Union and Confederate Armies, Series 1, Vol. III, by BVT. Lieut. Col. Robert N. Scott, Third U. S. Artillery (Washington, D. C.: Government Printing Office, 1881).
7. Official Army Register 1861-1865, Volume VI, by Adjutant General's Office (Gaithersburg, MD, Reprinted by Ron K. VanSickle Military Books, 1987).
8. The Civil War in Missouri Day by Day 1861-1865, by Carolyn M. Bartels (Independence, MO: Two Trails Publishing, 1992).

Chapter 2

1. The Good Old Days: Early History of Northeast Clark County, Missouri, by Kenney Dowd (Athens, MO: Reproduced by Athens Park Development Association, 1963).
2. Missouri State Gazetteer and Business Directory 1860, by James Sutherland and Henry N. McEvoy (St. Louis: Sutherland and McEvoy Publishers and Compilers, 1860).
3. McKee family Bible and genealogy tree furnished by Roger Boyd, Park ranger, Battle of Athens State Park, and Julia McKee Connelly, the great granddaughter of Col. William McKee. His brother, Major David McKee was born in 1823 and fought with the Seventh Missouri Cavalry. At least three unrelated families of McKees lived in and around Clark County; in addition to Robert McKee of St. Francisville, Edwin McKee, born August 31, 1842, in Knox County, Illinois, enlisted in Co. K, Iowa 1st Volunteer Infantry, but was discharged early because of wounds suffered in the battle of Wilson's Creek.
4. A History of Iowa, by Leland L. Sage (Ames: The Iowa State University Press, 1974).
5. History of Lewis, Clark, Knox and Scotland Counties, Missouri (Marceline, Mo: Walsworth Publishing Company, 1887). Robert A. McKee, born in 1805, married Amanda A. Lapsley. In 1835, after the birth of Robert S., the young physician in St. Francisville, they had left Kentucky when Amanda's father, John A. Lapsley decided to move west. Robert, Johnny's hero, always imparting knowledge, more than medical facts, to salve Johnny's insatiable curiosity, told Johnny the Lapsleys and McKees left after they heard a debate on slavery at Transylvania University in Lexington, Kentucky. One of the McKees had argued for slavery.

But his opponent argued so convincingly against slavery that the Lapsleys and McKees freed their slaves. Robert surmised that they settled in Clark County because their freed slaves could more easily remain with the family, free but as paid servants. Robert A. served as one of the first three judges in the county and had gained considerable wealth, owning large tracts of land.

6. A Guide to the Medicinal Plants of the United States, by Arnold Krochmal and Connie Krochmal (New York City: Quadrangle/New York Times Book Company, 1973).

7. Civil War Medicine, by Stewart Brooks (Springfield, Ill: Charles Thomas Co., 1966).

8. The Theory and Treatment of Fevers, by Dr. John Sappington (Arrow Rock, MO: Reprinted by The friends of Arrow Rock, Inc., 1971).

9. Organization and Administration of the Union Army 1861-1865, Vol. II, by Fred Albert Shannon (Cleveland: The Arthur H. Clark Company, 1928). In the spring of 1861 after war erupted, the army insisted that the United States Congress reconsider the status of the conscientious objector. After hours of debate, Congress concluded that all Quakers must join the army — they did not have to carry a gun — or they could pay for a substitute. In 1863 after Senator Garrett Davies of Kentucky said in referring to Quakers, Shakers, and clergy, "...fight, pay, or emigrate...," Senator John B. Henderson of Missouri said, "If I could put them in service from allowing them to escape by any payment whatever, I would put them there and let them fight the war; I would make them do the actual service in the field, and trust to God in the future that they would not bring such another war upon our hands." In the Congressional Globe, 38th Congress, 1st Session. But Lincoln and his Secretary of war were sympathetic to the conscientious objector.

10. Missouri Baptist Biography, by J.C. Maple, A.M.D.D., and R.P. Rider, A.M., Vol. I (Kansas City, MO: Western Baptist Publishing Co., 1914).

11. The Palimpsest, Vol. II, by John C. Parish, ed. (Iowa City: The State Historical Society of Iowa, 1921). The episode with Daggs' slaves occurred in 1849. A detailed and intriguing account of the story can be found in Iowa Journal of History and Politics: Vol. XXII, 1924. Editor Benjamin F. Shambaugh (Iowa City: Iowa State Historical Society, 1924).

12. Jenkins Family Book, by Robert E. Jenkins (Boston: New England Historic Genealogical Society, 1904).

13. A History of Iowa, by Leland L. Sage (Ames: The Iowa State University Press, 1974).

14. The Twenty-First Missouri: From Home Guard to Union Regiment, by Leslie Anders (Westport, Connecticut, London, England: Greenwood Press, 1975).

15. Grist Mills, by Elmer L. Smith (Lebanon, PA: Applied Arts Publishers, 1992).

16. Gate City of Keokuk, Iowa, January 9, 1922. "Another Account of the Battle of Athens, Aug. 5, 1861," by John T. McKee, 81 years old.

17. John M. Hiller to Dear Brother, Aug 5th, 1861, Hiller Family Papers, Mss 3856, folder 254, Western Manuscripts Collection, Joint Collection-State Historical Society of Missouri/University of Missouri, Ellis Library, The University of Missouri, Columbia. The letter was also printed July 23, 1964, in Keokuk's The Daily Gate City.

Chapter 3

1. Shelby County Herald, March 30,1997, "We were never licked, just overpowered, says Bethel Confederate Vet, "Uncle Pres." K. Walters was 86 years old when he recounted his role in the battle of Athens and then the battle of Lexington under Gen. Price.
2. History of Lewis, Clark, Knox and Scotland Counties, Missouri (Marceline, MO: Walsworth Publishing Company, 1887).
3. Missouri State Gazetteer and Business Directory 1860, by James Sutherland and Henry N. McEvoy (St. Louis: Sutherland and McEvoy Publishers and Compilers, 1860).
4. An Illustrated Historical Atlas of Lewis County, Missouri, by Edwards Brothers of Missouri (Philadelphia, PA: Edwards Brothers, 1878).
5. The Good Old Days: Early History of Northeast Clark County, Missouri, by Kenney Dowd (Athens, MO: Reproduced by Athens Park Development Association, 1963).
6. History of Marion County, Missouri, 1884, by R. I. Holcombe (Hannibal, MO: The Marion County Historical Society, 1979).

Chapter 4

1. The Good Old Days: Early History of Northeast Clark County, Missouri, by Kenney Dowd (Athens, MO: Reproduced by Athens Park Development Association, 1963).
2. History of Lewis, Clark, Knox and Scotland Counties, Missouri (Marceline, MO: Walsworth Publishing Company, 1887).

3. Annals of Iowa, Vol.6, by Sanford W. Huff, M.D. (Iowa City: State Historical Society of Iowa, 1868).
4. The Gate City of Keokuk, Iowa, January 9, 1922. "Another Account of Battle of Athens, Aug. 5, 1861," by John T. McKee, 81 years old.
5. Jenkins Family Book, by Robert E. Jenkins (Boston: New England Historic Genealogical Society, 1904).
6. From the records of Immanuel Methodist Church, Canton, Missouri. The first congregation was organized in 1832 and met at the home of Capt. William Pritchard. In 1843 it split over the slavery issue into M.E. Church North and M.E. Church South.

Chapter 5

1. Missouri Day by Day, Vol. I, by Floyd C. Shoemaker (Jefferson City: State Historical Society of Missouri, 1942).
2. Missouri State Gazetteer and Business Directory 1860, by James Sutherland and Henry N. McEvoy (St. Louis: Sutherland and McEvoy Publishers and Compilers, 1860).
3. The Twenty-First Missouri: From Home Guard to Union Regiment, by Leslie Anders (Westport, Connecticut, London, England: Greenwood Press, 1975).
4. Civil War Medicine, by Stewart Brooks (Springfield, Ill: Charles Thomas Co., 1966).
5. A Guide to the Medicinal Plants of the United States, by Arnold Krochmal and Connie Krochmal (New York City: Quadrangle/New York Times Book Company, 1973).

Chapter 6

1. The Twenty-First Missouri: From Home Guard to Union Regiment, by Leslie Anders (Westport, Connecticut, London, England: Greenwood Press, 1975).
2. History of Lewis, Clark, Knox and Scotland Counties, Missouri (Marceline, MO: Walsworth Publishing Company, 1887).
3. History of Monroe and Shelby Counties Missouri (St. Louis: National Historical Companies, 1884).
4. History of Adair County, by E. M. Violette (Kirksville: The Denslow Publishing Co., 1911).

Chapter 7

1. One Strong Voice, by Linda Flanagan (Kansas City, MO: The Lowell Press, 1976).
2. Civil War Medicine, by Stewart Brooks (Springfield, Ill: Charles C. Thomas Publishing Co., 1966).
3. Medical and Surgical History of the War of the Rebellion, Vol. I, by James K. Barnes, ed., surgeon general, U. S. Army (Washington, D.C.: Government Printing Service, 1870).
4. Encyclopedia of the History of St. Louis, Vol. IV, by William Hyde and Howard L. Conrad (New York, Louisville, St. Louis: The Southern History Co., 1899).
5. Lion of the Valley, St. Louis, Missouri, 1764-1980, by James Neal Primm (St. Louis: Missouri Historical Society Press, 1981).
6. St. Louis Missouri Republic, December 23, 1861.

Chapter 8

1. Hannibal Messenger, February 12 and 13, 1861. James S. Rollins's letter published in response to R.E. Dunn, esq., Marion County.
2. History of Boone County Missouri, by William F. Switzler (St. Louis: Western Historical Co., 1882).
3. Mary Rollins to My Dear Husband, November, 1861, James S. Rollins Collection, Mss 1026, folder 77, Western Manuscripts Collection, Joint Collection-State Historical Society of Missouri/University of Missouri, Ellis Library, The University of Missouri, Columbia. Mrs. Rollins tells her husband, "We got one more of our mules yesterday...".
4. James H. Rollins to My Dear Father, December 15, 1861, Mss 1026, folder 77, Western Manuscripts Collection, Joint Collection-State Historical Society of Missouri/University of Missouri, Ellis Library, The University of Missouri, Columbia.
   James was a cadet at West Point and wrote his father to express his disappointment that his father had not stopped by for a visit on his return to Washington.
5. Official Army Register 1861-1865, Vol. V, by Adjutant General's Office (Gaithersburg, MD: Reprinted by Ron K. VanSickle Military Books, 1987).
6. One Strong Voice, by Linda Flanagan (Kansas City, MO: The Lowell Press, 1976).
7. Abraham Lincoln's Philosophy of Commonsense, Part II, by Edward J. Kempf (New York: New York Academy of Science, 1965).
8. Missouri State Gazetteer and Business Directory 1860, by James Sutherland and Henry N. McEvoy (St. Louis: Sutherland and McEvoy Publishers and Compilers, 1860).
9. Missouri: Mother of the West, Vol. II, by Walter Williams and Floyd Calvin Shoemaker (Chicago, New

York: The American Historical Society, Inc., 1930).
10. History of Boone County, Missouri, by William F. Switzler (St. Louis: Western Historical Company, 1882).
11. Medical and Surgical History of the Civil War, Vol. VI, by James E. Barnes (Wilmington, North Carolina: Bradford Publishing Company, 1991).
12. Early Quaker Writings, edited by Hugh Barbour and Arthur O. Roberts (Grand Rapids, Michigan: William B. Erdmans Publishing Company, 1973).
13. St. Louis Missouri Republic, December 23, 1861.

Overview 1862

1. War of the Rebellion. Series 1, Vol. VII, by BVT. Lieut. Col. Robert N. Scott, Third U.S. Artillery (Washington: Government Printing Office, 1882).
2. War of the Rebellion, Series 1, Vol. X, Part I, by BVT. Lieut. Col. Robert N. Scott, Third U.S. Artillery (Washington: Government Printing Office, 1884).
3. The Time Chart of the Civil War, by James K. Arnold and Rebecca Wiener, Editorial Consultants (St. Paul, Minnesota: MBI Publishing Company, 2001). This pictorial book offers excellent time charts to give an overview of the war during struggles in northeast Missouri.
4. Battle Cry of Freedom, by James M. McPherson (New York: Ballantine Books, 1988).
5. War of the Rebellion, Series 1, Vol. XI, Part II, by BVT. Lieut. Col. Robert N. Scott, Third U.S. Artillery (Washington: Government Printing Office, 1884).
6. War of the Rebellion, Series 1, Vol. XIX, Part I and II, by The Late Lieut. Col. Robert N. Scott, Third U.S. Artillery (Washington: Government Printing Office, 1887).

7. War of the Rebellion, Series 1, Vol. VIII, by BVT. Lieut. Col. Robert N. Scott, Third U.S. Artillery (Washington: Government Printing Office, 1883).

Chapter 9

1. Battle Cry of Freedom, by James M. McPherson (New York: Ballantine Books, 1988).
2. History of St. Louis City and County, Vol. I, by J. Thomas Scharf (Philadelphia: Louis H. Everts Co., 1883).
3. History of Boone County Missouri, by William F. Switzler (St. Louis: Western Historical Co., 1882).
4. Mary Rollins to My Dear Husband, February 27, 1862, James S. Rollins Collection, Mss 1056, folder 79, Western Manuscripts Collection, Joint Collection-State Historical Society of Missouri/University of Missouri, Ellis Library, The University of Missouri, Columbia.
5. History of Lewis, Clark, Knox and Scotland Counties, Missouri (Marceline, MO: Walsworth Publishing Company, 1881).
6. The Twenty-First Missouri: From Home Guard to Union Regiment, by Leslie Anders (Westport, Connecticut, London, England: Greenwood Press, 1975).
7. With Porter in North Missouri, by Joseph A. Mudd (Washington, D.C.: The National Publishing Company, 1909).
8. A History of Northeast Missouri, Vol. I, by Walter Williams (Chicago, New York: The Lewis Publishing Company, 1931).
9. Writings of James Amzi Jenkins furnished by Joan Jenkins of Windsor, Colorado. Born in 1849, James wrote these recollections during the last years before he

died in 1927. In 1873 he married Mary Serena Hill, sister of the fictitious Serena.

10. The Forgotten Men: Missouri State Guard, by Carolyn M. Bartels (Shawnee Mission, KS: Two Trails Publishing, 1995).

Chapter 10

1. A History of Northeast Missouri, by Walter Williams (Chicago, New York: The Lewis Publishing Company, 1913).

2. Aesculapius Was a Mizzou Tiger, by Hugh E. Stephenson, M.D., Jr. (Columbia, Missouri: University of Missouri Medical School Foundation, Inc., 1998).

3. Quinine and Quarantine; Missouri Medicine through the Years, by Loren Humphrey (Columbia and London: The University of Missouri Press, 2000).

4. Missouri State Gazetteer and Business Directory 1860, by James Sutherland and Henry N. McEvoy (St. Louis: Sutherland and McEvoy Publishers and Compilers, 1860).

5. Centennial History of Missouri, Vol. I, by Walter B. Stevens (St. Louis, Chicago: The S. J. Clarke Publishing Company, 1921).

6. Medical and Surgical History of the War of the Rebellion, by James K. Barnes, ed., surgeon general, U. S. Army (Washington, D.C.: Government Printing Service, 1870).

7. Hardtack and Coffee, by John D. Billings (Lincoln and London: University of Nebraska Press, 1993).

8. History of Lewis, Clark, Knox and Scotland Counties, Missouri (Marceline, MO: Walsworth Publishing Company, 1881).

9. With Porter in North Missouri, by Joseph A. Mudd (Washington, D.C.: The National Publishing Company, 1909).

Chapter 11

1. With Porter in North Missouri, by Joseph A. Mudd (Washington, D.C.: The National Publishing Company, 1909).
2. War of the Rebellion: Official Records of the Union and Confederate Armies, Series 1, Vol. XIII, by Lieut. Col. Robert N. Scott, Third U.S. Artillery (Washington, D. C.: Government Printing Office, 1885).
3. The Civil War in Missouri Day by Day, 1861-1865, by Carolyn M. Bartels (Independence, MO: Two Trails Publishing) 1992).
4. Roger Boyd, ranger at the Athens State Park, states that many of the southern supporters around Athens believed Doctor Aylward amputated many confederate limbs needlessly. While the man on the street in those days might have seen wounds that did not appear so severe as to warrant amputation, the surgeon of that time amputated to prevent infection, that was certain to set in, from spreading and giving blood-poisoning.
5. History of Monroe and Shelby Counties, Missouri (St. Louis: Missouri National Historical Companies, 1884). Only one of the 21 advance guard escaped death and returned to the main force to sound the alert.
6. A History of Northeast Missouri, Vol. I, by Walter Williams (Chicago, New York: The Lewis Publishing Company, 1931).

Chapter 12

1. The Twenty-First Missouri: From Home Guard to Union Regiment, by Leslie Anders (Westport, Connecticut, London, England: Greenwood Press, 1975).
2. The Constitution (Keokuk), Keokuk Public Library, the Bickel Collection, Keokuk, Iowa, and History of Lewis, Clark, Knox and Scotland Counties, Missouri (Marceline, MO: Walsworth Publishing Company, 1881).
3. History of Adair County, by E. M. Violette (Kirksville: The Denslow Publishing Co., 1911).

Chapter 13

1. History of Adair County, by E. M. Violette (Kirksville: The Denslow Publishing Co., 1911).
2. A History of Northeast Missouri, by Walter Williams (Chicago, New York: The Lewis Publishing Company, 1913).
3. In 1862 Confederate soldiers received a small (3 X 43/4 inches) Bible published by Augusta: Confederate States Bible Society and printed by Wood, Hanleiter Rice and Co, Atlanta, GA. The religious conversion of many southern soldiers is recorded in Southern Stories, by Drew Gilpin Faust (Columbia and London: University Missouri Press, 1992). He states, "From the fall of 1862 until the last days of the Civil War, religious revivalism swept through Confederate forces with an intensity that led one Southerner to declare the armies had been nearly converted into churches."

Chapter 14

1. L. Hazel Bates from the Autobiography of "Bennie" Howell Drescher kindly furnished by Mrs. Ellen Cole of Sergeantsville, New Jersey.
2. History of Marion County, Missouri 1884, by R. I. Holcombe (Hannibal, MO: The Marion County Historical Society, 1979).
3. From the writings of Frank Sosey, former owner of the Palmyra Spectator, The Civil War In Marion County From 1860 to 1865, furnished by Eldon Mette, Palmyra.

Chapter 15

1. History of Marion County, Missouri 1884, by R. I. Holcombe (Hannibal, MO: The Marion County Historical Society, 1979).
2. Robert Devoy: A Tale of the Palmyra Massacre, by Frank H. Sosey (Palmyra, MO: Sosey Brothers Press, 1903).
3. The Kidnapping and Murder of Mr. Andrew Allsman by Ed. J. Schaeffer, March 1960; furnished by Eldon Mette.
4. Bakers Gone Home, by Leland Smith (Nashville, Tenn: Cherry Tree Publishers, 1978).
5. The Court Martial of William R. Strachan, by Jane Kiso (Jefferson City, MO: Mid-Missouri Genealogical Society, 1999).
6. History of Monroe and Shelby Counties Missouri (St. Louis: National Historical Companies, 1884).

Other available books written by Loren Humphrey

Medical Blemishes: Untrue Stories about Real Problems is a collection of 16 short stories. Allegorical with a surprise ending, each entertains while stimulating the reader's search for truth.

Order from Jenkins LTD for $12.35 ($9.95 plus $2.40 S/H)*

Extreme Cancers is a novel about hope. A pastor and his younger brother, a cancer surgeon, portray the age-old battle of God versus science as they minister to the cancer patient.

Order from Jenkins LTD for $15.55 ($12.95 plus $2.60 S/H)*

Embryo Factory: the Stem Cell Wars, co-authored with Richard Humphrey, is a novel about the controversy surrounding the use of stem cells from human embryos for research.

Order from Jenkins LTD for $12.35 ($9.95 plus $2.40 S/H)*

Quinine and Quarantine: Missouri Medicine through the Years, is the tenth in the Missouri Heritage Readers Series published by the University of Missouri Press. This unique book presents medical problems and advances that threatened the citizens of Missouri.

Order from University of Missouri Press (800) 828-4498 for $9.95

* Jenkins LTD, 503 Nifong #201, Columbia, MO 65201-3717

Johnny Come Home:
The Civil War in Northeast Missouri
Order Form

Postal Orders: Jenkins LTD
503 Nifong #201
Columbia, MO 65201-3717

Telephone Orders: (520) 548-1525

E-mail Orders: ljenks@centurytel.net

Please send *Johnny Come Home: The Civil War in Northeast Missouri* **to:**

Name _____

Address _____

City_____ State _____ Zip _____

Telephone (_____) _____

Book price: $12.95

Shipping: $2.60 for the first book and $1.00 for each additional book to cover shipping and handling within the U.S.. Canada and Mexico. International orders add $6.00 for the first book and $2.00 for each additional book.

Or contact your local bookstore